DATE DUE			
NOV 06			
MAR 01			
MAR 13			
MAR 27			
MAY 5			
MAY 16			
SEP 25			

Fic   88
Hah   Hahn, Mary Downing.
       The wind blows
       backward

GAYLORD M2

88

The Wind Blows Backward

MARY DOWNING HAHN

The Wind Blows Backward

Clarion Books~New York

Quotations from *Rain Makes Applesauce* by Julian Scheer used by permission of
Holiday House, Inc.

Quotations from *Owl at Home* by Arnold Lobel used by permission of
HarperCollins Publishers.

Clarion Books
a Houghton Mifflin Company imprint
215 Park Avenue South, New York, NY 10003
Text copyright © 1993 by Mary Downing Hahn

Printed in the U.S.A.

Library of Congress Cataloging-in-Publication Data

Hahn, Mary Downing.
The wind blows backward / by Mary Downing Hahn.
p.   cm.
Summary: Although they share a love of poetry and problems with their
parents, a shy high school senior's attraction to a popular classmate is tempered
by her fear of his moody, self-destructive side.
ISBN 0-395-62975-6
[1. Interpersonal relations — Fiction.   2. Emotional problems — Fiction.
3. Parent and child — Fiction.   4. Suicide — Fiction.]   I. Title.
PZ7.H1256Wi   1993
[Fic] — dc20   92-12245
CIP
AC

AGM   10   9   8   7   6   5   4   3   2   1

For Beth . . . who still talks silly talk

The Wind Blows Backward

~ Chapter One ~

ONE FEBRUARY AFTERNOON, I was leaning against a cart piled high with books, leafing through a collection of Emily Dickinson's poetry. Although I wasn't supposed to read while I was working, I couldn't put a book on the shelf without opening it first. Hiring me to work in a public library was like giving an alcoholic a job as a bartender. The temptation was more than I could handle.

Feeling sneaky, I glanced around to make sure Mrs. Jenkins wasn't watching me. The last time she caught me reading on library time, she gave me a warning. Once more, and I was in danger of losing my job, something I couldn't afford to let happen.

The aisle was empty. I was alone. Just me and hundreds of books — my idea of paradise.

In seconds, I forgot Mrs. Jenkins, forgot my job, forgot the library. Closing my ears to distant coughs and rustling pages, I sank into Dickinson. Solemn images filled my mind — a bird with eyes like frightened beads, the buzz of a fly in a room where someone lay dying, horses' heads turned toward eternity, lips covered up with moss.

I wasn't always sure what the poems meant, couldn't have paraphrased them for my English teacher, but I loved the way the words lifted from the page and took to the air, I loved the way they *tasted*. Like cool stones, I rolled them around in my mouth, whispered lines to myself, memorized my favorites.

Lost in Dickinson, I didn't notice Vanessa Blake until she cleared her throat to get my attention. Startled to see one of my worst enemies so close, I shut my book and slipped it quickly into its proper place on the shelf. If Vanessa had been Mrs. Jenkins, it would have been the end of my career.

But, as much as I would have hated to lose my job, facing Vanessa was worse. It was bad enough to sit in class with her. Did she have to ruin my Saturday, too?

Unfortunately, Spencer Adams was right behind her. I wanted to see him even less, but he turned up in at least one class every year. Senior English this time.

"Well, if it isn't Mouse," Vanessa said. "Do you work here?"

Feeling my face burn, I nodded. With one word, Vanessa had reduced me to my middle-school self. Trapped behind my cart of books, I was the mouse, and Vanessa was the cat. At the thrust of her paw, the old game began again.

Spencer's frayed running shoe moved forward and nudged Vanessa's foot. At the same time, he murmured something I couldn't hear.

Ignoring him, Vanessa asked, "Where's Robert Frost?"

I wanted to say he was dead and buried in New England, but the cat had my tongue. Without answering, I leaned over to grab a collection of Frost's poetry and bumped heads with Spencer, who was reaching for the same book. For a second, we were face to face, inches apart, staring into each other's eyes.

2

Keeping my balance with difficulty, I thrust the book at Vanessa. She turned to leave, but Spencer lingered to apologize.

"I didn't hurt you, did I?"

Without answering him, without looking at him, I shook my head. Nearby, I heard Vanessa let out a sigh, sharp-edged with impatience. Flustered by their presence, I picked up a volume of Walt Whitman's poetry and scanned the shelves for its place, but the numbers on the books' spines jumbled, inverted themselves, made me feel dyslexic. The very air belonged to Spencer and Vanessa. How could I think with them so near?

Spencer leaned closer and took the book out of my hand. For a second, his fingers touched mine. *"Leaves of Grass,"* he said. "Do you like Walt Whitman?"

Without looking at him, I nodded, but I couldn't think of anything to say, brilliant or otherwise. Spencer hadn't spoken to me since we graduated from middle school almost four years ago. Why was he talking to me now?

While Spencer leafed through "Song of Myself," Vanessa said, "Wasn't Whitman gay or perverted or something?"

"What's that got to do with his poetry?" Spencer asked. "Whitman was great. He said things most people were scared to talk about. Things that still scare people."

"Spare me, Spence." Vanessa glanced at me to see if I shared her opinion. Failing to get a response, she tossed her long hair to the side and sighed again, louder this time, as if to say that she, Vanessa Blake, had better things to do than hang around libraries.

"What poem are you writing about for Walker's class, Lauren?" Spencer asked me.

" 'A Certain Slant of Light.' " Still avoiding his eyes, I scanned the shelf, trying to find room for Edna St. Vincent

Millay. Walker had told us to write a short paper on a poem, any poem. It didn't matter which, as long as our ideas were original, all our own, no cheating with *Cliff Notes* or *Twentieth Century Views* or any other critical source. This was my favorite type of paper. I hated research. It always killed my ideas. Other people's thoughts had a way of coming between me and my feelings.

"That's a great poem," Spencer said. "It's so, so . . . well, you know, majestic. That last stanza — 'When it goes, 'tis like the distance/On the look of death' — somehow you know what she means, even if you can't put it into words."

Still unable to speak, I nodded. *Go away,* I thought, *don't talk to me. Leave me alone.*

Sweeping his hair nervously to the side, Spencer went right on. Even though I hadn't asked, hadn't said anything to suggest I was the least bit interested, he told me he'd picked "Stopping by Woods on a Snowy Evening."

"I thought about a few others," he said, talking too fast for anyone to interrupt. " 'Desert Places' and 'Acquainted With the Night,' but there's something about 'Stopping by Woods,' something I like. The snow, the woods, the pond . . ."

When he paused, I dared myself to look at him. Head lowered, he was fidgeting with the books on my cart. He still bit his nails, I noticed, right down to the quick.

"Emily Dickinson," he said. "She's right for you somehow."

While I wondered what he meant by that, Vanessa frowned and shifted her weight dramatically from one hip to the other. "Come on, Spence. We're supposed to meet Meg and the others at the mall."

"I have to find a book, Van." Spencer ran one finger along

a shelf as if he were checking for dust. "Give me five or ten minutes."

Vanessa pulled back her sleeve and made a show of studying her watch. "I'll wait for you at the checkout desk." Before she left, she added, "See you in Walker's class, Mouse."

Coming from her mouth, the words sounded threatening. In eighth grade, Vanessa had been able to scare me with a look, a remark, a smirk. After a comment like that, I would've stayed home from school to avoid her. Now she merely made me uncomfortable. It was consoling to think I'd gained at least a small degree of confidence.

Without raising my head, I watched her walk away. She paused once at the end of the aisle and frowned at Spencer. Then, with a toss of hair, she disappeared, leaving a trace of perfume in the quiet air.

Too embarrassed to look at Spencer, I examined the books on my cart as if I'd never seen them before. He'd leave soon, I was sure he would, but he stayed where he was, close enough for me to hear him breathing.

"Have you read 'Song of Myself'?" Spencer showed me the photograph of Walt Whitman on the cover. Old and white-haired, long beard, deep-set eyes, an authoritative nose.

While I stared at the picture, Spencer went on talking. "He looks like God, doesn't he? Or a prophet. Very wise — the kind of person you'd like to talk to."

He paused to take a breath, shifted his weight, bumped the cart. "Gandalf," he said, "That's who he reminds me of. Give him a long robe, a staff, a pointed hat, and he'd be a perfect wizard."

Spencer leaned against the shelves and waited for me to

agree. Once I would have, but I wasn't a naive eighth-grader anymore. He couldn't charm me with his smile, not now. I wouldn't give him the chance.

Instead of answering, I shrugged and went on working. If I paid no attention to him, maybe he'd take the hint and go away.

Near me, too near me, Spencer sighed. He cleared his throat, started to say something, changed his mind. For several minutes, he thumbed through books, pausing to read a poem here, a poem there. He turned pages loudly, he coughed, he even whistled a few notes of Beethoven's Ninth.

Spencer was hard to ignore, but I forced myself to continue shelving. It was what I was paid to do. My job. Slowly I moved away from him, towing my cart behind me.

Finally he said, "Well, it sure was fun talking to you, Lauren."

Catching the sarcasm in his voice, I looked up, but he was already walking away. The eagle on the back of his warm-up jacket stared at me with mad yellow eyes. At the end of the aisle, Spencer glanced over his shoulder and caught me watching him.

"Tell me someday what you think of Whitman." He didn't smile. His face gave nothing away.

The moment he disappeared, I thought of dozens of things I should have said and done, witty remarks, snide observations, ironic comments. But it was too late, I'd missed my chance, he was gone.

Taking a deep breath, I told myself not to be silly. Spencer meant nothing to me. He was an obnoxious jock, a snob — what did he know about Whitman or Frost or Beethoven?

But his presence lingered in the still air, distracting me, making it hard to concentrate, filling my head with a jumble of memories. Myself at thirteen, tall and thin and miserably self-conscious, walking into an eighth-grade language arts class. New to Adelphia, new to Oak Ridge Middle School, very scared. A total misfit, that's what I was. And smart enough to know it.

My high test scores put me in the talented and gifted program with the meanest and snobbiest kids in school, the "pushed and shoved," Mom called them. Vanessa Blake, Meg Foster, Melanie Gruber, Holly Bernstein, girls with perfect skin, perfect hair, perfect clothes. Girls with mean eyes and whispery voices and giggles sharp as broken glass. Girls waiting for the perfect victim to walk into their lives — me.

Even now, I remembered the notes they passed, the way they looked at me and snickered. They called me Mouse because I was shy, because my ears were pink around the edges, because I had a squeaky voice, because they knew I couldn't defend myself. I hated them, I hated myself.

But Spencer, I'd thought Spencer was different. In eighth grade, he was short and thin and very quiet. His braces were even more formidable than mine, and Vanessa called him Metal Mouth. In some ways, he was a misfit, too.

It didn't take us long to discover we both loved the same kind of books — fantasies and science fiction. That was all we read, trilogy after trilogy. We spent hours in the school media center talking about elves and dragons and wizards and magical quests. Space travel, time travel, alternate worlds, black holes. Rings of power, shape changers, good versus evil. We were both more at home in Middle Earth than the real world.

By the end of eighth grade, I thought I was in love with Spencer Adams. He didn't know, of course. It was one of those secret adolescent things. You tell your best girlfriend, you swear her to secrecy, you write his name in your notebook, but you'd die if he knew.

Something happened during summer vacation, though. Spencer grew taller, he got rid of his braces, he started hanging out with jocks like Ted Dillon and Kevin Evans. When we began high school in the fall, he was a different person, a stranger. Surrounded by his friends, he was the center of the crowd, laughing the loudest, talking the most, telling the funniest jokes. He was never quiet. Never still. He joined the cross-country track team and won the county championship, he had a string of girlfriends, he made the Honor Roll. He was Spencer Adams, Prince of Jocks.

He never spoke to me again. If he passed me in the hall, he pretended not to see me. I was an embarrassment, I guess, a reminder of his uncool middle-school self.

Without my friend Casey, I wouldn't have survived ninth grade. Every time I cried, she told me Spencer was a creep, a jerk, a snob. But no matter what she said, it still hurt to see him. I went though a lot of Kleenex that year.

Gradually, I stopped missing him, stopped crying, stopped watching him. I lost track of his girlfriends and his victories. I ignored him, refused to think about him or even look at him. Until this afternoon, nothing Spencer said or did interested me.

Now, standing alone in the silent aisle, I stared dumbly at a row of books. The titles might have been written in Japanese for all the sense they made. How could it be? After years of silence, all it took was a few well-chosen words from Spencer and I was as vulnerable as a middle-schooler.

The sound of footsteps startled me. For a moment, I hoped it was Spencer, but when I looked over my shoulder, I saw Mrs. Jenkins frowning at me.

"Haven't you finished shelving the eight-hundreds?" she

asked. "I have at least three carts of picture books taking up space at the check-in desk. When you finish here, please go to the Children's Room."

Before she left, she added, "The kids have made a real mess — dollhouse furniture everywhere, books on the floor, puzzles scattered all over the place. See if you can clean up before we close."

As soon as my cart was empty, I headed for the Children's Room. If Mrs. Jenkins thought she was punishing me, she was wrong. Most of the pages hated shelving picture books. They were skinny and slippery and you had to crawl along the floor to put them away. But I'd never outgrown them. I still loved Angus and Little Bear and Madeline.

Today there was an added benefit. I was sure the Prince of Jocks wouldn't be caught dead in kiddy lit land.

~ Chapter Two ~

As soon as the library closed, I crossed the street and headed for the mall. Casey was working at Mister Burger, and she'd promised to give me a ride home. I had an hour to wait, so I browsed in Waldenbooks to kill time. In the poetry section, I found a paperback edition of *Leaves of Grass.* Telling myself I wanted to read Whitman for my own pleasure, not because Spencer had thrust him at me, I bought the book and made my way through a crowd of shoppers to Mister Burger. Casey was too busy filling orders to talk, so I got a cup of coffee and found a table in the back.

Opening *Leaves of Grass,* I turned to "Song of Myself" and began to read. From the first page it was obvious my school anthology had only given me a carefully chosen taste of Whitman. Spencer was right — I was amazed that this poem had been written more than a hundred years ago.

"Potent stuff, isn't it?"

Startled, I looked up. Spencer was staring down at the open book.

Feeling my face burn, I read the words he was looking at: "I will go to the bank by the wood and become undisguised and naked, /I am mad for it to be in contact with me."

"So what do you think?" he asked.

With feigned indifference, I closed the book and tried to look more worldly than I was. If I smoked, I'd have lit a cigarette and stared scornfully into space. Unlike Whitman, I didn't want to be undisguised, I didn't want to be naked, I didn't want Spencer to think I was mad to be in contact with anything.

"Hey, Adams," somebody called, "over here."

To my relief, Spencer joined a crowd of jocks at a nearby table. The next time I raised my eyes from my book, I caught him staring at me. Vanessa was sitting on his lap, whispering in his ear, and he was stroking her hair idly, the way you might pet a cat, not really paying attention to her.

Disturbed by the expression in Spencer's eyes, I looked at Casey. She was leaning across the counter, talking to Jordan Grimes, one of Spencer's jock buddies. Her uniform, a dark-green polo shirt, clung to her breasts, and her red hair tumbled in waves to her shoulders. I knew she liked Jordan, she'd told me more than once. It was obvious their hormones were in high gear.

A burst of laughter drew my attention back to the crowd surrounding Spencer. Although I doubted many of them knew me, I knew them. Like Vanessa and Spencer, they lived in High Meadow Estates, a community of huge, expensive houses just outside Adelphia. Like rich kids everywhere, they ran high school just as they'd run middle school, just as they'd probably run college.

"Meadows," Casey called them. Boring and predictable.

As shallow as the one-hundred-dollar bill she'd once seen Vanessa hand a clerk in a clothing store. And Spencer was their prince, according to her.

While I watched, Vanessa shoved Spencer's hair out of his eyes and said something I couldn't hear. He was angry, I could see that from where I sat. Tossing his head, he scowled at Vanessa. "Leave it alone," he said in a voice loud enough to make people at other tables stare.

"Maybe I'll leave you alone, too." Vanessa slid off Spencer's lap so fast she knocked over his soda. Leaving him to mop it up, she eased herself onto Kevin's lap and stroked his short hair.

Without looking at Spencer, Kevin let Vanessa kiss his cheek. That surprised me — I'd always thought he was one of the prince's favorites. Along with Ted, they were always together. The Three Musketeers, Casey called them.

Slumped in his seat, arms folded across his chest, Spencer ignored Vanessa. She looked at him, giggled, and kissed Kevin again — on the mouth this time.

Ted frowned and said something to Spencer, but he merely shrugged and looked at me.

Mortified at being caught again, I tried to hide my red face by bending my head over my book. I felt him staring at me, I heard Vanessa's laughter, but I kept my eyes on the black type wiggling meaninglessly across the page. Was Vanessa about to dump the Prince of Jocks? Usually it was Spencer who shed his old girlfriends like a snake getting rid of its skin. It would serve him right to be on the receiving end for once. *Break his heart, Vanessa, smash it, make him feel as small as he once made me feel.* Oh, I was savage — Miss Havisham in *Great Expectations,* that was who I was, telling Estella to hurt Pip.

To keep myself from looking at Spencer, I forced myself to continue reading "Song of Myself":

> *I mind how once we lay such a transparent*
> *   summer morning,*
> *How you settled your head athwart my hips and*
> *   gently turn'd over upon me,*
> *And parted the shirt from my bosom-bone, and*
> *   plunged your tongue to my bare-stript heart.*

Those lines certainly hadn't been in my anthology of American literature. If Walker had read them out loud, the boys would have laughed so loud the principal would have heard the uproar in his office. No wonder we'd studied "O Captain! My Captain!" instead of "Song of Myself."

The next time I looked up, Spencer's group was gone, and Casey was standing beside me.

"Ground Control to Lauren," she said. "Ground Control to Lauren — are you there?"

It was one of Casey's favorite jokes — I was in outer space, floating free, millions of miles from earth, and she was calling me back.

"I'm off," she said. "Let's go."

Outside in the misty night, Casey said, "Doesn't Jordan have a great body?"

"But not many brains."

Casey laughed. "At least he's not stuck on himself like some of his jock buddies."

Unlocking her old Ford Escort, she slid in and reached across to open my door. Before she started the engine, she lit a cigarette. "Did you notice the prince tonight?"

"Spencer?" Faking indifference, I shrugged. "It looks like things aren't going very well with him and Vanessa."

"That's an understatement." Casey tromped on the gas and played with the clutch pedal. The car wheezed, sputtered, died.

"It's more than that," Casey said. "He's been acting weird all year. Haven't you noticed?"

"He actually spoke to me twice today — that was pretty strange."

Casey exhaled a cloud of smoke. "Jordan told me Spencer's not going out for cross-country this spring. His grades are too low."

"What are you talking about? He's on the Honor Roll. There's a bumper sticker on his car to prove it — 'PROUD PARENTS OF AN HONOR STUDENT AT STEVENS FOREST HIGH.' "

"It must be an old one," Casey said. "He's in two of my classes — calculus and psychology. He doesn't do anything in either one. Just sleeps. At the rate he's going, he'll be lucky to graduate."

While Casey cranked the engine, cursed it, and begged it to start, I was shocked into thinking about my English class. It was true. Spencer never said a word. If Walker called on him, he shrugged and mumbled something. He slept, he stared out the window, he jiggled one leg, he gnawed his fingernails.

It astonished me to realize I'd been sitting a few seats away from him for months without giving his behavior any thought. Last year he'd raised his hand, he'd spoken up, he'd always known the right answer — French, algebra two, chemistry. The prince had been brilliant.

Casey was too busy punching the dashboard and swearing at the car to notice my silence. Running through the scene in the library again, I remembered how tense Spencer had been. Why had he talked to me? What had he wanted?

"Start!" Casey yelled at the car. "Start, dammit!" The Escort coughed, choked, and reluctantly obeyed. Making a victory gesture, Casey pressed the accelerator and sped out of the mall parking lot.

"What are you doing tonight?" she asked.

"It's Mom's birthday. I made a reservation for dinner at Clyde's."

Obviously impressed, Casey stared at me. "Well, that sure is nice of you. Even if I could afford a place like that, I wouldn't treat my mother to Mister Burger's. Nag, nag, nag — she drives me nuts."

Casey fiddled with the radio till she found a song she liked. "I was hoping to talk you into going to a party with me."

I shrugged, glad I had an excuse. I'd been to enough parties with Casey to know what to expect — beer, pot, big crowds, lots of shoving, guys hitting on you. Not my idea of fun. "Even if I didn't have a date with Mom, I couldn't — I have to study for a French exam."

Casey made a face. "You're such a prude sometimes, Lauren, I swear you are. You never go anywhere, you never do anything. Your social life is absolutely terminal."

We'd been over this before, and I knew my lines by heart. "I'm not good at parties. I never know what to say, what to do. I can't dance, I don't drink, I don't smoke — I'm a totally boring person."

"Bull," Casey said. "There's nothing wrong with you. It's all in your head."

Refusing to give up, she added, "It's in High Meadow, at Jeff Hughes's house. His parents went to Bermuda or someplace and left him home alone. Everybody knows about it. The whole school will be there."

A traffic light she hadn't seen startled Casey. As we fish-tailed to a stop, I clung to the little strap over the door, sure we were about to hit the car in front of us. When I thought it was safe to open my eyes, I glanced at her. She was puffing her cigarette nonchalantly and singing along with the Cowboy Junkies.

What was it like to be Casey? As far as I could tell, nothing bothered her, nothing worried her, nothing scared her. Or at least if it did, she refused to acknowledge it. To her, life was an adventure. School, cars, parties, boys — she didn't take any of it seriously, never saw the dangers I saw, didn't worry about big questions like death and God and the meaning of life. While I stood on the shore shivering, she plunged into the waves and came up laughing.

By the time Casey pulled into Mayfaire Court, I thought she'd forgotten the party, but, as I got out of the car, she said, "If you change your mind, let me know. I'm not leaving till nine or nine-thirty."

. I gave her a quick nod. Then, jumping a puddle, I ran toward the door and dashed up three flights of steps to our apartment.

"Hi, honey," Mom called from the bathroom. "Just putting on my face."

Dumping my book pack on a chair, I walked down the hall to the bathroom. "Hurry up, Mom. We're supposed to be at Clyde's at seven."

"Clyde's?" Mom spritzed her hair, scrunching it in her hand to encourage the curl.

"You didn't forget, did you?"

"Oh, my God." Mom stared at my reflection in the mirror. "It slipped my mind completely. Joanna's picking me up in five minutes. She's taking me to this club in Baltimore, a new place."

16

"Can't you tell Joanna you'll meet her later?"

"She's counting on me, Lally. Her boyfriend's going to be there with this guy she wants me to meet."

Mom smiled winningly, but using my baby name didn't take the sting out of her words. "I was counting on you, too," I said.

"We'll do it another time, honey, I promise." Mom smiled again. "It's Saturday night. Go somewhere with Casey, have fun. You don't want to hang out with an old lady like me."

"But it's your birthday."

"Don't remind me," Mom said. "Thirty-seven — God, I should be wearing black." Frowning at her reflection, Mom lifted the skin on her cheekbones. "See how the wrinkles disappear when you do that? Maybe I should start saving for a facelift. What do you think?"

I frowned at her face in the mirror. Knowing I was being snide, I said, "Wrinkles are part of life. Why don't you just accept them?"

"Tell me that when *you're* thirty-seven." Giving me a quick kiss, Mom crossed the hall and went into her bedroom. From the doorway, I watched her pull a slinky blue dress over her head and shake it into place.

"What do you think?" she asked. "Does my stomach stick out?"

Eyeing her reflection anxiously, Mom twirled around in front of her mirror. "How about my rear end? Do I look fat?"

Without waiting for an answer, she grabbed her purse and her raincoat. "I told Joanna I'd wait for her in the vestibule. She hates climbing our steps."

Still angry, I followed Mom to the door. If Joanna lost a few pounds, stairs wouldn't be such an obstacle.

"What about my dinner?" I called after her. "What am I supposed to eat?"

From the second-floor landing, Mom looked up at me. "There's some stuff in the freezer, Lally. A couple of chicken things, a pizza. Just stick one in the microwave."

Going to the window, I watched her run across the sidewalk and hop into Joanna's racy little Nissan. Behind me, the refrigerator hummed a tune. The kitchen faucet dripped. The furnace came on and blew hot air out of the vent in the ceiling. Downstairs, a baby cried, a door slammed. Outside, the mist made halos around the lights.

Mom and Joanna saw each other every day at Stockman Electronics. You'd think she could spare me one night. Just one. After all, I was the only kid she had. And she wouldn't have me much longer. Soon I'd be away at college, and she could move in with Joanna if she liked her so much.

I sighed. Mom was Mom — I shouldn't have expected her to give up a chance to meet a man. She'd established her priorities a long time ago. As Casey had once pointed out, we were both victims of our mothers' benign neglect.

Benign. I wrote the word on the steamy windowpane. What was so benign about neglect?

While my pizza nuked in the microwave, I found myself thinking about Spencer. Against my will, I saw his face, heard his voice. Suppose I went to the party with Casey, suppose he was there, suppose he — I shook my head.

"Don't be stupid, Lauren," I muttered to my reflection in the oven's glass door. "When it comes to Spencer Adams, you're as bad as your mother."

~ *Chapter Three* ~

AFTER I'D EATEN MY PIZZA, I went to the window again and watched the rain fall on Mayfaire Court. "Garden apartments," that was what they were called, but in the four years I'd lived here, I hadn't seen any flowers. Just abandoned shopping carts, junked cars, and downtrodden grass. It wasn't a bad place to live, if you didn't mind outbursts of domestic violence in neighboring apartments or an occasional drug bust.

Behind me, the empty rooms were full of shadows. I didn't want to study French, I didn't want to read, I didn't want to watch TV. It wasn't just boredom, it was loneliness. How many Saturday nights had I stood at this window wondering where Mom was, worrying about her, waiting to see her headlights, hoping to hear her key turning in the lock?

On an impulse, I dialed Casey's number. Her phone rang once, twice, three times. Just as I was about to hang up, she answered.

*　　*　　*

By the time Casey picked me up, I was wearing the white silk blouse I'd planned to give Mom. As far as I was concerned, she no longer deserved a birthday present.

Casey agreed. "That's what I love about you, Lauren. Me — I'd just buy it for myself in the first place, but everybody knows how selfish I am. Just ask Mom, she'll tell you."

High Meadow Estates was on the other side of Adelphia from Mayfaire Court, but it might as well have been on the other side of the moon — maybe on another planet altogether. Built on pastures where cows used to graze, the houses sat on two-acre lots. Custom-built, they were wrapped in decks and surrounded by terraced lawns. The darkest night couldn't hide their splendor.

"How much do you have to earn to buy a place like that?" Casey asked as we passed a house big enough for three families.

"More than we'll ever earn," I said.

"Drug money," she said. "I bet they sell cocaine."

Casey drove slowly, pointing out swimming pools and tennis courts. When we passed the same house twice, I asked her if she knew where Jeff lived.

"It's around here somewhere." Casey frowned and lit a cigarette. "In the dark, it's hard to see where we're going."

Ignoring my suggestion that we give up and go to a movie, Casey peered through the drizzle. "Isn't that Spencer's house?"

I glanced at the big brick home and felt my throat tighten. On a whim, I'd once asked Mom to drive past it. As I remembered the incident, I'd hidden on the floor of the car and taken one quick look before telling her to speed away.

"He should be at the party," Casey said. "With Vanessa or without her."

I mumbled something about not caring who or what he

20

came with, but, as we left his house behind, I was swamped with conflicting emotions. I wanted to see Spencer, I didn't want to see Spencer, yes I did, no I didn't. Why hadn't I stayed home and studied French?

"There it is." Casey slammed on her brakes and made a sharp turn. Ahead of us, the street was lined with cars. BMWs, Audis, Mercedes, Jeeps — nothing in the class of Casey's rust-pitted Escort.

With her usual insouciance, Casey hopped out of the car and urged me to hurry. The rain had changed to a thin mist, and the wind lifted her coat in swirls. Anchoring her little felt hat with one hand, she ran toward Jeff's house.

I followed her slowly, reluctantly. Kids milled around in the street, surged up the driveway, and pushed their way toward the house. The air was pungent with marijuana smoke. In the darkness, a girl shrieked with laughter, a boy yelled something. After years of avoiding Vanessa and Spencer, I was walking straight into their territory. A mouse entering the cat's lair, that was me.

Clinging to Casey for protection, I let her tow me toward a group of hulking forms blocking the driveway, big guys, football players. In the darkness, they were more menacing than usual. One of them broke away and shoved his way toward us.

"It's about time." Jordan slung his arm around Casey. "I was beginning to think you'd stood me up."

Casey laughed and kissed him. *Stupid, stupid me — I should have known this would happen.* It always did. Casey would persuade me to go somewhere, a guy would appear, and all of a sudden, I'd be on my own. I was her back-up, a friend to leave with if things didn't work out.

Feeling used, I grabbed her sleeve. "Can I talk to you?"

"Later, Lauren." Turning her head so quickly she swatted

my face with her hair, Casey took a sip from Jordan's beer can and kissed him again.

Slumping against the car beside her, I folded my arms across my chest. What was I going to do now? Inside the house, kids were dancing to an ancient Stones song turned up full blast. If I went in there, I'd probably find myself face to face with Spencer and Vanessa. He might think I was following him because he'd spoken a few words to me, something he'd probably done just to irritate Vanessa. Cold as I was in the driveway, the darkness hid me. I might see him, but he wouldn't see me. With any luck, he'd never know I was here.

Staring at the lighted windows, I thought I saw Spencer's dark hair, but the room was so crowded, it was hard to be sure.

When someone called my name, I spun around, afraid it was Spencer, wishing it was Spencer. Troy Van Dusen was stumbling toward me. Already drunk, he was holding two cans of beer over his head, sloshing people as he shoved past them.

"Have a beer, Mouse," he said.

Pushing the can away, I shook my head. If there was one person I really detested, it was Troy. Last year he slept his way through French in the seat next to me, waking up long enough to copy from my paper every time we had a test. Once he actually grabbed my hand and moved it to see what I'd written. He was so conceited, it never occurred to him I didn't like him.

"This is a party." Troy was so close I could smell beer on his breath. "You're supposed to have a good time — smile, be happy, get drunk. Hey, it's Saturday night."

Leaning toward me, he slopped beer from the can. "Whoops," he said. "Sorry, got some on you."

Troy pawed at my denim jacket, pretending to brush away the beer he'd spilled. I shoved his hand aside and tried to put some distance between us. Although this was my first experience with him, I'd heard enough to know he made passes at every girl unfortunate enough to get near him.

Setting his beer can on the roof of a car, he grabbed my arm and pressed his mouth against mine so hard his teeth hurt my lips.

"What's the matter, Mousie?"

I pushed him away and looked for Casey. She was gone. Dark shapes hemmed me in, blocking the driveway. "Leave me alone," I said.

But he wouldn't. He muttered and murmured and pressed himself against me. The more I twisted and turned and struggled, the tighter he held me.

"Don't be so cold," Troy mumbled. He drew back, tried to smile, and lost his balance. "Whoa," he said, "something's the matter here. Just a minute, Mouse, just a minute now. Don't go away."

When Troy turned his back and started vomiting in the bushes, I didn't hang around waiting for him to feel better. Ducking and dodging faceless shapes in the dark, I ran to the end of the driveway. Where was Casey?

The only solution was to wait for her in the car, but when I opened the Escort's door, I saw Casey and Jordan making out in the backseat. Jordan muttered something and Casey stared at me.

"Sorry." I shut the door fast.

"Now what? Behind me, the party split the night with noise, but ahead was silence. In the murk, the trees glistened, and beads of water hung from their bare limbs. It was starting to rain again. Toward the west, the sky glowed pink from the neon signs on Route Forty.

Turning my back on the party, I ran into the darkness. With luck, I'd find my way home before dawn.

Less than a block from Jeff's house, the headlights of a car sent my shadow racing ahead of me. I moved to the shoulder to let it pass, but its brake lights flashed red and it slid to a stop a few feet down the road.

Convinced it was Troy, I tried to jump a grassy ditch beside the road. I planned to hide in the shadows on the other side, but I slipped on the wet ground and landed in the mud at the bottom.

Above me, the car door opened, and a dark form looked down at me. "Lauren, what are you doing? Are you all right?"

It was Spencer. The person I most wanted to see, the person I least wanted to see. Three times in one day was three times too many. Scrambling to my feet, I wiped my hands on the seat of my jeans and scowled at him. "I thought you were going to run over me."

When he saw me slip on the side of the ditch, Spencer held out his hand. Ignoring him, I managed to climb out by myself. I didn't need his help. Didn't want it, either.

"Were you at Jeff's?" he asked. We stood eye to eye, a few feet apart.

"Briefly."

"I didn't see you."

"I didn't see you, either."

Spencer ran a hand through his hair. Beads of mist clung to it, tiny droplets shining like diamonds. "Who did you come with?"

"Casey Fulton."

"I saw her get in a car with Jordan."

I turned away. "That's why I'm walking."

"Wait, I'll give you a ride."

"No, thanks." I started running again, slow and easy, a good pace that would get me back to Mayfaire Court on my own.

Spencer drew up beside me in the car and leaned across the passenger's seat. "Don't be dumb, Lauren," he said. "It's almost midnight."

Unsmiling, he gripped the steering wheel and stared at me. The car radio was playing "Riders on the Storm," an old Doors song recorded before either one of us was born. The music was dark, moody, intense, full of menace. So were the words. I knew them by heart.

"You better get in," Spencer said quietly.

Glancing over my shoulder, I saw what he saw. Two county police cars had just turned the corner several blocks away. They were heading in our direction.

Without another word, I slid into the car beside Spencer. He turned off the lights and pulled into a driveway. In a few seconds, the cops sped past, sweeping silently toward Jeff's house.

"Well," Spencer said, "it looks like we left just in time."

"What should we do?"

"Sit here till they leave." He spoke as if he'd experienced this before.

In the silence, the car made little pinging sounds as the engine cooled. Water dripped on the roof. From a block away, we heard people yelling. The police were breaking up the party.

Huddled against the door, I glanced at Spencer. He was chewing his thumbnail and staring into the darkness. Groping for something to say, I asked him where Vanessa was.

Without looking at me, he said, "The last time I saw her she was in the backseat of Kevin's car, too drunk to care who she was with. That's her way of getting back at me."

"Getting back at you?" I stared at Spencer. "For what?"

"For letting her down, for not being who she thought I was." His hands tightened on the steering wheel. "I seem to have that effect on people."

The night closed around us again, dark and misty. Cars passed the end of the driveway, their headlights raking our faces. The party was over. It was safe to leave.

Putting the BMW into gear, Spencer backed out. The road he took to Adelphia was dark and narrow. It twisted around curves posted with warning signs and snaked over hills. Ignoring the suggested speed limit, he hit sixty. If I hadn't been wearing my safety belt, I'd have been thrown from side to side like a rag doll.

"Do you always drive like this?" I asked. "If you're drunk, you can let me out right now."

Spencer slowed down. Tipping his head back for a moment, he gripped the steering wheel. "I drive fast," he said, "but I don't drink. Not ever."

Lit by the dashboard, his face was a study in dark and light. Several minutes passed. He said nothing, I said nothing. Trapped in the car with him, I was aware of the scent of after-shave and shampoo.

I felt like rolling the window down to escape the good smell of him. Instead, I watched the scenery slip by. We passed a dark farm, one of the last, and then we were on the outskirts of Adelphia.

At a traffic light, Spencer said, "I could really go for something to eat. How about you?"

When I shook my head, he sighed. "You don't trust me, do you?"

"Should I?"

The light turned green, and Spencer accelerated so quickly the car fishtailed. "I'd really like to talk with you, Lauren."

26

"About what?"

He frowned. "I don't know. Just things, stuff I've been thinking about."

Things, just things — what kind of things, I wondered. *Safe things? Dangerous things?* I hesitated, afraid to say yes, afraid to say no.

Spencer's eyes swept over me, and my skin tingled as if he'd touched me. Clasping my hands between my knees, I stared at the taillights of the cars ahead of us. Off to the right was my apartment, its rooms dark and cold and empty.

"We could go to McDonald's," he said.

"Okay." I spoke so softly I had to repeat it. Maybe I'd regret it, probably I would, but I wanted to hear what Spencer Adams had to say.

~Chapter Four~

AT A TABLE BESIDE A WINDOW, Spencer and I faced each other, our food spread out between us — Quarter Pounders oozing sauce and cheese, french fries, coffee.

Spencer opened the bun and removed the pickle. Holding it up to the light, he eyed it with disgust and laid it back on the burger. "I really picked a great place, but when all you have is five bucks, you don't have a lot of choice."

Bending my head, I poked at the food I'd let him talk me into ordering. The longer I stared at it, the more inedible it seemed. Tension knotted my insides, my stomach hurt. Why couldn't I think of something to say?

I sneaked a look across the table. Spencer wasn't eating, either. Head half turned, he was staring out the window. Bored, he was bored, I was boring him to death. He was sorry he'd picked me up, sorry he'd brought me here, sorry Vanessa was with Kevin and not him.

My eyes shifted from Spencer to my own reflection. The harsh fluorescent light bleached the color from my skin, my hair was tangled, my face was pale and shadowed. If only

I looked like Casey or Vanessa — then maybe he wouldn't notice how boring I was.

I sipped my coffee, but it had the flat bitter taste that comes from sitting too long in the pot. I dumped sugar into it — one pack, two, three, four. Nothing helped. It cloyed my mouth with sweetness, but the bitterness was still there, just under the surface.

Suddenly Spencer said, "You look like you're bored to death."

I was so surprised I almost dropped my coffee. "I was just thinking the same thing — about you I mean." Had I said that right? I tried again. "I thought *I* was boring *you*."

He shook his head. "It's just strange being with you after all this time. We never used to have any trouble talking — remember?"

When I didn't say anything, Spencer leaned toward me, a burger in one hand, a cup of coffee in the other. "Do you still read Tolkien and LeGuin?"

He waited for me to answer, his face a foot or so from mine. I'd forgotten how unusual his eyes were. The iris was pale green and rimmed in black, as if it had been outlined with a fine-tipped drawing pen. Around the pupil, the color changed to yellow. Like a cat's eyes, they hid everything, revealed nothing.

"Not anymore," I said. "The library has a classics paperback rack — Jane Austen, the Brontës, Hardy, Dickens, Eliot, Tolstoy. I'm in the middle of *War and Peace* now."

Hearing myself, I cringed. I sounded like a show-off, a phony, someone pathetically eager to impress people. Ashamed of myself, I fidgeted with the empty sugar packets.

Although I had no intention of telling him, Spencer was the reason I'd quit reading fantasies. The heroes had always worn his face. He was Strider facing the powers of darkness, he was the elf warrior Legolas, he was Ged in flight from the evil he'd summoned.

When Spencer turned his back on me, when he left Middle Earth, he took all the magic with him.

"I just read the Earthsea series again," Spencer was saying. "The first is still my favorite — Ged coming into his power, getting his true name, fleeing, then chasing the shadow, finally realizing he's been running from himself. You see more in some books when you're older, stuff you miss the first time."

While he talked, he shredded his empty coffee cup. With great concentration, he arranged the pieces in patterns on the tabletop. Lines, curves, semicircles, he moved them around with his finger.

"You're the only person I've ever been able to talk to," he said. "Did you know that?"

He studied the design he was making. I watched his hands move deftly from one piece to the next. His nails were so short, his fingertips swelled over them, soft, fleshy, almost deformed. They were little blind creatures, vulnerable and helpless. It was all I could do to keep myself from touching them.

Spencer raised his head for a moment. His face was unguarded, his eyes shadowed by worry. "I must have hurt you, Lauren."

I shrugged and made patterns of my own in the sugar I'd spilled all over the table. "It was a long time ago, we were kids playing kids' games, daydreaming about magic, living in fantasy worlds."

Affecting a cynicism I didn't feel, I was trying to put distance between myself and the thirteen-year-old I'd been. Pink-eared Mouse was gone. And I wanted her to stay gone.

"I don't know what happened," Spencer said. "When I started high school, my mother really pressured me. All she could think about was college. Study, get good grades, score high on the SATs, run, win, achieve. Be happy, be like everybody else."

He rearranged the cup pieces on the tabletop and sighed. "It sounds dumb now, but I thought the answer to everything was to do what Ted and Kevin did. They were always laughing and joking. Nothing bothered them. If it worked for them, it would work for me. I'd be happy, too — or at least people would *think* I was happy."

He hesitated. "And you," he said, "you — well, you . . ."

I waited for him to go on, to tell me what he meant, but he was gazing out the window again, jiggling one leg. I finished the sentence for him. "I didn't fit in, I was all wrong."

Spencer looked at me then. "I felt bad every time I saw you, but I didn't know what to do."

He paused, but I didn't raise my head. Was he waiting for me to say it was okay, I hadn't cared? I stared at the food I couldn't eat, at the coffee growing cold in my cup. All I wanted was to go home, get into bed, close my eyes, sleep. If I had to sit in this brightly lit place much longer, I'd cry.

Spencer sighed so hard he scattered the cup pieces. With one finger, he started a new pattern. "I've missed talking with you, Lauren."

"Really." My heart sped up, adrenaline pumped through my blood. Did he actually expect me to believe him?

"I mean it." Spencer gnawed at what was left of his thumbnail, watching me while he spoke. "I can't talk to girls like Vanessa. They aren't interested in how people feel, it makes them uncomfortable or something. They end up thinking I'm weird."

He returned his attention to the bits of cup littering the table like white petals. "Ted and Kevin just tell me to lighten up. All they care about are sports, getting into a good college, finding a job that pays big bucks. Econ, business management, how to get swanky cars and clothes, stuff like that."

He glanced at me. "But you, the things you say in Walker's class, they just blow me away sometimes. It's like you're putting *my* thoughts into *your* words, making them clear, helping me understand the sounds in my head."

Before I realized what he was doing, Spencer grabbed my hand. "Can we be friends, Lauren? Can we talk like we used to?"

His grip was so tight my hand hurt. "Not just Middle Earth and time travel and poetry. Other things — things nobody knows, nobody understands. Stuff I've never told anyone, stuff that's just eating me up inside."

Letting my hand go as quickly as he'd grabbed it, he threw himself back in his chair, arms outspread in a gesture of resignation. "I sound like a lunatic. You must think I'm crazy, out of my mind, a raving maniac."

To keep myself from reaching out to him, I clasped my hands. "I know how you feel, Spencer. It's the same with me." I hesitated a moment and he leaned toward me, watching me, waiting for me to go on.

"Casey's been my best friend since middle school," I said.

"She's funny, she's smart, she makes me laugh, but we're so different. She just doesn't understand the way I feel, the things that bother me, worry me, scare me. If I get too serious, she teases me."

Suddenly embarrassed, I sat back, amazed at the words spilling out of me. I hadn't realized how much it hurt when Casey teased me. "Guys don't like serious girls," she always said. "Laugh, say something funny for God's sake. At a party, nobody wants to talk about holes in the ozone layer."

"What about your parents?" Spencer asked. "Do they listen? Or are they like mine? 'No bad news, Spence — let us think you're happy. Put on a good show.' "

Realizing how little we knew about each other, I said, "I never talk to my mother about anything important. She tells me how she feels, what she needs, what she thinks, but she never has time to listen to me. She's so caught up in her own problems, I'd be surprised if she notices whether I'm happy or sad."

Spencer's hand stole across the table and touched mine again. His fingers were soft, tender. The look in his eyes warmed my whole body.

Scared of the sudden intimacy, I pulled my hand away and frowned at my Quarter Pounder. "I'm sorry, but I just can't eat this."

Spencer swept the little cup pieces into the palm of his hand. Dumping them into my empty coffee cup, he said, "I don't want mine either. Let's get out of here."

By the time we got to Mayfaire Court, it was raining hard. On the third floor, my windows were dark. No surprise — if Mom was having a good time, she might not be home till dawn, maybe not even then.

Spencer turned sideways in his seat and leaned against the

driver's door. Stretching one arm along the back of the seat toward me, he smiled. Accidentally or deliberately, his fingers touched my hair. He was so close, too close, he filled the whole car. I heard him breathing. I smelled the woodsy scent of his shampoo again and the damp wool of his jacket.

To keep from suffocating, I reached for the car door.

"Wait." Spencer leaned toward me. "Don't go yet."

Rain drummed on the car's roof. It sluiced down the windshield, it made watery patterns on my lap and hands. I felt like I was in a submarine sinking to the bottom of the sea.

"If I promise to act like a normal person, will you go to Baltimore with me tomorrow?" he asked. "No crazy talk, I promise. I'll take you to the Science Center. Have you ever been there?"

Talking too fast for me to interrupt, he rushed on. "There's a planetarium, an IMAX movie, and all these things you can do — games, mazes, experiments. It's like being a little kid on an educational TV show. Mr. Wizard or something."

Without giving me a chance to say yes or no, Spencer reached into his pocket and pulled out a small spiral notebook. "What's your phone number?"

Trying to keep my voice steady, I watched him write it down.

"I'll call you tomorrow morning." Before I realized what he was doing, Spencer moved closer. His lips brushed mine as lightly as a butterfly's wings. "Thanks for putting up with me," he whispered.

When I started to pull away, he kissed me again. "For tomorrow — promise you won't change your mind?"

"Tomorrow." I stared into his cat's eyes. Something glowed in their shadowy depths — something that made my knees weak, heated my face, jolted my heart. I fumbled for the door handle, jumped out of the car, and ran to the safety of the apartment building.

Taking the stairs two at a time, I stopped on the landing and looked down at the BMW. Spencer flashed the headlights and backed out. By the time I got to the living room window, he was gone.

In my bedroom, I searched my closet for a scrapbook I'd made in eighth grade. Spencer's name was scribbled all over the cover. Inside were maps he'd drawn of imaginary kingdoms and notes he'd written in runes, things I'd saved for years but hadn't looked at for a long time. Turning the pages slowly, I studied them for clues.

Coming to a clipping from the *Adelphia Flier,* I read the caption under a grainy photograph: "Spencer Adams crosses the finish line, breaking his own record and snaring the county cross-country title for the second year."

The photographer had caught Spencer with his head back, his eyes shut, his teeth clenched. Wet with perspiration, his dark hair clung to his skull. The tendons in his neck stood out like ropes under his skin. He looked as if he were in terrible pain.

Staring at the picture, I ran Spencer's words back and forth through my mind, trying to understand what he'd said, how he felt, but it was no use. To me, he had everything I'd always wanted — mother, father, brother, sister: a real family. I'd seen them together at the mall, at the lake, at the park. Once, I'd actually followed them, hiding behind trees, devouring them, longing to be with them.

So his parents pushed and shoved and expected him to

perform. That meant they cared about him, they loved him, they wanted him to do well and be happy. Spencer didn't know how lucky he was.

Closing the scrapbook, shutting the Prince of Jocks inside, I undressed and got into bed. Lying alone in the dark, I wondered what a kiss meant to a boy like Spencer. A lot less than it meant to a girl like me.

~ Chapter Five ~

WHEN I WOKE UP, I lay still for a moment, hovering on the edge of a dream. Did I really have a date with Spencer Adams today? Impossible. Talking about poetry in the library, riding in the BMW, stopping at McDonald's — it couldn't have happened the way I remembered it.

But it had, I knew it had. Last night Spencer Adams let me see the lonely person hiding in the depths of his eyes. He'd apologized for hurting me, he'd held my hand, he'd asked me to be his friend — he'd kissed me. I touched my mouth cautiously so as not to disturb any evidence that might still linger on my lips.

Gradually, the real world took shape and form around me. I was lying in bed, wearing red long johns, staring at the gray light slanting through my venetian blinds. Across the room, Mikhail Baryshnikov smiled at me from a poster I'd found in a library trash can. The white silk blouse hung on the back of my desk chair, my jeans lay on the the floor.

Sunday, it was Sunday morning. I smelled coffee brewing, I heard Mom laugh. An unfamiliar voice rumbled a response — a masculine voice.

Oh, God, who had Mom dragged home? Burrowing under the covers, I decided to stay in bed until he left. I wasn't in the mood to make polite conversation with a stranger. Not this morning — I wanted to think about Spencer. I had plans to make, conversations to invent, witty lines to rehearse.

But this was not to be. In a few minutes, my door opened, and Mom tiptoed across my room. Even with my eyes shut, I felt her looking at me. "Lally?" She shook my shoulder. "Lally, are you awake? Are you alive?"

I opened one eye. "Who's in the kitchen?"

Flopping down on the bed beside me, Mom said, "Somebody I want you to meet — Paul Duvall, the guy Joanna introduced me to. For once she was right. He's the nicest man I've ever met."

I groaned inwardly. Every guy was the nicest man Mom had ever met — until he left her crying by a silent telephone. Aloud I said, "Did he spend the night?"

"Of course not, Lally. I just met him."

I studied her face for signs she was lying, but Mom was smiling at me, her eyes as wide and candid as a child's. She looked so vulnerable perched on the edge of my mattress, watching me, waiting for me to smile, to be happy.

When I didn't say anything, Mom laughed. "You won't believe this, but we were talking about breakfast last night. When I told him we usually have bagels and coffee, he offered to come over and fix us oatmeal the old-fashioned way. He's making bran muffins too."

"You've met a health-food freak?"

Mom clapped a hand over her mouth. "Thank God you reminded me. Don't say a word about meat, okay? He's a vegetarian. I told him we are, too."

"What about the hot dogs in the refrigerator?"

"I got up early and hid all the incriminating evidence. Including my cigarettes. I don't smoke, okay? I gave it up years ago. My lungs are as pink as a newborn baby's."

Bending close, Mom nuzzled my face and kissed me. "Take your shower and put on something nice. Breakfast will be ready in twenty minutes."

In the shower, I let hot water pour on me till my skin turned pink. *Oh, please let Paul be nice,* I prayed. *Don't let him hurt her, don't let her fall in love too fast* — my mother, myself.

When I was dressed, I walked down the hall to the kitchen. Like it or not, I couldn't avoid meeting Paul, unless I was willing to climb out my bedroom window and drop three floors to the ground. To please Mom, I'd smile and be polite and hope he'd stick around long enough to learn my name — *Lauren,* not Laura, not Lori, not Laurel.

They were sitting at the table reading the Sunday paper. Paul had the sports section, and Mom was poring over the latest reports of accidents, murders, rapes, and armed robberies. She hoped to protect herself by avoiding intersections where killer dump trucks ran red lights and killed the occupants of small cars, city streets where people were shot because other drivers didn't like their choice of music, parks where women were murdered or raped or both. According to Mom, it was a dangerous world and you needed all the information you could get just to stay alive.

When he saw me, Paul jumped to his feet and stuck out his hand. He was a tall bear of a man with a beard and a deep voice and a rumbly laugh, a big improvement over Mom's last boyfriend, who parted his hair just above his ear in a futile effort to hide his bald spot.

"Glad to meet you, Lauren," he said, earning immediate points for getting my name right. "You're just as pretty as your mother."

I blushed and glanced at Mom, but she was gazing at Paul with the sort of adoration you see in old photographs of girls watching the Beatles. It looked like romance with a capital *R,* and I braced myself. If things followed the usual pattern, she'd be out with him every night, and I'd be living on a diet of frozen pizza.

Telling me to sit down, Paul dished up bowls of oatmeal and set them in front of us. Next, he produced bran muffins, jam, glasses of orange juice, cups of coffee. When his back was turned, Mom whispered, "Isn't he wonderful? Don't you just love him?"

While we ate, Paul entertained us with stories about his job. He was a librarian at the county detention center, and he soon had us laughing at his experiences with the inmates.

"And then this guy wants to know why he can't get the *Anarchist's Cookbook* through interlibrary loan," Paul was saying when the phone rang.

"I'll get it." Jumping up from the table so fast I knocked my chair over, I ran to my room and picked up the extension. *Let it be him, let it be him, let it be him.*

Spencer's voice sounded unfamiliar in my ear, strange, unsure. "Do you still want to go to the Science Center?"

I nodded, then remembered he couldn't see me. "Yes," I said, "if you do — still, I mean."

"Did you think I'd change my mind overnight?" The voice sounded more like Spencer's. "I'll be right over."

When I told Mom I was going to the Science Center with a guy from my English class, Paul said, "That's a great place. Before my ex-wife moved to St. Louis, I used to take my kids there."

The conversation faltered on the word "ex-wife," and Mom said, "When will you be back, Lally?"

"I don't know, probably around six." Grabbing my jacket, I started toward the door. If Mom hadn't been so interested in Paul, she would have asked who this mysterious guy was. She'd never actually met Spencer, but I'd talked about him so much, I knew she'd remember his name. And how much I'd cried over him.

"He'll be here any minute," I said. "I'll wait downstairs for him." Then, remembering Mom's departure the night before, and her comment about Joanna, I added, "I'm sure he wouldn't want to climb three flights of steps."

I loaded the remark about the steps with sarcasm, but Mom didn't notice. "Have fun, sweetie" was all she said.

Spencer drove up in a big station wagon, the kind you see everywhere in Adelphia — usually full of kids wielding hockey sticks like death weapons and driven by mothers who look like they wish they'd stayed on the pill.

"Pardon the locker-room smell," Spencer said. "Mom carpools my brother's soccer team. God knows when they take showers or change their sweat socks."

I was so happy to see him I didn't care what we rode in — a dump truck, a tank, a cement mixer. Anything that had Spencer in the driver's seat and me beside him was fine.

Turning his head to back out of the parking place, Spencer said, "I was planning to knock on your door like a civilized person. I thought your mother might want to see who was whisking her daughter off to Baltimore."

"She trusts my judgment." Suddenly uncomfortable, I fumbled with my seat belt. It hadn't occurred to me that Spencer would want to meet Mom. Wasn't that awfully old-fashioned? I was sure Casey never introduced her boy-friends to her mother. And besides, how would I have explained Paul?

"Well, maybe next time." Spencer smiled at me and drove out of Mayfaire Court. He hit the speed bumps halfway up the hill so hard my head grazed the ceiling.

By the time we left Adelphia, we were talking like old friends — telling each other about movies, laughing at things we remembered from middle school, arguing about music, discovering we both liked Hitchcock thrillers but hated horror films.

In other words, we stuck to safe subjects — no confessions, no apologies. Today, Spencer was the boy I saw at school, laughing at jokes, smiling at the girl beside him, tilting his head and widening his eyes at just the right moment to give her the full impact of his charm.

Now I was the girl. Caught off balance by the glow in those disturbing eyes, I forgot the Spencer I'd glimpsed last night. Who could believe the Prince of Jocks had ever been lonely or sad?

Heading north on the Interstate, Spencer drove the station wagon like a racing car, moving swiftly from lane to lane, passing trucks, changing gears, accelerating to seventy, seventy-five, eighty. He held the wheel in a relaxed grip, his long fingers curled loosely. His foot moved rhythmically from gas pedal to brake and back. Sometimes his eyes met mine in the rearview mirror, sometimes his hand brushed my leg when he shifted.

An old song was playing on the radio, one I remembered from middle school. The singer's voice was husky, sensual, full of longing and desire. I knew the words by heart — in ninth grade I'd worn out my tape playing the song again and again, crying over Spencer.

Fearing he'd guess the music's significance, I glanced at him, but his attention was concentrated on the truck he was passing. Could I really trust him? What if he was just playing a game? I didn't know the rules, I had no protection. The song said it all — I didn't want to fall in love, I didn't want to be hurt.

Unaware of my thoughts, Spencer started talking about the Science Center. While he described some of his favorite exhibits, I stared at his profile. Except for a tiny bump at the bridge, his nose was straight. His cheekbones were high and prominent, his jaw strong, his lower lip full and soft. His hair drifted over his eyes and almost hid the small silver ring he wore in one ear.

Shifting the subject to the IMAX movie, he said, "The screen is five stories high, so the picture is huge. It fills up your whole field of vision, you can't see anything else. When you watch it, you feel like you're falling into it. Your heart speeds up, you can hardly breathe."

My heart was already racing, and I was having trouble breathing. Sitting close to him in a dark theater, I'd probably die of coronary arrest.

When Spencer left the Interstate, he took the curving exit ramp so fast I closed my eyes, sure we were about to fly over the concrete barrier. To slow the car, he downshifted and braked hard. The rear wheels slid for a moment and the brakes squealed.

Getting the car under control, Spencer said, "Sorry, Lauren. I forgot the wagon doesn't handle curves like the BMW."

We parked in a neighborhood of narrow houses leaning together like old folks propping each other up. Cats watched us from marble steps. Pigeons strutted on the brick sidewalk, and seagulls coasted over the rooftops.

When we reached Conway Street, Spencer pointed to the harbor. "Race you to the Science Center, Lauren."

Off he went in a long, steady cross-country lope with me behind him. In no time, he was half a block ahead, running backward, laughing at me. The wind blew his hair into his eyes and he flipped it aside with a toss of his head. "Come on, slowpoke!"

Dodging tourists and babies in strollers, we dashed across Light Street. At the water's edge, the wind whipped our faces and filled our nostrils with the fresh salt smell of the Chesapeake Bay, gray green under the cloudy sky.

Still ahead, Spencer reached the Science Center first. Pretending to trip, he let me run past him. "You win," he shouted. "You win."

Inside, he led me from room to room, floor to floor, pushing buttons, pulling levers, looking through peepholes. We saw the planetarium show, we watched the IMAX movie, we bought holographic key rings in the gift shop.

Outside again, we strolled along the edge of the harbor. Crying like hungry cats, hundreds of sea gulls circled and wheeled over the bay. Others, as still as decoys, perched on pilings, light poles, and boat masts.

Tipping his head to watch one gull soar past, Spencer said, "They make it look so easy. Just spread your arms and off you go."

Like a little kid, Spencer ran after the gull, flapping his arms and laughing. I watched him jump into the air and land with a thud on the edge of the harbor. He teetered and I closed my eyes, scared he'd fall into the bay.

"Come on, Lauren," Spencer shouted. "It's your turn to try."

Three old women in down coats were sitting on a bench

watching. Perplexed, puzzled, disapproving, they chattered to one another without taking their eyes off us.

"Let's give them a thrill." Spencer put his arms around me and kissed me. His nose was as cold as a puppy's, but his lips were warm and soft.

Forgetting the women on the bench, I clung to Spencer for a moment and let myself enjoy the feel of his mouth on mine. Long before I was ready to let him go, a gull dipped over our heads and startled us with a loud squawk.

Full of jittery energy, Spencer danced away on the balls of his feet as lightly as Baryshnikov. "All of a sudden, I'm starving. How about going inside for a hamburger?"

I was hungry, too — so hungry my bones felt hollow, my body weightless. Chasing Spencer through the crowd, I lifted my feet effortlessly. For a moment, I thought I really could fly.

"Look," I called, "look!"

Spencer watched me run toward him. When I caught up with him, he hugged me again. "Keep trying," he whispered. "We'll go to Never-Never Land someday. Just you and me, Lauren."

~ Chapter Six ~

IN THE LIGHT STREET PAVILION, Spencer and I found a table overlooking the harbor. Too hungry to talk, we devoured our hamburgers.

When I reached for my coffee, Spencer grabbed my hand. "Can I ask you a question?"

"Sure." Leaving my hand in his, I stared at him. He was so handsome I had to force myself not to gaze into his eyes like a lovesick teenager.

Head tilted, Spencer watched me, his face serious. "I've been thinking about something you said last night."

With my free hand, I picked up my coffee and took a sip. We'd said so much — what was he going to ask me?

"You were talking about your mother, but you never mentioned your father. Not once. I was just wondering what happened to him."

Pulling my hand away, I dumped three or four packs of sugar into my coffee. "When I was five years old, my wonderful dad met this woman in Kmart. It was Valentine's Day, of all things, and he was buying a card for Mom. At the last minute, of course. The woman was looking for a Valentine, too — for her husband."

Leaving out a lot of details, I made a long story short by saying, "They got to talking, one thing led to another, and a couple of months later they ran away together."

"Do you ever see him?"

"No. I don't even remember what he looks like. After he left, Mom burned every single picture of him."

Spencer ate a cookie and finished his coffee. Soon he was tearing the cup into pieces just as he had last night.

Thinking I'd satisfied his curiosity, I watched a couple of kids on the promenade tossing popcorn to the gulls while their father took pictures. I wondered where their mother was.

Spencer raised his head and looked at me. "How do you feel about your father? Do you miss him?"

Puzzled by his interest, I hesitated. How could I explain my tangled emotions to him? Spencer had never lived through a divorce. He didn't know what it was like to lose a parent.

"I hate him," I said. "He hurt my mother, he hurt me. Nothing was the same after he left. Nothing."

I looked at Spencer. There was something about the way he listened to me, really listened, that made me trust him with things I usually kept to myself. "I'd never tell my mother this," I said, "but sometimes I wish my father would write to me or call me, maybe even drop by for a visit. I'm seventeen — doesn't he ever wonder how I turned out, what I'm like? Has he forgotten all about me?"

To my embarrassment, my eyes filled with tears. Before I could brush them away, one fell on the table and lay on the vinyl between us. Spencer took my hand again and held it gently. His thumb caressed mine, his eyes reflected my own unhappiness.

"You can't imagine what it's like to lose your dad," I said, "to think he didn't love you enough to stick around."

Without saying anything, Spencer closed his eyes for a moment and squeezed my hand. "Maybe I know more than you realize, Lauren."

"What do you mean?"

"I'll tell you someday," he said, "but not now. We're supposed to be having fun, remember?"

His eyes scanned my face and lingered on my mouth. They promised things his lips hadn't said, they warmed my whole body, they made me forget my father.

"There," he said, "that's better. You're so pretty when you smile."

I opened my mouth to say I wasn't, but he silenced me with a kiss. "Come on, finish your coffee, and we'll go see the seals."

The seals lived in a pool beside the National Aquarium. Spencer and I found a space in the crowd and watched them swim round and round, changing direction, chasing one another, playing like kids. They swam on their stomachs, they flipped over and swam on their backs, they heaved themselves out of the water and floundered clumsily across the rocks.

"Remember our eighth-grade endangered-wildlife project?" Spencer asked. "You and I picked the seals because they were being slaughtered for their fur."

"I still have the report we wrote," I said. "We got an A-plus on it."

"When you had to tell about the hunters clubbing the baby seals, you cried in front of the whole class. I wanted to kiss you." Putting his arm around my shoulders, Spencer drew me against his side. "What would you have done if I had?"

I wanted to tell him the truth, but I was too embarrassed. Instead of admitting I would've kissed him back, I shrugged and pretended I didn't know.

A recorded message saved me from giving myself away. While it warned us not to feed the seals, not to throw anything into the water, not to climb on the railing, Spencer toyed with a long strand of my hair.

"I hate to see them swim round and round and never get anywhere," he said. "I wish there was a way to set them free. They should live their lives the way they want to."

Keeping me close, Spencer turned and studied the wide pavement separating the pool from the bay. Plastic cups, beer cans, bottles, and other bits of trash washed up and down on the waves. Oil slicked the surface of the water.

"Maybe they're better off where they are," he said slowly. "They'd never make it to the ocean. Not through that muck."

Spencer sighed and examined my earrings. The wind had tangled the tiny chains and stars, and he carefully straightened them. His fingers were deft and gentle. While he worked, I watched his face.

"You must think I'm a real basket case," he murmured. "Worrying about seals, making you freeze your butt off in the cold. What is it about you, Lauren? I usually keep stuff like this to myself."

Taking my hand, he led me away from the harbor. On the corner of Light Street and Conway, a man was selling helium-filled balloons shaped like hearts. While we waited for the light to change, I watched him hand a pink one to a little girl.

"Hold tight," her father warned. "If you're not careful, it'll get away."

She looked up at him, and he added, "You don't want to lose your heart, sweetie."

We crossed the street behind them. The balloon danced above the little girl's head, blown this way and that by the wind. She held the string with one hand and her father's hand with the other. Inside my jacket pocket, I crossed my fingers and hoped she wouldn't let go. You could lose things so fast. In seconds they were gone beyond your reach.

Spencer poked my side. "You look sad again. What do I have to do to make you smile?"

Without waiting for me to answer, he twisted his perfect features into a hideous grimace, crossed his eyes, and wiggled his ears. "Can you do that?"

The sidewalk was crowded, and a couple of people stared at us. Embarrassed, I shook my head. I didn't want to make myself ugly, not in front of Spencer.

"I bet you can." He made another face, more hideous than the one before. "Come on," he said, "try it."

When I backed away, he startled me by turning upside down and walking around me on his hands. As quarters tumbled out of his pockets, he looked at me, his face red, and stuck out his tongue. "I won't quit till you smile."

He looked so comical, I had to laugh. "Stop," I begged, "Stop."

While passersby paused to watch, Spencer did a couple of back flips, three or four handsprings, and finally came to a halt, right side up, a few inches from my nose. "Tell me I make you happy," he said.

"You make me happy."

Spotting the balloon man, Spencer said, "How about one of those? Would a big red heart make you even happier?"

50

Before I could stop him, he ran back to the corner. In a few seconds he was handing me a balloon. "Here you are, Lauren, the world on a string. It's all yours — just remember, I gave it to you."

Hand in hand, we walked along, telling each other sad balloon stories — ones that got away, ones that shrank overnight, ones that burst, ones we wanted but didn't get. The sadder the story, the more we laughed.

Right in the middle of a birthday party tragedy, Spencer stopped talking and stared at a motorcycle parked by the curb. Running a finger lightly over the frame, he read the FOR SALE sign taped to the handlebars.

"Isn't this a beauty?" he asked.

To me a motorcycle was a motorcycle was a motorcycle. One of Mom's old boyfriends owned one, and I remembered watching her ride away on the back, waving at me as the distance between us widened. I'd been scared I'd never see her again.

Bending over the bike, Spencer examined the wheels, the tires, the lights, the chain, everything he could see. "It's in good shape," he said, "and they're asking a fair price."

He ran a hand through his hair and sighed. "There's only one problem — my mother. No matter how many magazine articles I show her, no matter what I say about safety, she's dead set against motorcycles."

Head tipped, Spencer studied the bike from every angle. Forgotten, I shifted my weight from one foot to the other, trying to keep warm. The sun was almost gone and the wind cut right through my clothes.

Suddenly, he turned to me, hope lighting his face. "I've got a great idea. Suppose I kept it in your parking lot? My mother would never know I had it."

I stared at the motorcycle. Sleek, black, and slightly sinister, it said dark roads, moonlit nights, wind in your face. It said Spencer.

Seizing my shoulders, he peered into my eyes. The wind lifted his hair in dark wings, his body was wound tight with excitement. "Just think, we could take a trip this summer, we could ride all the way across America. Have you ever been to California?"

I shook my head. Missouri, I'd been as far west as Missouri to see my Aunt Joan. "I've never even seen the Grand Canyon."

"We can stop there on the way," he said. "My grandparents live in San Diego. It's beautiful, Lauren, you'd love it."

While he described the Pacific, the cliffs, the birds, the beaches, he shaped maps in the air with his hands. In the winter dusk, he was thirteen again, talking about other worlds and what it might be like to travel through space and time. I wouldn't have been surprised to hear him say the motorcycle would take us to the Forever Place where things never changed and you were happy every day.

"Say yes, Lauren, say yes. Make this the best day of my whole entire life."

"Yes," I whispered, "yes."

Spencer grinned and tipped his head back. Spreading his arms, he jumped into the air and yelled, "Whoopee!"

When he came down, he kissed me. This time he didn't just brush his lips against mine. His mouth was warm and soft, it tasted good, even his tongue was sweet.

When he finally let me go, we stared at each other. I'd never been kissed like that, never. I didn't know what to say, what to do.

Taking a step backward, Spencer widened his eyes, tipped

52

his head, looked at the sky. "Oh, no," he said. "Your balloon."

He jumped and grabbed at the string, but he was too late. My beautiful red heart was floating upward, growing smaller and smaller as it rose into the darkening sky. We watched till it shrank to a black dot.

"I'll buy you another one." Spencer was ready to turn and run back to Conway Street.

"No." I remembered the seals swimming round and round, round and round. "We set it free, we liberated it."

"Another balloon story," Spencer said, "the best one yet."

With our arms around each other's waists, we walked slowly down the sidewalk, hips bumping with every step, pausing every now and then to kiss each other. Part of me was floating free, just like the balloon, going up, up, up into the clouds. How far, I wondered, and for how long? Nobody escaped the law of gravity.

~ *Chapter Seven* ~

"I HAVE TO GO HOME," Spencer whispered in my ear, "I don't want to, but my mother will kill me if I get the station wagon back late."

We were parked at a dark end of Mayfaire Court near the dumpster. We'd been making out so long the windows were opaque with condensation, and the car had a warm, fusty smell, a combination of wool and hair and shampoo. My legs felt weak from kissing, and I wasn't sure I had the strength to open the car door, let alone climb three flights of stairs to my apartment.

"I had a wonderful time, Lauren."

"Me, too." I kissed him again. On the nose, on both cheeks, on his ears, on his forehead, and, last of all, on his lips.

"Where did you learn to kiss like that?" Spencer asked.

I drew back, embarrassed. What could I say? I hadn't learned it. It came naturally.

Spencer tipped my face up. "Did I say something wrong?"

I shook my head. I wanted to tell him I'd learned just

now, from him, but maybe it would be better to let him think I was a woman of experience. More mysterious.

He kissed me again and again. The winter wind nudged the car, shook it a little, and we slowly let each other go.

"My mother," Spencer said. "I have to get the car home." His voice was slow, husky, sexy; his eyes were shadowed, his lids heavy.

I opened the door, and the cold air slapped my face. I turned back to say goodnight again.

Spencer leaned across the seat. "I'll see you in school," he said. "Sit next to me in Walker's class."

While I watched, he backed out of the parking place, turned, and drove away. As the wagon's taillights flashed red over the speed bump, I ran upstairs to my apartment. I was thinking I'd talk to Mom — maybe I'd ask her how you knew you were in love, maybe I'd tell her about Spencer, maybe she'd explain him to me — but the first thing I noticed when I opened our apartment was the smell of dinner cooking. Not something nuking in the microwave, but real food.

"Lauren, is that you?" Mom poked her head out of the kitchen and beckoned to me.

Paul looked up and smiled when he saw me, then returned his attention to the pot on the stove. "Vegetable chili," he said. "My specialty."

"Paul's been telling me what horrible things they do to cattle before they slaughter them," Mom said. "I'm so glad we gave up meat." I knew she was reminding me that we were vegetarians, so I smiled and tried not to think about the hamburger I'd eaten. Could vegetarians smell meat on your breath? To be safe, I lingered in the kitchen doorway and watched her and Paul. Everything he said amused her, everything she said amused him.

Making an effort to be included, I said, "Poor little vegetables — how do you know potatoes don't suffer when you yank them out of their beds in the warm, dark ground and throw them into pots of boiling water?"

"Don't be silly, Lauren." Mom glanced at Paul to see if I'd offended him, but he laughed.

Making a menacing gesture with his knife, he hovered over the cutting board. "Watch out, zucchini," he said to the helpless vegetables huddled there. "Your time is up. No one gets out alive."

At the dinner table, Mom gave most of her attention to Paul, leaving me free to think about Spencer. I imagined him at home, surrounded by his family. His little brother and sister, his mother and father, the dog I'd seen in his car once. They were sitting at a big table, lit by candlelight, laughing at a funny story the little brother was telling. The dog was mooching food from the little sister.

And Spencer — what was he doing? Was he laughing like the others or was he sitting there silently, his hair hiding his eyes, poking at his food?

The imaginary scene reminded me of a puzzle in a kid's magazine: "What's wrong with this picture?" At first glance, everything seemed perfect, but then you noticed little things. The curtains didn't really match, a portrait was upside down, a bird was in the fishbowl, a fish was in the bird cage, and so on.

"Did you have fun in Baltimore?" Mom asked.

My mouth was full of corn bread, another of Paul's specialties, so all I could do was nod. The moment for telling Mom about Spencer had passed. I wanted to keep him to myself, not share him with anyone. Suppose he changed again? What if he ignored me in school?

"Oh, before I forget," Mom said. "Casey called three times while you were out."

"Did you tell her where I was?"

Mom nodded. "She asked who you were with, but all I could tell her was some boy from school."

After dinner, I left Mom and Paul in the kitchen. They said they'd wash dishes, but the radio was tuned to a golden-oldie station, and, from the sounds of it, they were dancing to "Crocodile Rock."

When Casey answered the phone, the first thing she said was, "I knew you'd like Troy."

For a moment I stared at the receiver. *Troy?* What was she talking about?

"I saw you making out with him," she went on, "so I figured he took you home. You didn't get picked up by the cops, did you? I was scared when I saw the lights. Jordan and I were still in my car, and it was like oh, my God, let's get out of here. Have you ever tried to drive and button your shirt at the same time?"

When Casey stopped talking to laugh, I said, "Troy is a total jerk."

She must not have heard me because she wanted to know where we went. "Your mother said the Science Center, what a joke. I can't imagine Troy going there, it's much too intellectual for him. What did you really do?"

"Casey, will you shut up and listen for once?" I yelled into the phone. "I didn't go anywhere with Troy. If you hadn't disappeared with Jordan, you would've seen him barfing in the bushes and me walking home."

"You walked home? Lauren, are you crazy?"

Overcoming the temptation to lie and make Casey feel guilty, I admitted I'd gotten a ride.

"With who?"

Twirling the phone cord around my finger, I wondered what to tell her. How much, how little.

"Are you still there, Lauren?" Casey asked.

"Spencer picked me up," I said casually, "just about the time the cops arrived."

"Spencer Adams?" Casey paused to inhale. When she exhaled, I could almost smell the tobacco smoke. "I should have guessed. He was staring at you the whole time he was in Mister Burger."

While I doodled Spencer's name on a piece of notebook paper, Casey said, "So you went to Baltimore with the prince himself."

Before I could stop myself I was telling her about the Science Center, the seals, the balloon. While I talked, I saw Spencer's face, his eyes, the clouds blowing across the sky, the gulls wheeling over our heads, the balloon floating free. How could I make Casey understand what it was like to be with him, to hold his hand, to kiss him?

"The way he talks, Casey, the things he says, the way he *listens* — I've never known anybody like him." It was inadequate, I couldn't put my feelings into words without sounding corny and dumb.

Casey took a long drag on her cigarette and I drew patterns of fancy *S*'s and *A*'s up and down the margins of my paper — something I hadn't done since eighth grade. I wanted to tell Casey I was in love, really in love, I wanted her to be happy for me, I wanted her to say Spencer was great, wonderful, handsome, kind, sensitive.

Instead, she launched into one of her Ann Landers routines. She didn't think it was such a good idea to get involved with Spencer. Slow down, take it easy, be careful. I knew what he was like, how he treated girls, dated them and dumped them and moved on to someone else. And then there were his grades, his hair, his general attitude.

"Do you know what Jordan calls him?"

Before I could tell Casey I didn't care what a dumb jock called Spencer, she said, "Zombie Man." They all call him that, Ted and Kevin, too. It's kind of a joke, I guess, but he's got problems, Lauren. I don't know what they are, but I wouldn't rush into any big romance."

Casey went on talking about something Jordan had told her, but I wasn't listening. One word hung in my ear — *problems*. Spencer had problems. Everyone thought so, even a person as obtuse as Jordan Grimes.

"You don't know Spencer," I said at last, "and neither does Jordan. He's not like Ted and Kevin and those other jocks. He's, he's, well, he's different . . ."

My voice trailed off. Suddenly I was tired, too tired to talk to Casey, too tired to worry about Spencer, too tired to listen to Mom and Paul in the kitchen singing "I Want to Hold Your Hand."

Casey sighed into the phone. "You still love him, you never stopped. He's treated you like dirt for almost four years and you forgive him the minute he's nice to you. God, Lauren, how naive can you get?"

Holding the receiver a foot from my ear, I glared at it. From far away, Casey was warning me — I'd be sorry, I was asking for trouble, and so on and so on and so on.

Finally I said, "Are you finished?"

"I'm telling you this for your own good!"

"Thanks, but I have to study." Slamming the receiver down, I sat on the floor and stared at my notebook. Like my eighth-grade scrapbook, it was covered with Spencer's name. Loops and flourishes linked it with mine. Lauren and Spencer, Spencer and Lauren, over and over again.

Embarrassed by my immaturity, I tore the sheet out of my notebook, crumpled it into a ball, and threw it toward the wastebasket. It fell to the floor several inches short of the target, and I watched the wad of paper slowly open with a secret rustling noise. *Spencer and Lauren,* it said, *Lauren and Spencer.*

The happiness I'd felt earlier was wearing off like anesthesia after surgery. Casey's unwanted opinions clouded my thoughts, made me doubt and worry. When I'd been with Spencer, I'd believed every look, smile, word, kiss — but suppose Casey was right and I was just naive and lonely, unused to attention from a boy like him. Maybe all he really wanted was a place to keep his motorcycle.

The phone rang and I jumped. Picking it up before Mom grabbed the one in the kitchen, I heard Spencer's voice in my ear.

"I can't talk long," he said, "but I wanted to tell you again how much fun I had today."

I heard Beethoven in the background, the same symphony Spencer had been humming in the library. I pictured him lying on his bed, his dark hair drifting across his pale face. What was his room like, I wondered. What color was his blanket?

"I had fun, too," I whispered.

"You have the sexiest voice," he said.

Even though Spencer couldn't know what I'd been thinking, I felt my neck and chest prickle with embarrassment. What was the matter with me?

"I wish I were with you right now," he added, "kissing you again."

By the time I hung up, my knees were weak. Maybe it was going to be all right. Strange as it sounded, maybe

Spencer really liked me. He'd spent a whole day with me, he'd asked me to sit next to him in English, he'd called to say goodnight.

What did Casey know about someone as complex as Spencer? She might have had more boyfriends than I'd had, more experience, but she'd never dated anybody like him. He was unique. Even if he broke my heart, it wouldn't matter. A boy like Spencer didn't dance into a person's life every day.

Opening my French book, I stared at a page of irregular verbs, but Spencer's face floated between the text and me. With my head cradled in my arms, I fell asleep at my desk thinking about love — *amour, faire l'amour* — and kiss — *baiser, embrasser.*

~Chapter Eight~

EVEN IF I'D WANTED TO TALK to Mom about Spencer,
I wouldn't have had a chance. In the morning, all she did
was rave about Paul — how nice he was, really nice, not
like that jerk Steve, not like that loser Doug. No, Paul was
different, he liked women, he respected them. On and on —
Paul, Paul, Paul. When she wasn't talking, she was singing
old Beatles songs. By the time she left for work, I was
exhausted.

With a headful of worries about seeing Spencer at school,
I left the apartment building. Casey was waiting for me as
usual at the top of the hill. The wind gave her hair a life of
its own. It lifted in tendrils, dropped, swirled around her
face. She looked like Botticelli's Venus, earthbound and fully
clothed.

"You're not mad, are you?" she asked. "About what I
said last night?"

"I don't want to talk about it." I slid into the Escort and
watched Casey go through the morning ritual of getting the
engine to turn over.

With a bad-natured sputter, the car finally started, and

Casey lit a cigarette. Faking a cough, I opened my window. "I'll probably die of lung cancer thirty years from now and it'll be all your fault."

"I knew it," Casey said. "You're pissed off."

Instead of answering, I fiddled with the radio dial till I found some music I could stand. Slumped in my seat, I watched the split levels and colonials glide past, each house a slight variation of the one next to it. Adelphia was a monotonous place, dreary and brown under the dull sky. Bare trees, bare bushes, no color anywhere. Very different from Spencer's description of California — warm and sunny, flowers all year round, red-tiled roofs climbing the mountainsides. Pelicans instead of starlings.

Casey patted my knee to get my attention. "I'm sorry, okay? I said too much, I always do. You know how I am. I say what I think."

"Didn't you hear what I just told you?" I glared at Casey. "I don't want to talk about it, I don't want to hear your opinions, I'm not going to take your advice. Like I said, you don't know Spencer. Neither does Jordan."

"And you do?" Casey exhaled a cloud of cigarette smoke. "After one date you know him?"

When I didn't respond, Casey started complaining about her mother. It was a familiar morning subject, one that required little from me but sympathetic sounds and head nods at appropriate moments.

In the school parking lot, I turned to Casey, suddenly frightened. "What if he doesn't speak to me? What if he walks right past like he used to?"

Casey pointed at the side door. Hands in his pockets, shoulders hunched against the wind, Spencer was leaning against the wall and grinning at me.

"Good luck," she called as I got out of the car.

"I thought you'd never get here." Spencer opened the door and ushered me into the crowded hall.

All around us, kids shoved and pushed, yelled and laughed. Locker doors slammed, a hat flew past my nose, a teacher shouted. Ignoring everything, Spencer leaned against my locker. His hands rested on my shoulders, his eyes searched my face and lingered on my lips till I thought I'd die if he didn't kiss me. Reading my mind, he pulled me close and covered my mouth with his.

"Hey, Spence, you'll be late for P.E."

The kiss ended abruptly. Ted and Kevin were standing a few feet away staring at us. From the expression on their faces, it was obvious they were puzzled to see Spencer with me, Mouse.

Spencer nodded at them. He kept his arms around me, and I felt his body tense. "I'll be there in a few minutes," he said.

Keven mumbled something and walked off, but Ted shoved his hands in the pockets of his jeans and rocked back and forth on his heels, light and swift as a cat. Tall and lean, he had a sharp-nosed, narrow face and blond hair. His eyes were close set, cold, unfriendly.

Of all the jocks, he was the one who scared me most. In middle school, he'd teased me mercilessly about my height, my nose, my ears, my figure. Like Vanessa, he'd ignored me in high school — I was too unimportant to notice. But now, standing a few feet away, he was looking at me as if he were seeing me for the first time. And not liking what he saw.

"How's it going, Mouse?" he asked.

"Okay." To my embarrassment, my reply came out high and squeaky.

"Her name is Lauren." Spencer's voice was knife-edged, cold enough to make me shiver. His arm tightened and pulled me closer to his side.

Ted shrugged. "You coming to P.E. or not?"

"Go on, I'll see you later." Spencer watched Ted disappear into the crowd. "Asshole," he mumbled so low I barely heard him.

Catching me looking at him, he brushed his hair aside and shrugged. "Sorry, it just slipped out. But it's true. He's got a real attitude problem."

Spencer hugged me, kissed me, held me at arm's length, gave me the full benefit of his eyes. "See you this afternoon, Lauren."

As soon as I walked into English, Spencer grinned and grabbed my hand. "Sit down next to me."

Caught off balance, I dropped into the seat with an embarrassing thud. From the other side of the room, I felt Vanessa's laser eyes bore into my back.

Spencer's leg bumped mine. "I missed you all day."

I smiled, but I was too nervous to talk. Just on the edge of hearing, Vanessa and Meg were whispering to each other. The hiss of their voices numbed my brain.

Walker ended their conversation by walking into the room and perching Indian-style on his desk. He was about thirty, handsome in an intellectual way, and I'd been half in love with him since the beginning of the year — the result, Casey claimed, of my father fixation, a handy term she'd picked up in psychology class.

As Walker called roll, I watched his face. Would he notice the new seating arrangement? I thought his eyes lingered on Spencer and me for a moment, but not with approval;

if anything, it was the opposite. Suddenly embarrassed, I bent my head and wrote the day's date at the top of a blank page in my notebook.

I planned to pay attention the way I always did, but Spencer distracted me every time he moved. His leg brushed mine, his fingers tapped his desk, he sighed. My notes turned to doodles, my thoughts drifted.

From somewhere in space, I heard Walker droning on and on about irony. At the sound of chalk skittering across the blackboard, I looked up.

"Irony of situation." Walker was repeating the words he'd scrawled. "In other words, given a certain situation, you expect one thing to happen, but the opposite occurs."

"For example, listen to this poem by Edwin Arlington Robinson." Clearing his throat, Walker began:

> Whenever Richard Cory went down town,
> We people on the pavement looked at him:
> He was a gentleman from sole to crown,
> Clean favored, and imperially slim.

As Walker read, a picture formed in my head. I saw a man with Spencer's face, a man who "glittered when he walked," a man "richer than a king," a man who had everything, the envy of all.

I didn't know the poem, but I was caught by the language, pure and clean and clear as glass. When Walker paused, I held my breath, waiting to hear the ending.

Sure of our attention, Walker closed the book and recited the last lines:

> So on we worked, and waited for the light,
> And went without the meat, and cursed the bread;

And Richard Cory, one calm summer night,
Went home and put a bullet through his head.

For a moment, no one moved. Stunned, we waited for
Walker to go on, to read the rest, to explain, but he said
nothing.

Finally, Scott Burns raised his hand. "Is that all?"

"That's it," Walker said. "The townspeople envied a man
who was miserable. They were so caught up in their own
struggle to survive, they never saw the pain beneath his
polished surface. They had no idea. Like so many of us,
they thought money and good looks and charm make people
happy."

Walker paused to make it clear he was including us among
the townspeople. Not himself, of course. "Irony of situation," he repeated.

Vanessa's hand shot up. "Why is so much poetry about
death?" Her voice was high and childish and filled with
dismay. "Why do we have to think about stuff like that?
It's morbid and depressing."

A murmur of agreement ran around the room. In response, Walker launched himself from the desk and began
to pace back and forth. The great mysteries of life were the
poet's subjects, he said. Love, sex, and death, death most
of all — the greatest mystery. We couldn't understand life
unless we understood death. Death, the great leveler.

"Who remembers the poem we read by William Cullen
Bryant?" he asked.

Meg and I raised our hands and Walker called on me.
" 'Thanatopsis,' " I said.

"And what does that mean?"

"A meditation on death," Meg said, eager to prove she
knew as much as I did.

67

"And?" Walker looked at me as if he were playing us against each other.

"It comes from Thanatos, the ancient Greek god of death, but it can also mean death wish, the urge to kill yourself."

Walker smiled. "Very good, Lauren." Scanning the rest of the class, he said, "Thanatos comes for us all. Like it or not, we have to think about dying, we have to prepare ourselves for it, we have to accept what Camus called 'the dark wind from the future.'"

Somebody in the back of the room muttered, "I die, you die, we all die," and another voice added, "Don't breathe on me, you have thanatosis." People laughed, coughed, desks squeaked.

Brent Fitzhue wanted Walker to explain the death wish. "Why would anyone want to die?" he asked. "I know people kill themselves, but I just don't get it. No matter how awful your life is, it's better than dying."

Walker adjusted his glasses and shifted his position on the desk. "Thanatos exists in subtle forms," he said. "Self-destructive behavior, for instance — taking drugs, drinking and driving, speeding, dangerous sports like sky diving or bungee jumping. To many people, the risk of dying gives their lives an edge, a thrill."

I glanced at Spencer, wondering what he was thinking, but he had his head on his desk like a little kid at nap time. I nudged his leg with mine, but he didn't move. He was so still, I thought he must be asleep.

Steering us away from death, Walker began a discussion of Robinson's language: "sole to crown," "imperially slim," "glittered when he walked" — words chosen to set Richard Cory apart from the common man, to show his apparent nobility, to make the simplicity of the last two lines all the more shocking.

Dutifully, I took notes, sure Walker would include his analysis of "Richard Cory" on an exam, but Spencer didn't move. Looking at him, I felt an aching tenderness for his white neck, his long, silky hair, his bitten fingernails, his faded jeans, his ragged running shoes. "Zombie man," Casey had called him. "The walking dead." Well, she should have seen him yesterday. He was wide awake then. And more alive than anyone I'd ever known.

~ *Chapter Nine* ~

AFTER CLASS, Spencer walked me to the mall for a cup of coffee before I went to work at the library. Sitting at a small table in the Food Court, we watched the shoppers and made up stories about them. The prim middle-aged lady eating a salad at a nearby table had just embezzled all the money from her office. She was going to spend it on clothes and a plane ticket for Hong Kong. The balding man who joined her was her lover, and the woman in sunglasses a few yards away was the private detective his wife had hired.

Suddenly changing the subject, Spencer took my hand. "What did you think about that poem?"

" 'Richard Cory'?" I shivered. "It scared me."

"You never read it before?"

When I shook my head, Spencer told me he'd come across it years ago. "Walker really played up the shock value," he said. "I hate it when a teacher does that."

"All he did was read — he didn't make up the ending."

"It was the way he recited the last verse, the way he closed the book and paused and looked at everybody — 'And Richard Cory, one calm summer night, /Went home and put a bullet through his head.' "

It was a perfect imitation of Walker's voice. I would have laughed if Spencer had been joking, but he wasn't trying to be funny.

"I'm surprised he didn't pull a toy pistol out of his pocket and pretend to shoot himself." Spencer pointed his finger at his head. "Bang! — wouldn't that have increased the drama?"

I wanted to defend Walker, but how could I explain the way I felt? The romantic things he said about poetry, the timbre of his voice when he read aloud, the haunted look in his brown eyes, his tweed jackets, his jeans, the ascot he tucked in his shirt — Spencer would think I had a crush on him.

"What I really like about poetry is its ambiguity," Spencer said. "Symbols, metaphors, images — you read a poem and think you understand it, but the next time you look at it, it's just words on paper. Then it shifts again, and you see something new, like tricks with mirrors. You never know exactly what it means. Even the poet can't tell you."

Spencer tipped his head back to drink the rest of his coffee. I started to say something, but he wasn't finished with Walker. "That pompous ass imposes his interpretation on everything we read. Or else he makes it an example of something like 'irony of situation.' "

Spencer leaned across the table. "Do you really believe Robinson wrote 'Richard Cory' just to illustrate irony? Can you imagine him sitting at his desk, pen in hand, and saying, 'Let's see, today I'll write a poem for all those English teachers who need a good example of irony'?"

Balancing his chair on two legs, Spencer frowned at me as if I'd defended Walker. "It's all crap," he said. "The man's a phony, he doesn't understand anything."

"If you don't like what Walker says, why don't you raise your hand and tell him what *you* think? I bet he'd love to get a good discussion going."

"Don't kid yourself. I'd never trust him with my own personal feelings about anything. Wearing that ascot, reading poetry like he's trying out for a part in a play, spouting clichés about love and beauty and death — the only thing he wants to hear is his own echo. That's why girls like Meg get A's. They're good parrots."

Worried he was silently including me among the parrots, I said, "That's not fair. Mr. Walker cares about us, he's interested in what we do, how we feel. I'm going to major in English because of him. I might even go to graduate school and get my M.A., maybe a Ph.D. He thinks I could do it."

Out of breath, I stumbled to a stop and looked at Spencer. I was afraid he'd laugh. I'd never told anyone, not even Casey, that I was thinking about going for a Ph.D.

Spencer tipped his chair back farther. "It sounds like Walker's got your whole life planned."

"Not really," I said, faltering, unsure, hurt by his sarcasm. "Maybe I won't like English. I could end up doing something entirely different. Archeology, philosophy, history."

When Spencer didn't say anything, I asked him what he was going to major in.

"Damned if I know." Silencing me with the expression in his eyes, he picked up our empty cups and dumped them in the trash can. "We'd better go. You'll be late for work."

Without waiting for me, he strode toward the exit. A lump as sharp as glass filled my throat — what had I said, what had I done to make him so angry?

72

In the parking lot, he walked beside me like a stranger I'd accidentally fallen into step with, his face closed, his hands jammed in the pockets of his warm-up jacket.

Suddenly, he turned to me. "What Walker said about Thanatos, the death wish — do you believe that?"

The question took me by surprise. Spencer wasn't angry after all, I could see that, but something was wrong, something was disturbing him. Feeling confused and inadequate, I said the first thing that came to mind.

"I don't like to think about dying. It scares me."

"Why?"

"Why does dying scare me?" I stared at him, perplexed by the intensity in his voice. "It just does."

"Don't you ever think of it as a release? An escape from pain?" Spencer ran his hands through his hair, smoothing it back, revealing the silver hoop in his ear. " 'All goes onward and outward, nothing collapses,/And to die is different from what anyone supposed, and luckier.' "

When I didn't react, he said, "I told you to read Whitman. The things he says can change your whole outlook, make you see life differently, electrify you."

Spencer reached for my hand and held it as we walked. "Walker said one thing today that made sense. Death is the greatest mystery. That's what makes it so fascinating."

I was glad when he changed the subject to a book he was reading about the universe. While he spoke of black holes, supernovas, pulsars, and the death of stars, we crossed Warfield Parkway. Despite the clouds, the wind was soft-edged. In the flower bed edging the sidewalk, daffodil shoots pierced the earth. The crocuses were already blooming. Soon it would be March.

Near the library entrance, Spencer said, "I'll give you a ride home when you get off work."

*   *   *

A couple of hours before closing time, Mrs. Jenkins sent me to the Children's Room to shelve. A child was banging a xylophone while his mother talked to the librarian about her older son's homework assignment. A toddler was pulling books off the shelf and throwing them on the floor. Two little girls were engaged in a loud dollhouse game. A typical evening in kiddy lit land.

Every time a person entered the room, I looked up, hoping to see Spencer. Suppose he forgot? It was a long walk home, and I'd already told Casey I didn't need a ride.

While I was organizing my third cart of picture books, I heard someone cough. On the other side of the shelf, Spencer was making faces at me. I laughed, and he pulled me around the corner. His lips tasted as fresh and cold as the winter night.

When he let me go, he told me he had a surprise for me, but he wouldn't give me a clue. "You'll see," was all he'd say.

Catching the librarian's eye, I tried to concentrate on shelving, but with Spencer so close, I dropped books, put them in the wrong places, forgot what I was doing, where I was.

It didn't help when he began showing me his favorites. Opening *Bedtime for Frances,* he turned to the page where Frances mistook a pile of clothes on her chair for a monster. "When I was little," he said, "I used to see a wolf behind my door. He was so real I could smell him."

There was also a witch under his bed, a monster in his closet, and a bear who crept upstairs at night.

"But the worst one of all lived in the tree outside my bedroom window," Spencer said. "The clown bird. It used to fly right up to the glass and look in at me. Its eyes were huge and it had big sharp claws. I could never understand why nobody but me ever saw it."

I told him about the monster who hid in our bathroom and made noises like a toilet flushing all night long. "He was covered with scales and he had a huge mouth full of long, sharp teeth." What I didn't tell him was how often I'd wet my bed because I was scared to go to the bathroom at night.

"Remember this?" Spencer held up *Owl Alone*. In a mournful voice, he read from the scene where Owl was thinking of sad things to make himself cry:

> *Chairs with broken legs. Songs that cannot be sung . . . because the words have been forgotten. . . . Books that cannot be read . . . because some of the pages have been torn out. . . . Mornings nobody saw because everybody was sleeping. . . . Mashed potatoes left on a plate. . . . Pencils that are too short to use.*

Closing the book, Spencer looked at me. "Do you think anyone could really cry a cupful of tears?"

I'd certainly been sad, I'd certainly cried, I'd soaked pillows with my tears, but a whole cupful? No, I didn't think the saddest person in the world could cry that much.

"You're right," Spencer said. "I tried once." He tapped his forehead and made a funny face. "Even when I was a little kid I was totally wacko."

Leaning across my cart of books, he kissed me. "I better let you get some work done."

When the library closed, Spencer led me to a dark corner of the parking lot to show me his surprise. "What do you think?"

The motorcycle's handlebars gleamed in the moonlight, and it cast a sharp shadow on the asphalt.

"You got it already?"

"When I want something, I don't fool around." Glancing at me, he added, "That includes you, Lauren Anderson."

Turning away, he ran his hand over the seat, caressing the vinyl as if it were skin. By the time he looked at me, I was still struggling to control my feelings. It wasn't what he'd said as much as the tone in his voice, dark and sweet and exciting.

"I called the owner last night, just before I talked to you," Spencer said, his ordinary words at variance with the expression in his eyes. Like yesterday, they roamed my face, my body, suggesting things that tightened my throat. "He was anxious to get rid of it — his new girlfriend hates motorcycles."

"But your license, your registration." Like Spencer, I was trying hard to sound casual, but I wondered if he saw the same thing in my eyes that I saw in his. A sort of hunger, a need, a warmth that made my bones melt.

"Ted's brother John taught me to ride last summer. As soon as I turned eighteen, he took me over to Glen Burnie to get my license." Spencer flipped his wallet open to show me the proof. "We're going to Motor Vehicles tomorrow to take care of the tags and registration. Don't worry, John's twenty-one — we'll be legal."

Pulling two helmets out of the saddlebag, he handed one to me. "My own mother won't recognize me with this on, not even if I pull up beside her at a traffic light."

He was right. The black helmets were designed to cover your head, even your eyes if you pulled the visor down. They were cold and hard and shiny, something an evil alien might wear in a science fiction movie.

"The guy threw this in free." Spencer held up a black leather jacket. The color emphasized the whiteness of his skin, the darkness of his hair, the contours of his cheek and jaw. "Mad Max — right?"

He looked more like Hamlet in some bizarre updated production of the play — Claudius as the head of the Pagans, Gertrude as his old lady, the whole cast roaring around the theater on motorcycles while they declaimed their lines.

Straddling the bike, Spencer patted the seat behind him. "Get your butt on here."

"Don't go too fast," I yelled, but he was already accelerating. With a sickening lurch of speed, we headed away from the library, away from Mayfaire Court, away from Adelphia. Shopping centers, gas stations, and apartments fell behind, taking neon signs and traffic lights with them. Following the twists and turns of dark, narrow roads, the motorcycle plunged through woods and streaked past moonlit fields, roared over one-lane bridges, leaned into curves, shattered the quiet night. The trees were huge, their trunks massive in the beam of the headlight. We were going fast, too fast to see, too fast to breathe.

Cresting the top of a hill, I shut my eyes. At the bottom was a long, narrow bridge over a reservoir. We shot toward it, picking up speed, and I bit my lip to keep from screaming.

Gradually, the motorcycle slowed to a stop, and I opened my eyes, surprised to find I was still alive.

Spencer cut the engine and pulled off his helmet. "Wasn't that great?"

My face was so stiff with fear I couldn't open my mouth to answer. To avoid looking at him, I fumbled with my helmet. I didn't want Spencer to know how scared I'd been, not when he was so happy. On shaky legs, I followed him to the middle of the bridge.

Waving his arm at the sky, he took in the moon and the stars, the whole night. "It was like flying, breaking out, leaving the world." He kissed me as if he were never going to stop. I couldn't breathe, couldn't move, couldn't do anything but press my mouth against his, loving him, wanting him to love me.

Spencer drew back and peered into my eyes. "I didn't scare you, did I?"

"Just a little." My heart was racing, but not from fright. Not now. Not after the way he'd kissed me.

"You'll get used to it," he said. "It's like riding a roller coaster. The first time, you're terrified — you're sure you'll die, but the second time, it's not so bad. Before you know it, you're holding your hands over your head, you're yelling, 'Faster, faster.' "

While Spencer talked, I listened, but I wasn't about to admit that I'd ridden a roller coaster exactly once in my whole life. Afterward, one of Mom's boyfriends had to pry my hands off the safety bar and help me out of my seat. Unlike Spencer, I'd never wanted to go on another one.

~ *Chapter Ten* ~

"I BETTER LEAVE WHILE I STILL CAN," Spencer murmured against my mouth. We were leaning against the dumpster in the parking lot. Beside us, the motorcycle shone in the moonlight. We were home safe, we'd survived.

"If you park the motorcycle here, how are you going to get home?"

"It's only three or four miles, an easy run." He smiled at me. "I know all the shortcuts. Besides, I like running. Not on a team — just for my own pleasure. It gives me time to think."

"About what?" I stared at him, wondering.

"You, for one thing. And the bike — the wind in my face, your arms around me, the dark road, the woods, the moon. And poetry — sometimes I think about poetry."

"Walt Whitman?"

Spencer ran his finger down my cheek, toyed with my tangled earrings, kissed me. "Whitman, Robinson, Frost. There's one poem of Frost's especially — 'Desert Places.' Do you know it?"

When I shook my head, he said, "It's about loneliness,

feeling you don't fit in anywhere, you just don't count, and then you look up and see the stars and the empty space between them."

Spencer glanced at the sky. "What's worse are the black holes in your own mind, the 'desert places' in your head."

His hands rested lightly on my shoulders. Together we looked at the stars dusting the sky, blurred by the neon glow of Route Forty.

"When I was little, I tried to imagine the universe stretching out to infinity," he said, "but it scared me to think of all that endless emptiness. Now, like the poem, it's my own head that scares me. 'My own desert places.' "

He said it quietly, but his eyes probed mine, searching for signs I understood. I did, of course I did — I'd been living in desert places all my life, lonely and scared, set apart.

But it was hard to believe Spencer knew that kind of loneliness. His old facade, the one I'd believed in for so many years, refused to fade completely. The Prince of Jocks, the golden boy, sheltered from pain by a picture-book family — how could he talk of desert places?

Suddenly, Spencer pulled me close, kissed me hard, and drove my questions right out of my head. When he let me go, he whispered, "The loneliness isn't so bad now."

Without giving me a chance to say anything, he danced backward across the parking lot, waving to me, blowing kisses, smiling. Reluctant to let him go, I watched him run up the sidewalk, appearing and disappearing in pools of light cast by street lamps. At the top of the hill, he turned and waved one last time. Then he was gone.

While I trudged upstairs, I pictured Spencer jogging along a footpath, the bare trees swaying over his head, dead leaves chasing him. What was that other Frost poem? I thought a moment, trying to remember. Yes, Spencer was one acquainted with the night. He'd outrun "the furthest city light."

Lost in thought, I was surprised to find Mom stretched out on the couch, reading a book. I'd expected her to be out with Paul or over at Joanna's. It wasn't often she was home. And rare that she waited up for me.

"Where have you been, Lauren?" Mom asked. "It's almost midnight."

"Spencer gave me a ride." I said his name without thinking. "The boy in my English class," I added when she looked puzzled, "the one I went to Baltimore with."

When I started to walk past her, Mom patted the couch. "Sit a minute, Lally. I haven't seen much of you lately."

I flopped down beside her. *Whose fault was that?* I wondered. She was the one who was never here, not me.

Giving me a hug and a kiss, she said, "Your face feels so cold." Her eyes narrowed as she took in my tangled hair. "Did you come home on the motorcycle I heard?"

When I nodded, Mom asked if Spencer lived in Mayfaire Court. "I didn't hear him drive away."

"He's keeping the motorcycle in our parking lot." Without raising my eyes, I added the explanation we'd invented. "He lives in High Meadow and his parents don't want a bike in their driveway. They think it's an eyesore."

Mom studied my face for a moment and I blushed, sure she suspected I was lying. "This isn't the same Spencer you were so crazy about in middle school, is it? The one you used to cry over?"

Pulling at a loose thread in the couch cushion, I said, "We started talking in the library a couple of days ago. He's changed, he's not like he was. He . . ."

I couldn't finish the sentence. What could I tell Mom about Spencer? How could I explain him? My own feelings were so tangled and confused. Loving him, scared of loving him. Trusting him, afraid to trust him. Understanding him, puzzled by him. He shifted and changed shape and slipped away from me, an enigma.

"He what?" Mom asked.

I shrugged and toyed with the thread. "He likes me," I said finally, "at least I think he does, he *says* he does, he *acts* like he does, but I don't know why."

Wondering if she understood, I glanced at Mom. "Casey thinks it's weird that he's going out with me. He's always dated girls like Vanessa Blake. You know the type — cheerleaders, really popular, pretty . . ."

"What does Casey know?" Mom frowned. "She's probably mad because Spencer didn't ask her out. Remember the time she went home from a dance with *your* date? Some friend."

Not only did Mom misunderstand, but she was getting off the track. I didn't want to talk about Casey. Interrupting her account of an incident I preferred to forget, I said, "Do you think I'm pretty?"

"Of course I do," she said. "You're much better-looking than Casey."

"Mom, can we please leave Casey out of this? Do you really think I'm pretty or are you just saying it because you're my mother?"

"Lally, Lally," Mom said. "Can't you just take my word for it?"

"My teeth aren't too big?"

She shook her head.

"How about my ears? Do they stick out?"

Mom stared at me. "You haven't worried about your ears since middle school." Smoothing my hair back, she added, "You didn't look like a mouse then and you don't look like one now. Those girls were jealous because you were smarter and prettier than they were."

Slumped against Mom's side, I tried to imagine Vanessa or Meg envying me. What a laugh. My mother certainly didn't remember much about middle school.

"All you need," Mom said, "is a haircut and some new clothes. A little makeup wouldn't hurt, either. Boys like girls to look good."

It wasn't the advice I was hoping for. Instantly on the defensive, I said, "What's wrong with my hair?"

Mom ran her fingers through it, lifting strands, frowning. "Your face is long and thin, and your hair drags it down, makes you look sad. It should be shorter, fluffier."

I jerked my head away, tossed my hair. "I like it the way it is."

"Well, a new outfit then," Mom said. "Something bright. A pretty pink sweater maybe. For instance, that dress I wore the night I met Paul. He just loved it, he said the color attracted his attention. The blue matched my eyes, made him notice how big they were."

It was incredible. In a few seconds, Mom had managed to change the subject to Paul.

Not caring if it was rude or not, I yawned and got to my feet. "I'm really tired, Mom."

"Try a darker lipstick, one of those deep mauves," she called after me. "Paul thinks makeup is sexy."

Alone in my room, I undressed in the dark and got into bed. Tired as I was, I couldn't fall asleep. I'd really wanted to talk to Mom, but all I'd gotten was advice on hair, clothes, and makeup. And, of course, a monologue on Paul. To Paul or not to Paul — that was the only question.

Staring at the ceiling, I pictured Spencer running silently

toward home, his head full of Whitman, Robinson, and Frost, passing fields silvered by moonlight, his shadow following him. Suddenly, I was on the motorcycle again watching tree trunks and telephone poles leap out of the darkness, feeling the narrow road twist and turn. At the bottom of the hill, I saw the bridge, the black water, the woods. I held tight and felt Spencer's body tense with pleasure as we flew over the top and roared downward faster and faster.

A tiny dry voice whispered, "Thanatos." In the back of my mind, in a desert place, Walker spoke of the death wish, self-destructive behavior, danger, risk, excitement, but I didn't want to listen to him. Pompous ass, that was what Spencer called him. Maybe he was right — what did an English teacher know about real life? Plenty of people owned motorcycles, drove too fast, took chances. It didn't mean they wanted to die.

Changing position, I curled up under the covers and thought about the feel of Spencer's lips on mine, the sound of his voice in my ear, the smell of his leather jacket.

But no matter what I did, I still heard Walker's voice repeating Thanatos, Thanatos, Thanatos. The next time Spencer and I were together, I'd make him tell me what was bothering him. It couldn't be anything too serious. Maybe it was just a bad case of senior slump. Or a role he enjoyed playing. A tragic pose, the romantic hero, Lord Byron on a motorcycle.

~ *Chapter Eleven* ~

THE NEXT DAY, Spencer skipped school to register the motorcycle. Without him to protect me, I was careful to avoid his friends. Catching a glimpse of Ted in the hall, I ducked into the girls' room. To dodge Kevin, I took a different route to a couple of my classes, and, in English, I made a point of paying attention to Walker, answering questions, and ignoring the hiss of voices behind me.

By the time I met Casey in the school parking lot, I was exhausted. The first thing she said was "Spencer cut psychology today."

"He had something more important to do," I told her. Before she could ask any more questions, I switched the subject to Jordan. Like Mom, Casey enjoyed talking about her love life, and she entertained me all the way home with an account of Jordan's clumsy attempt to seduce her in the backseat of the Escort.

When we pulled into Mayfaire Court, the first thing we saw was the motorcycle. His back to us, Spencer was polishing the chrome. The very sight of him made me feel like a girl in a love song, all silly and light-headed.

Casey grabbed my arm. "When did Spencer get that Honda?"

"Yesterday," I said. "He's keeping it here because his parents don't want it in their driveway."

It was what I'd told Mom, but Casey narrowed her eyes as if she suspected I was lying. She opened her mouth to say something, but, at the same moment, Spencer turned around, saw me, and waved.

"Thanks for the ride, Casey." Without looking back, I ran down the hill to meet him.

"Am I happy to see you." He gave me a big hug. "Take me into your nice warm apartment — it's cold out here."

For a moment, I hesitated, suddenly unsure. Mom wouldn't be home for a couple of hours. I'd be alone with Spencer.

"It's a mess," I said nervously, thinking of the breakfast dishes I'd left in the sink, the newspaper on the table, the laundry basket full of unfolded clothes sitting on the coffee table.

"I don't care what it looks like, just so it's warm." Grabbing my hand, Spencer ran toward my building, raced me upstairs, watched me fumble with my key.

Inside, things I'd ignored in the morning looked much worse — Mom's high-heeled boots in the middle of the living room floor, her paperback romance open face down beside the couch, a coat slung over a chair, a philodendron turning yellow on the windowsill, a faint, undefinable odor from the garbage can. I was sure Spencer's house never looked — or smelled — like this.

"Do you want something to eat?" What it would be I wasn't sure. Moldy cheese? A brown banana? A peanut butter sandwich, a frozen pizza? Mom never kept much in the refrigerator.

Putting his arms around me, Spencer shook his head. "I'd rather see your room."

In the gray afternoon silence, my mind raced round and round in circles. I knew Casey took boys to her room, sometimes even let them sleep over, but I'd never had that kind of relationship with a boy, never even been close to it.

Mouth-to-mouth with Spencer, I remembered a phone conversation I'd overheard last summer — Mom telling Joanna she never worried about leaving me home alone, bringing boys in, having sex, getting pregnant. "Lauren's such a brain," she'd whispered, "I don't think she knows she has a body, much less what to do with it."

Unflattering as they were, Mom's words had given me a certain grim satisfaction. At least I wasn't like her — so desperate to be loved I'd sleep with anyone who gave the slightest hint of calling back.

Spencer drew away and stared into my eyes. Waiting, I guess, for me to lead him down the hall.

"It's just a room," I said. "Boring, ordinary, there's nothing in it worth looking at."

Without listening, Spencer maneuvered me to the door. At first, he seemed content to stand on the threshold and study my posters — Mikhail Baryshnikov smiling over a stack of books, a unicorn beside a moonlit lake, views of Notre Dame, the Eiffel Tower, a castle in Spain, prints from the National Gallery of Art, some postcard-size drawings by William Blake.

When he turned his attention to my graffiti wall, I tugged his sleeve. "That's just stuff Casey and I wrote — don't read it, it's kind of personal."

Ignoring me, Spencer stared at the wall as if it were the most amazing thing he'd ever seen. Looked at with his eyes, it must have seemed pretty strange. When we were in middle

87

school, Casey and I had started writing boys' names on it. Mom didn't notice, so we added other things — words from our favorite songs, rainbows, unicorns, shooting stars, insults and put-downs, cartoons and caricatures, quotes from poetry and novels, anything that interested or amused us. By the time Mom realized what we were doing, it was too late to object. The whole wall was covered with graffiti.

Now with Spencer beside me, I held my breath and prayed he wouldn't see his name. Don't let him recognize my caricature of Vanessa, don't let him realize practically everything on the wall has something to do with him.

"My mother won't even let me stick a thumbtack in my walls," Spencer was saying. "She gets my posters framed, and then the GSF hangs them with mathematical precision. If I did something like this, she'd have a heart attack."

"The *GSF*?"

"Short for the Great Stone Face. If you ever meet him you'll see why — he looks just like the rock formation in New Hampshire, the one Hawthorne wrote about."

"Your father?"

Spencer shrugged. "Who else?"

Brushing past me, he walked to my window and looked out. For a few minutes he stood there motionless, his back to me. The eagle on his warm-up jacket gazed at me, its beak open. Outside, thick, gray clouds massed above the treetops, a crow flew past, a gust of wind shook the glass and spattered a few raindrops against it.

From the threshold, I watched Spencer slowly turn and smile at me. He paused by my desk and looked at the jumble of books. *"Leaves of Grass,"* he said. "Did you finish reading 'Song of Myself'?"

When I nodded, Spencer fell backward on my bed and closed his eyes. For a few seconds, he didn't move. Then, without getting up, he beckoned. "As Walt says, 'I am mad for you to be in contact with me.'"

Like a sleepwalker, I crossed the room and let him pull me down beside him. "When's your mother coming home?" he whispered.

"I don't know — soon probably."

His hands crept over my body, his lips moved over my face, touching my eyelids, moving against my mouth, sweet and soft. My heart thudded aginst my ribs — I was mad to be in contact with him, too — but I couldn't let it happen, not now, not so fast.

"What's the matter?" Spencer's lids drooped over his cat's eyes. One hand reached out to touch my face, my breast, the other caressed my thigh.

Forcing myself to sit up, I moved to the edge of the bed, my bed, the bed no one but me had ever slept in. To speak, I had to push my voice through a throatful of fog. "This just isn't a good idea."

Without letting Spencer touch me again, I got to my feet and ran out of the room. Sure he was angry, I braced myself for what I thought would happen next — he'd storm past me, he'd leave, he'd slam the door behind him. Why had I dared think Spencer Adams liked me? Hadn't Casey warned me?

I was already crying when Spencer turned me around to face him. "I'm sorry, Lauren," he whispered. "Don't be mad, please don't be mad."

He kissed my tears away one by one, then he kissed my lips. When he hugged me, I felt him tremble. "I was scared you were going to kick my butt out of here," he said.

"I thought *you* were mad at *me*."

"I *am* mad." Spencer twirled a finger beside his temple and made one of his hideous gargoyle faces. "'Mad call I it, for to define true madness, /What is't but to be nothing else but mad?' "

I stared at him, puzzled, and Spencer laughed. "That's poor old Polonius trying to explain Hamlet's state of mind. Didn't you study Shakespeare for your SATs?"

Kissing me again, he said, "Is it too late to change my mind about having something to eat?"

By the time Mom came running up the steps, Spencer and I were sitting on the couch watching *Sesame Street* — his idea. Bert and Ernie, Oscar and Big Bird were still his favorite TV stars, though he admitted Ernie wasn't quite the same since Jim Henson died.

Embarrassed to have been caught laughing at a kids' show, I wanted to run to the TV and switch the channel. But, before I could move, Spencer leapt up and introduced himself. He actually held out his hand, and Mom shook it. Then, his face flushed, he took the grocery bag she was carrying and set it down on the kitchen counter.

Turning off Ernie in the middle of a song, I followed Mom and Spencer to the kitchen. She was already busy filling the kettle for tea, and Spencer was setting cups on the counter.

"I always loved *Sesame Street*," Mom was saying. "Lally and I watched it every afternoon. She used to think it was a real place."

While Mom babbled, I aimed a silent message at her. *Please shut up, be quiet, stop talking,* but mental telepathy didn't work on her. Nothing did. She went right on.

"We went to Baltimore once," she told Spencer, "and Lally saw a neighborhood that looked just like Sesame Street. We parked the car and walked around for a while, but Oscar didn't pop out of the garbarge cans, Big Bird didn't come strolling around a corner. No Susan, no Gordon, no Cookie Monster, no Bert, no Ernie — what a bummer."

Mom laughed and ruffled my hair. "Sometimes I think Lally's still trying to get to Sesame Street."

Mortified, I ducked away, and Mom smiled at Spencer. "I always tell her that's what mothers are for — to embarrass their daughters." She laughed. "I'm real good at it, just ask Lauren."

Thank goodness the kettle whistled, and Mom turned away to fix our tea. While her back was turned, Spencer kissed me and whispered, "It *is* a real place. Stick with me, Lally, and I'll tell you how to get to Sesame Street."

Once we were settled at the table, Mom gave Spencer her full attention. First she asked him what his favorite subject was. When he said he didn't have one, she told him she'd loved science. Especially biology — all those neat little squiggly things you saw through the microscope — weren't they just fascinating?

Failing to get more than a smile for a response, Mom asked Spencer about the cross-country team. "Do you still run?"

"Just for myself," he said. "I dropped off the team."

"But you were county champion," Mom said. "Lauren used to cut pictures of you out of the *Flier*. We kept them on the refrigerator door. Let me tell you, you were famous around here."

Spencer glanced at me. He seemed pleased, but I was too embarrassed to look at him. Next Mom would tell him I cried over him. I didn't think I could stand that.

Instead, she asked him why he quit.

"I got tired of it," he said.

Mom stared at Spencer as if she expected him to say more,

but he was drinking his tea, his face hidden by a fall of straight dark hair. It was very quiet. The clock ticked, the rain hissed at the windows, the refrigerator's motor started up with a thump loud enough to make me jump.

My mother was the sort of person who hated silence. Ignoring the tension her questions were generating, she asked another one. "Where are you going to college?"

Without raising his eyes, Spencer said, "My mother wants me to go to Lehigh — that's where she went, her father, too. Even her grandfather."

When Mom asked him what he was going to major in, I waited to hear his answer.

Caught gnawing his thumbnail, Spencer laid his hand on the table and covered it gently with the other. "I haven't decided."

"Lehigh has an excellent engineering school," Mom said helpfully.

"That's what my father studied." Spencer didn't look at either of us. His leg jiggled up and down. It made a thumping rhythm against the table.

"Very practical," Mom said, "You'll be sure of a job when you graduate. A decent salary. With the economy what it is, you have to think of things like that, boring as they are."

Spencer shrugged. "I guess so." He sounded like someone discussing his own funeral.

Switching the conversation to herself, Mom said, "I went to a little college in Virginia — Martha Washington. But I met Lauren's dad at a party at U.VA. and got married at the end of my freshman year. What a mistake. I never did finish my degree, but I might someday, I just might."

I stared at Mom. She'd never said anything to me about going back to college.

"If I had a degree," she went on, "I wouldn't be wasting my life typing order forms, entering data, putting up with a lot of crap from stupid people. Like today — you wouldn't believe this man in our office."

While Mom launched into an account of her arch enemy's latest efforts to make her look bad, Spencer bumped my leg under the table. For a moment, his hand caressed my thigh, then darted away. Hoping Mom's drill was over, I tried to relax.

Finishing her story, Mom smiled at Spencer. "What sign are you?"

Startled out of his own thoughts, he stared at Mom. "Sign?"

"When's your birthday?"

"January twenty-sixth."

"Aquarius — I knew it." Mom smiled again, pleased with herself. "I'm a Pisces, but Lauren's a Sagittarius — very compatible with Aquarius."

Oh, Mom, please! I muttered silently.

When Spencer stood up to leave, I followed him down to the vestibule to say good-bye in private.

"Does your mother always ask so many questions?" he said. "I felt like I was on trial or something. She should go to law school, become a prosecuting attorney."

I agreed. "Too bad she missed the Spanish Inquisition."

In the harsh overhead light, Spencer looked pale and sad. Pulling me close, he leaned against the mailboxes and kissed me.

"I don't know what I'd do if you stopped talking to me," he said, "if you treated me the way I treated you. It scares me to think about losing you."

For an answer, I hugged him as hard as I could. I wanted to tell him he'd never lose me, couldn't if he tried, I loved him, loved him, loved him, but I wasn't brave enough to say all that. Instead of speaking, I looked at him and hoped he'd read my thoughts in my eyes.

In my arms, his body was tense and unyielding. His eyes were shadowed, unreadable. There was no joy in them.

"What do *I* have to do to make *you* smile?" Gathering my courage, I made a face as hideous as the one he'd showed me at the harbor. If I looked ugly enough, maybe he'd laugh.

A tiny smile lifted the corners of his mouth, but it didn't reach his eyes. "I'm sorry, Lauren. Your mom's questions — everybody asks the same ones. When you're eighteen, you're supposed to know the answers, but I don't."

His voice trailed off, and he held me so tightly I could hardly breathe. When I tried to tell him nobody knew the answers, he silenced me with kisses — hard, desperate kisses.

Suddenly, he released me, stepped back, stared at me, no happier than before. "It's after seven," he said. "I have to go home."

Without another word, he turned and ran. The wind whipped past him into the vestibule. Covering my mouth with my hand to keep from calling him back, I stood in the doorway and watched him vanish into the darkness.

~ *Chapter Twelve* ~

WHEN I LET MYSELF into the apartment, I found Mom standing in front of the refrigerator, staring into the freezer. Pulling out two Budget Gourmet dinners, she said, "Which do you want, Lally? Chicken Cacciatore or Flounder Florentine?"

"You pick. They both sound awful." I scowled at her, but she was too busy punching holes in the tops of the packages to notice. Didn't she realize she'd upset Spencer?

As usual, Mom appeared to be totally unaware of my feelings. Without looking at me, she set the timer on the microwave. "So that was Spencer," she said.

"Why did you ask him so many questions? Couldn't you see you were making him uncomfortable?"

Startled by the anger in my voice, Mom spun around to face me. "What do you mean?" She was the picture of innocence, wide-eyed, incredulous. "I was just being friendly, Lally. I wanted to know more about him. Is there anything wrong with that?"

"Mom, you embarrassed him, you made him nervous."

Watching our dinners slowly revolve in the microwave,

Mom said, "All I wanted to do was get a conversation going."

She had the pouty look of a person who didn't want to admit she'd made a mistake. I sighed and gazed at the ceiling. What was the use?

Turning her back, Mom switched on the radio. Anything was better than silence — commercials for diet soda, the weather, golden oldies. This time it was John Lennon singing "Imagine," one of her many favorites.

I knew better than to talk while she was singing, so I set the table and waited for the song to end. I had more to say.

But so did Mom. The minute the disc jockey turned the show over to the traffic reporter for news of the latest accidents, she said, "Spencer reminds me of boys I knew when I was your age, back in the seventies. You don't see many of them anymore, those lost, needy kids. Maybe they hide it better now."

Deliberately misinterpreting her, I said, "Spencer's as far from needy as you can get."

"I'm not talking about money, Lally." The microwave beeped, and Mom opened the door. Removing our dinners, she turned back to me.

"Spencer's very insecure," she said. "Don't tell me you haven't noticed his fingernails. They're bitten right down to the quick. It hurts to look at them."

The image of Spencer's fingernails broke my defenses. I remembered the way his hands crept toward mine that night in McDonald's, I saw his eyes, heard the unhappiness in his voice. Maybe I was wrong about Mom, maybe I could talk to her about him, maybe she'd help me understand him. After all, she'd had a lot more experience than I'd had. She must have learned something about men, boys. How to help them, how to make them happy.

Mom handed me the Flounder Florentine, and I carried it to the table. Sitting across from her, I glanced at the chair Spencer had occupied earlier. It made me sad to think of him sitting there looking so unhappy.

"Spencer," I said to Mom, "Spencer . . ." I didn't know how to go on, what to say next. How could I explain him? What could I tell Mom?

She leaned toward me, her eyes probing mine, waiting for me to continue. When I didn't say more, she asked, "What's bothering him?"

"I don't know," I said slowly. "He lives in a big, beautiful house. He's got a mother and father, a brother and sister. A dog." Now that I'd started, I couldn't stop talking. For once, I had Mom's full attention. She was actually listening to me, instead of trying to change the subject to Paul.

"Till this year, he was one of the most popular guys in school," I went on. "The Prince of Jocks, that's what Casey and I called him. Now it's like that was all a pose, a role he played. Casey calls him Zombie Man, but when he's out of school, when he's with me, he's funny and smart. But sad, unhappy — something's wrong, but he won't tell me what it is."

Mom took a bite of chicken, chewed, thought a while. "Living in a big house doesn't mean anything," she finally said. "People with money know how to hide things better, that's all."

I ran the back of my hand across my eyes, but Mom saw my tears and patted my arm.

"It's not drugs, is it?" she asked.

The mood of intimacy shattered and I glared at her, furious. How could she think something that awful about Spencer? "Of course it's not drugs! He doesn't even drink!"

Mom drew back as if I'd slapped her. Immediately on the

defensive, she said, "He has all the symptoms. I still remember those pamphlets you used to bring home from middle school, the ones that described the warning signs. God, I learned them by heart."

While she recited them, I stared at her in disbelief. Did she really believe someone like Spencer would mess up his body or his mind with drugs?

Then, as if she hadn't said enough already, Mom added, "I don't think it's a good idea for you and Spencer to be alone in the apartment."

"What are you trying to say?" Was she suggesting that I, the sexless bookworm, was about to metamorphose into the sort of girl who might get pregnant?

Avoiding my eyes, Mom poked at the chicken on her plate. "Well, things can happen, Lally."

"If you think I'm going to sleep with Spencer, if that's what's bothering you, you can stop worrying. I don't have any intention of following your example!"

"Don't talk to me like that!" Mom leapt to her feet. "I just don't want you to get into a situation you can't handle."

"I'm seventeen years old." Flushed with anger, I sidestepped her and headed to the sink with my dishes. "I've been taking care of myself since I was ten. Don't start playing mother now!"

She followed me, but I wouldn't look at her, wouldn't talk to her. When she took my arm, I pulled away. "Leave me alone!"

Mom slammed her plate onto the counter so hard the plastic cracked with a little pinging sound. "All right, all right. Find out for yourself, Lauren. That's the only way people learn."

Turning my back, I went to my room and slammed the door. Sex, sex, sex — was that all my mother ever thought about? She couldn't say no herself, she thought everybody was like her, but she was wrong. I could have done it this afternoon, but I hadn't. And I wasn't going to. The last thing I wanted was to repeat my mother's life — get pregnant, get married, get divorced, be a single parent. Not me — I was going to college, to graduate school, I had plans.

I sat down at my desk, opened my literature anthology, and confronted Walker's assignment — several pages of excerpts from Ralph Waldo Emerson's essays. Small print, double columns. Not the sort of reading to keep my thoughts from wandering.

Instead of making the effort the great transcendentalist required, I stared at my graffiti wall. Although he hadn't mentioned it, Spencer must have seen his name. From where I sat, it leapt out from dozens of places. In purple ink, in green, in red, the letters wriggled across the wall — *Spencer, Spencer, Spencer,* a name scrawled by a thirteen-year-old who never imagined he'd see her handiwork someday.

A quotation from an old Simon and Garfunkel song caught my eye. I remembered writing it on my wall, crying, thinking about Spencer. I was going to be a rock, I'd said, I was going to be an island. I'd protect myself with books and poetry, I'd never touch anyone, no one would touch me. I'd be safe.

It hadn't worked in the ninth grade, and it wasn't working now. With a few words, a few kisses, Spencer had destroyed the walls I'd built so carefully. He'd been in my room, he'd read my graffiti, he'd touched my books, he'd lain on my bed. His presence lingered, subtly altering everything. My possessions were no longer mine, they belonged to him, too. He'd penetrated the core of my being.

Mom's voice broke into my reverie. Without opening my

door, she yelled, "I'm going over to Joanna's for a while. We might go out for a drink or something. If Paul calls, tell him I'll be home by midnight."

Her high heels clattered away. The front door slammed behind her. She was gone — probably to repeat the entire dinner conversation to Joanna. With embellishments that would turn everything in her favor. I'd look bad, she'd look good. Joanna would listen, sympathize, take Mom's side.

It was so typical. Sure I'd be my old self tomorrow, my mother always left when things got unpleasant. Complacent little Lally — that was how she saw me. Sweet, forgiving, a good sport, not a sulker.

And sure enough, I was already telling myself to forget it. Mom was Mom. I'd never be able to count on her, I'd never be able to talk to her, never be close the way I wanted to be. She shared intimacies with her friends and lovers — not with her daughter.

Forcing myself to concentrate on "Self-Reliance," I tried to forget Mom — and Spencer, too. But while I was puzzling over Emerson, I saw my hand writing "Spencer Adams" in the margin of my notebook paper.

In despair, I slammed my book shut and put my head on my folded arms. Was this what love did to people?

~ *Chapter Thirteen* ~

I WOKE UP IN THE MORNING thinking about love, I fell asleep at night thinking about love, and during all the hours in between, I found myself thinking about love — in calculus, in French, in history, in English, especially in English. Sitting beside Spencer, feeling his leg nudge mine, I was taken over by emotions I didn't understand, couldn't control.

Overnight, I changed into the sort of girl I'd once disdained. Like my mother, I waited for the phone to ring. I measured out my life in love poems. Dark, tragic, intense love poems. My heroines were Juliet, Ophelia, Tess, Anna Karenina, women who came to sad ends. Like them, I'd be destroyed. Spencer would break my heart, he'd leave me, I knew he would, yet I couldn't stop loving him.

Hoping for clues, I watched Mom and Paul. When they were together, they devoured each other with their eyes, they touched whenever they had a chance, they gave off a powerful aura.

I watched Casey and Jordan, too. The same things happened — they looked, they touched, they glowed.

And Spencer — whenever our eyes met, a current shot back and forth between us. Our bodies were electric, "instant conductors," as Whitman said, "flames and ether . . . flesh and blood playing out lightning." We touched, we were mad to be in contact with each other.

As for the aura that envelops people in love — both Casey and Mom saw it. At first they worried. Like me, they thought Spencer would break my heart. But as the weeks passed and he showed no signs of dropping me, they both lightened up.

Mom more than Casey — she enjoyed having a boy around, especially one as handy as Spencer. He kept her old Beetle running, showed her how to work the VCR Paul gave her, hung pictures so they wouldn't fall off the wall in the middle of the night. Pretty soon, she was treating him like a kid brother, teasing him, laughing at his jokes, making sure we always had a box of his favorite cookies in the cupboard.

Casey wasn't as enthusiastic. Although she stopped calling him Zombie Man, she wasn't convinced Spencer was the right boy for me. We tried double-dating a few times, but it didn't work out very well. Jordan loved action films — car chases, shoot-outs, Arnold Schwarzenegger saying, "Hasta la vista, baby." Spencer liked moody foreign films, the kind you had to go to Washington to see. If Jordan drove, we were subjected to heavy metal, the louder the better. If Spencer drove, we listened to brooding, intense music about the end of the world.

As for conversation, the things Jordan talked about — sports, parties, cars, bands — didn't interest Spencer. Slumped beside me, he didn't even make an effort to be sociable. Staring into space, he left the talking to me.

After four or five fun-filled evenings, Casey stopped inviting Spencer and me to go places with her and Jordan. We didn't care. As long as we had each other, we didn't need anyone else.

One afternoon, Casey and I were sitting in the swings behind Mayfaire Court, rocking back and forth. Spencer was running errands for his mother, Jordan had track practice, and neither one of us was scheduled to work. It was the first time in weeks we'd had a chance to be together, just the two of us.

The March sun was warm on our backs, and it was hard to pay attention to Casey's description of a new band. Her voice blended with bird songs and the sound of traffic on Thunder Valley Road. Losing interest, I drifted off into a daydream. Spencer and I were riding west on the motorcycle, crossing mountains, rivers, and deserts. Just as we reached the Pacific, I realized Casey was telling me something important.

"I started sleeping with Jordan last week." She said it so casually I'd almost missed it.

For a moment, I was speechless. Casey had begun dating Jordan the night Spencer drove me home from Jeff's house. She wasn't a virgin, I knew that, but still — how could she make a decision like that in seven weeks? I certainly wasn't ready to sleep with Spencer.

"You're shocked, aren't you?" Casey tipped her head back and pointed her little red pumps at the sky. Her breasts strained against her T-shirt, her hair sparkled like fire. She was laughing at me, her prudish little friend.

"Just surprised," I said, but it was a lie. Casey was right, I was shocked, but I knew she'd tease me if I admitted it. "Do you love him?"

"What's that got to do with it?"

"I can't imagine sleeping with someone I didn't love."

Turning my head, I let my hair blow across my face like a curtain. If Casey saw my eyes, she'd guess I was thinking about Spencer, maybe even wondering what it was like to do it.

"Jordan's sweet," she said, "he's got a great body, he's good in bed. But you know what I think of love."

Indeed I did know — she'd told me dozens of times. She, Cassandra Louise Fulton, had no intention of falling in love. She had bigger plans, better plans. Lovers by the dozen, but no husband, no kids. Girls who thought they were in love got hurt, got trapped, ended up in rotten marriages. "Look at our mothers," she was fond of saying. "Perfect examples."

Except for the part about lovers, I'd always agreed with her. Love was a lie kept alive in songs and poems, movies and books. But that was before Spencer.

Casey aimed her swing toward mine and bumped it to get my attention. "Remember when we were in ninth grade and I asked what you'd do if you only had twenty-four hours to live?"

"I said I'd write a poem."

"And I told you I'd find some good-looking guy so I wouldn't die a virgin," Casey went on. "I'll never forget the expression on your face."

"I was only fourteen."

"So was I." Casey laughed and spun her swing, twisting the chains, whirling faster and faster till she was a blur of motion.

"You'll make yourself even dizzier than you already are," I warned her.

"Oh, Lauren, don't be such a grump. I swear, you're getting as gloomy as the prince — it must be catching."

Perceiving Casey's comment as an insult, I leapt to Spencer's defense. While I was mentioning things like his sensitivity and intelligence, Casey coasted to a stop and stared at me.

"Pardon my curiosity," she said, "but what do you do when you're together, besides ride around on that motorcycle?"

Annoyed by her tone of voice, I shrugged. "We go into D.C. and watch gloomy movies, we go to art galleries and look at gloomy paintings, we go to museums and see gloomy exhibits, we go to restaurants and eat gloomy food — "

"Okay, Lauren, okay," Casey interrupted. Grabbing the chain of my swing, she pulled me toward her. She was so close, I could count every freckle on her face. "What I meant was — are you sleeping with him?"

When I shook my head, she asked me if I planned to stay a virgin all my life.

"What do you think?" I tried to make the question sound casual, rhetorical even, but I honestly wanted her opinion. She knew me better than anyone else did. Maybe even better than I knew myself.

Casey studied my face. "You take life so seriously," she said. "What's okay for me might not be the best thing for you. And Spencer, well, he's, he's . . ."

"He's what?" I eyed her warily.

"I just wish he wasn't so intense. You'd be better off with a guy like Jordan, somebody cute and dumb and funny who'd make you laugh."

"But he *does* make me laugh," I said. "Spencer's different when we're together, Casey, honest he is." Taking a deep breath, I added, "Anyway, I love him."

Casey sighed. "I know."

We looked at each other, and Casey grinned. "Hey, why

are we making such a big deal out of sex? Be like Molly Bloom. Say 'Yes' to life, Lauren, say 'Yes.' "

I laughed. When we were in ninth grade, Casey checked *Ulysses* out of the library. A great classic, she said, something we should read to prepare ourselves for an intellectual and sophisticated adulthood. Almost immediately, we got lost in James Joyce's prose. Skipping to the end, Casey read Molly Bloom's famous soliloquy out loud. She giggled so much, I had to read it myself to make sense of it.

Casey pumped harder, her swing flew higher, she dared me to keep up with her, but my stomach started fluttering and I dragged my feet in the dirt to stop myself. I was no Molly Bloom. "Maybe" was about as positive as I could get — I could say "Maybe" to life.

A few days later, Spencer and I rode out to the reservoir. It was after six, and the sun had dropped below the trees. We leaned against the bridge railing and watched the color slowly fade from the sky and the water. The wind murmured in the woods, and, in the distance, the cars on the Interstate sounded like waves breaking on a beach.

A hawk flew past, crying once, and Spencer threw his head back. "Yahoo," he yelled, "yahoo!"

I jumped at the unexpected sound, and the startled trees sent back his echo.

"What was that for?"

Spencer's answer was to yell again. Laughing, he turned to me. "It's my 'barbaric yawp,' " he said. " 'I too am not a bit tamed, I too am untranslatable, /I sound my barbaric yawp over the roofs of the world.' "

"Whitman — right?" I knew "Song of Myself" well enough now to recognize the lines.

Spencer put his arms around me and smiled. "You do it, Lauren," he said. "Sound your barbaric yawp."

I laughed, but he was serious. "Go on," he urged. "Express yourself. Get it all out — anger, unhappiness, whatever. Your primal scream."

I didn't want to yell, I never yelled. I made a little yawp, an unimpressive sound, not the least barbaric.

"You can do better than that." Spencer stood up tall and shouted again. "Yawp like you mean it. Make it echo, let the whole world know you're here."

After three tries, Spencer put his arm around my shoulders and drew me up tall beside him. "Take a deep breath," he said, "fill your lungs. I'll count to three, and we'll yawp together. I know you can do it."

This time I yawped as barbarically as Spencer. "Again," he shouted, "again!"

We yawped till we laughed, till we were hoarse, till the trees were too tired to echo our voices. Suddenly, Spencer hugged me. "I love you, Lauren," he whispered, "I really love you."

"I love you, too."

We stared at each other. I'd never said "I love you" to anyone but my mother. The words burned like fire on my lips, and I shivered when Spencer kissed me and murmured, "I love you, I love you" against my mouth and into my ears.

"I think about you all the time," he whispered, "what it would be like to be in bed with you. I want to sleep with you so much."

Frightened by the intensity in his voice, I drew back, but he pulled me closer. His face was level with mine and so near, all I could see were his eyes, his disturbing cat's eyes. They probed mine, hungry to swallow me up.

"Why are you so afraid?" he asked. "I'd never hurt you."

Turning my head, I let the wind blow my hair between us like a veil. Groping for reasons, I said, "There's a lot to be scared of. AIDS, getting pregnant . . ." Embarrassed, I let the silence fill in the details.

Spencer brushed my hair aside, seeking my eyes. "But you can protect yourself," he said. "Condoms, the pill. You won't get AIDS from me, but pregnant — well, I can't guarantee that wouldn't happen. But if it did, if I got you pregnant, I'd marry you, I swear I would."

I didn't look at him, I didn't speak. The thought of being pregnant with Spencer's child took my breath away. I stood still and stared down at the water. Whose face did I see reflected — mine or my mother's?

Spencer toyed with my hair, untangling the knots the wind had made. I felt him watching me, waiting for me to speak, but I couldn't face him — he'd know my traitor body was melting. I wanted him, too, I couldn't help it, but I was too scared to tell him. He mustn't know, he mustn't.

"Lauren," he murmured into my hair, "Lauren." His breath tickled my ear, his body was warm against mine, his hands caressed me.

"Stop," I whispered. "Please stop."

Spencer drew back and cold air rushed in to fill the space between our bodies. The light was gone now. The wind roughened the black water, and its surface glittered with fragments of moon silver.

For a while, neither of us spoke. Finally, Spencer put one arm around my shoulders and hugged me. "I'm sorry, Lauren."

"It's not you," I said. "It's me, it's . . ." I wiped my eyes with the back of my hand.

"It's what?" Spencer lifted a tear from my cheek, held it on his finger, kissed it.

How could I tell him, what could I say? I was scared to do it — scared to let him see me without my clothes, scared I wouldn't like it, scared I *would* like it.

While Spencer waited for me to explain, I remembered what Casey had said about girls who believed in love. They grew up to be women like our mothers, sleeping with men, looking for love in strangers' beds. If I gave in to Spencer, if I said yes, where would I be a year from now, ten years from now? I saw Mom staring at a silent phone, her eyes sad and empty.

Without thinking, I said, "I don't want to be like my mother."

Spencer sighed and turned away. His hands tightened on the railing, and he stared into the black water as if it were full of secrets.

"Nobody wants to be like their parents." His voice was so low I barely heard him.

"But how can you be sure you won't be?" I asked him. "Maybe it's in your genes, maybe you can't help doing what they do."

Spencer whirled around to stare at me. His face was as white and alien as the moon's. "Don't say that," he shouted. "Don't ever say that again!"

I backed away, scared of his eyes, of his raised voice, of his anger. I'd seen Spencer unhappy, moody, but never like this. He was a stranger, a boy I didn't know.

Spencer shut his eyes, grimaced, struck his open hand with his fist. Turning to the railing, he stared down at the water again, his body rigid.

For a moment he didn't move. Didn't speak. Just clung to the railing as if it were all that stood between him and destruction. Without looking at me, he said, "I'm sorry. I didn't mean to yell. I shouldn't have."

"What's wrong?" I whispered. "What did I say?"

"Nothing, Lauren, nothing." He grabbed me, held me close, trembled. "Just love me," he murmured. "Just love me."

He kissed me, hugged me, clung to me till he stopped shivering. "Sometimes I feel like I can't hold on much longer, I feel like I'm losing my grip." He studied my face. "Do you know what I mean? It's a mood, it comes and goes, I get to the edge and stare into the pit, then I pull back, things get better, the mood passes."

He'd told me things like this before, but tonight with the moon shining on the black water, his words sounded more convincing.

Spencer must have realized he'd frightened me. "Hey," he said, "don't look at me like that. I'm fine, honest I am."

Before I knew what he was doing, Spencer was standing on his hands on the railing. Scared to speak, scared to touch him, I watched him walk hand over hand across the bridge, his feet pointed at the stars, the reservoir far below. At one point his body wavered, his legs tilted toward the water. Then he straightened, continued the rest of the way, and jumped onto the bridge as if he'd just finished a gymnastic routine.

"Perfect balance," he said. "Perfect control."

~ Chapter Fourteen ~

THE NEXT DAY something happened in English that almost made me forget Spencer's behavior on the bridge. Walker had finally graded the essays we'd written weeks ago. After taking roll, he handed them out. He'd given mine an A-plus, and written "Excellent work, very insightful" at the bottom.

I was so pleased by the comments he'd scribbled in the margins, that I didn't notice Spencer's grade. When I glanced at him, I saw he'd shoved his paper into his notebook. Avoiding my eyes, he stared out the window, his mind elsewhere.

Some of us had done very well, Walker said, but others either hadn't followed directions or had misunderstood the assignment.

"I thought we'd talk about one poem in particular," he said, "because so many of you chose to write about it."

He opened his anthology and looked around the room. His eyes lingered for a moment on Spencer, then moved on.

"This was to be an original paper," he said. "I didn't want

you to read critical opinions, only the poem itself." Clearing his throat, he took his usual perch on the desk and read "Stopping by Woods on a Snowy Evening" aloud.

When he finished, he turned to Vanessa. "Since you were one of the many who picked this poem, please tell us what you think Frost is saying."

Vanessa stole a look at Spencer before she began to speak. "Well, he's describing this man who stops in the woods to watch the snow. They aren't his woods, but he knows the owner won't see him because he lives in town. It's very cold and his horse thinks it's odd to stop there by the pond, so he shakes his bells."

She hesitated and stared at her open book. "The man would like to stay there a while, but he has things to do. 'Promises to keep.' So he leaves."

Walker peered at Vanessa and raised his eyebrows. "Do you see anything else?"

Vanessa sighed. "Why can't it just be a poem about winter? Why does it have to have some weird hidden meaning?"

As usual, several people nodded their heads in agreement with Vanessa. Ever since we'd begun studying poetry, Walker had stressed the importance of symbolism, but he'd had a hard time convincing most of our class that it had any value. Practically everyone thought Mr. Walker took sadistic pleasure in forcing us to see things that weren't there.

Walker leaned toward her. "How many times do I have to tell you? That's the beauty of poetry, Vanessa, the skill of the poet. He tells you things indirectly. He lets you figure it out. If you want to read the words without thinking, it's a nice little story. But there's more to it."

Walker turned to Meg. "How about sharing your thoughts with us? You had some good insights."

Her voice ringing with its usual superiority, Meg said Frost was writing about the conflict between duty and pleasure. "As a poet, he'd like to stay where he is and enjoy the beauty of nature. But he has responsibilities, obligations, 'promises to keep.' He can't neglect them. It would be selfish. So he goes on."

Vanessa frowned as if she felt betrayed by her friend, but Meg was too pleased with herself to notice. She actually shot a snide look in my direction as if she were daring me to top her interpretation. I ignored her. Let Meg think of me as her major rival for the role of Walker's top student. I doubted her neatly written paper had received better comments than mine.

Walker smiled at Meg. "The conflict between the artist's needs and his obligations is certainly the next level of meaning," he said. "It should be quite obvious to anyone who gives the poem more than a cursory reading."

That must have deflated Meg's ego. "Obvious" and "cursory" were not the compliments she'd probably been hoping to receive. Shifting my position, I caught her scowling at me. Not so long ago, I would have been scared of the dislike I saw in her face, but not anymore. Pink-eared Mouse was gone. I wouldn't allow myself to be Meg or Vanessa's victim again.

"But there's a third level," Walker was saying. "Deeper, darker. It has something to do with the last stanza, the way it's worded, the way the last two lines are repeated."

Getting to his feet, Walker strode back and forth across the front of the room. As he recited, images of woods, snow, and silence filled my mind. I saw the beauty, felt the cold, understood the speaker's temptation to linger far from the village . . .

"Only one of you noticed what I'm speaking of." Walker turned to Spencer. "Tell the class what you wrote," he said. "Without looking at your paper."

Something in Walker's tone of voice set off an alarm in my head, and I glanced at Spencer. His face was paler than usual, and he gripped the sides of his desk.

Without raising his head, he said, "I think Frost is trying to say something about life and death and the choices you make when you're all alone."

Walker watched him intently, fingers steepled under his chin, glasses sliding down his nose.

Still avoiding Walker's eyes, Spencer swallowed hard and went on in a low voice. "The narrator starts out in the woods, far from other people. It's dark, it's cold. There's no sound till the horse shakes its harness bells."

When Spencer hesitated, I wanted to reach out and touch him, hold his hand, reassure him.

"The sound brings the narrator back from death," Spencer said. "It reminds him he can't stay in the dark woods, he can't die yet. He has 'promises to keep,' things to do before he sleeps, before he dies."

He paused again. "If it weren't for the horse, if he hadn't heard the harness bells . . ."

Spencer's voice trailed off into doubt and uncertainty. He chewed his thumbnail and stared at his open book.

For a moment, no one spoke. The room was so quiet, I heard the P.E. teacher yelling at somebody in the gym.

Walker took off his glasses and polished one lens with his handkerchief. Carefully setting them back on his nose, he said, "Where did you get that idea?"

"What do you mean?" Spencer asked.

"What critic, what source?"

I stared at Walker. Was he suggesting Spencer had cheated,

114

that he'd taken his idea from a book the way Meg probably had? I'd seen him write that paper, word by painful word. The only book he'd used was his old copy of Frost's poetry, so dog-eared, its pages were falling out.

"No critic, no source," Spencer said. He leaned back in his chair, his arms folded across his chest, and looked Walker in the eye.

"Do you expect me to believe you came up with that interpretation all by yourself?" Walker asked. "A student who never raises his hand, who submits no homework, who has failed every examination I've given?"

Astonished, I turned to Spencer, expecting him to defend himself, but he said nothing. He simply sat there, his face expressionless.

"See me after class," Walker said. Turning away from Spencer, he ran his eyes over the rest of us. "That's the level I meant," he said.

Jenny Watson sneezed. Meg cleared her throat. The P.E. teacher yelled, "Come on, pick up those feet, move it!"

"No matter what Vanessa thinks," Walker said sarcastically, "this isn't a sweet story about a man and his little horse. Don't be deceived. Dig deep, find what the poet is really telling you. In many poems snow, cold, silence, woods, the sound of wind in trees, the call of a bird suggest death — Thanatos. Keats's 'Ode to a Nightingale,' for instance."

Gazing past Spencer's bent head, Walker struck a pose:

> Darkling I listen; and for many a time
> I have been half in love with easeful Death,
> Called him soft names in many a mused rhyme,
> To take into the air my quiet breath;
> Now more than ever seems it rich to die,

115

To cease upon the midnight with no pain,
While thou art pouring forth thy soul abroad
In such an ecstasy!

Walker turned to us. "Like Frost, Keats does not follow the nightingale into the woods. He realizes the bird would continue its song long after he had ears to hear its 'high requiem.' "

He didn't look at Spencer's lowered head. He didn't see Vanessa roll her eyes. He paid no attention to the yawns and coughs and sqeaking seats.

When no one responded to his little monologue, Walker asked Colleen O'Neil to share her opinion of "The Road Not Taken."

Furious, I scribbled a nasty comment about Walker on the corner of a piece of notebook paper and nudged Spencer. He didn't look at me or read the words I'd scrawled. Until the bell rang, he sat as still as stone and stared at his desktop.

Without waiting for me, Spencer pushed his way out of the room and elbowed through the crowded hall. Ignoring the protests of the people I bumped into, I hurried after him. Hadn't he heard Walker ask him to stay after class?

Finally, I was close enough to grab his arm. "Where are you going, Spencer?"

Frightened by the expression in his eyes, I stepped back, bumped into someone, almost dropped my books. The stranger I'd seen on the bridge was back, cold and distant.

"Didn't I tell you this would happen?" Spencer said. Without another word, he left me standing alone in the hall.

All that stopped me from running after him was Vanessa. From a few feet away, she was watching, hoping to see me make a fool of myself. Fighting tears, I forced myself to go

116

to my locker, get my jacket, and walk calmly out of the building.

When I was on the footpath, I let myself cry, but I didn't slow down. Soon I was running toward the library. With every step, I thought about Spencer. I'd encouraged him to write that paper and I'd seen him working on it at the library, filling page after page with his cramped handwriting. Although I'd been shelving books a few feet away, he hadn't let me read it. It was an experiment, a test, he said. He was sure he'd found something in the poem Walker hadn't guessed at.

"You'll think it's stupid," he said, "and so will he. Just wait — he'll cut me down. Only Walker, the priest of poetry, knows the true meaning."

When I tried to sneak a look over his shoulder, he had covered his words with his hand and waved me away.

We'd talked about the poem, but he'd never hinted at his interpretation. As I recalled our conversation, it was my voice I heard, the future English major prattling about imagery and meter, the conflict between art and duty, the responsibility of the poet.

While I'd tried to impress Spencer with my brilliance, he'd been sitting there seeing something I missed altogether — Thanatos luring the poet into the woods to lie down in the snow and forget the miles, the promises, the obligations of living. To die.

And, just as Spencer had predicted, Walker had cut him down — not because he was wrong, but because he was right.

I walked faster, my heart beat loudly, hatred surged through my veins like black bile. How could I have admired Walker? How could I have thought I loved him? Looking back to the beginning of the year, I saw myself as a child, totally naive, imagining Walker falling in love with me, taking me to Paris, kissing me beside the Seine at sunset. What a stupid girl I'd been. Looking at him with Spencer's eyes, I despised my teacher.

And myself, too — I was the one who'd said Spencer was being unfair to Walker, I was the one who'd persuaded him to write his true thoughts down and trust them to a pedant. No wonder Spencer was angry with me. Without meaning to, I'd set him up to be humiliated.

By the time I signed in at the library, I'd stopped crying, but I dreaded the long lonely hours of shelving. Spencer was usually nearby, following me down the aisles, making faces at me, kissing me, finding books, reading things to me. But this afternoon, I had no idea where he was, what he was doing.

Pushing a cart of books toward the reading room, I pictured Spencer roaring down Ten Oaks Road toward the reservoir, a solitary figure on a motorcycle. Locked in a mood as black as the jacket he wore, his face hidden by his helmet, I saw him accelerate, lean into curves, fly over hills. What did he see in the silent woods? What did he hear?

Alone in the quiet library, I wished Spencer hadn't written that paper. Like a Rorschach test, Frost's images revealed something about Spencer I wasn't sure I wanted to know.

~ *Chapter Fifteen* ~

ALTHOUGH I EXPECTED HIM, looked for him, waited for him, Spencer didn't come to the library. The only person I saw was Casey. She found me shelving mysteries.

After she'd picked a few of the most gruesome books on my cart, Casey got around to the real reason for her visit. "What's all this crap about Spencer?" she asked. "Did he really punch Walker and walk out of class?"

"Where did you hear that?"

"It's all over school. Jordan said he's been suspended, they might not even let him graduate."

Taking a deep breath, I told Casey what actually happened. "Maybe he *should* have hit Walker," I said. "Spencer wrote that paper all by himself, I saw him. He didn't cheat."

"Don't you think it's kind of a strange interpretation?" Casey asked. "Be honest — would you have seen that poem as a death wish?"

"Walker thought it was valid. Snow's a symbol of death, so's cold, stillness, woods . . ."

"But we all know Walker is totally nuts," Casey said. "Did he ever tell your class what Hamlet was really about?"

When I shook my head, Casey laughed. "Ask him about it, get him to digress. He loves talking about sex and incest and strange desires. Believe me, if Jordan saw the same thing in a poem that Walker saw, I'd be worried."

I looked at Casey, but she was leafing through another thriller. I wanted to tell her about the way Spencer had acted on the bridge, but while I was trying to find words, Casey said, "Do you know what he did in psychology yesterday?"

"Jordan?"

Casey shook her head. "Spencer — Jordan's too dumb to be weird. We were doing a unit on suicide, and Goldstein was talking about Ernest Hemingway. He said he shot himself in the head just like his father had. In fact, Hemingway even used the same gun."

Casey paused while a woman selected a book from my cart. When we were alone again, she told me Spencer asked a question without even raising his hand, just blurted it out.

"Which is strange in itself — he hasn't said one word all year. He wanted to know if Goldstein thought suicide ran in families."

Casey looked at me. "He was so intense, Lauren, like it was really important."

"What did Goldstein say?"

"If one of your parents kills himself, it definitely ups the ante. Like alcoholism or drug abuse, it puts you in a high-risk group."

Casey watched me shove a thick mystery into a skinny space on the shelf. When I didn't say anything, she told me that everybody stared at Spencer. "You know how it is, the room got real quiet. He put his head on his desk, but he wasn't asleep, I could tell, because he was jiggling his leg in that nervous way he has."

Casey grabbed my arm and forced me to face her. "After

class, Goldstein gave him a referral slip. He wants him to talk to Mr. Shaw."

"How do you know?"

She handed me a wrinkled piece of paper. "I found this in the hall."

I stared at the slip. Casey was right. Mr. Goldstein had referred Spencer to the school psychologist.

"If he won't see Shaw," Casey said, "you better make him talk to you. Something's really wrong, Lauren, and it's not getting better."

The tears I'd been fighting filled my eyes. "His parents put so much pressure on him, they're always on his back," I said. "He doesn't know what he's going to do when he graduates, he gets in these moods."

Turning away to hide my face, I felt Casey's hand pat my arm gently. "I don't even know where he is," I sobbed. "He walked out on me after class. He was so upset, Casey. Walker was horrible, awful, I can't believe what he said, how he treated Spencer."

Like a mother, Casey led me to the women's room and made me wash my face and blow my nose. When she thought I was calm enough to face my cart of books, she walked back to the mystery section with me.

While I shelved, she entertained me with wry cracks about a movie she'd seen with Jordan. "The producers must have spent a fortune on cars," she said. "I tried to keep track of how many went up in flames, but after ten I lost count."

I knew she was trying to take my mind off Spencer, but I was glad when she squeezed my arm and said, "Here comes Jordan. Smile, look happy. You don't want him to think there's anything wrong."

Jordan slung an arm around Casey and kissed her before

turning to me with a question. "So where's Spence? Is he coming back to school or what?"

Casey hissed something at Jordan, a warning to shut up, I guessed, and he popped the gum he was chewing. "I just wondered," he said.

"You have the subtlety of a polar bear," Casey said, but she kissed him so affectionately Jordan didn't know whether he'd been insulted or complimented.

"Let's go, Case." Jordan nuzzled her cheek and winked at me. "It's past my bedtime."

I watched them leave — Casey a swirl of red hair, Jordan caressing her rear end. Nothing seemed to bother either one of them. They floated on the surface, never worrying how deep the water was, how dark, how dangerous.

When the library closed, Spencer wasn't waiting for me. I hung around for fifteen minutes and finally walked home, running most of the way because the dark places between the street lights scared me.

In Mayfaire Court, the space beside the dumpster was empty. The motorcycle was gone. For a moment, I listened for the sound of its engine, but all I heard was the traffic on Thunder Valley Road.

I trudged upstairs and let myself in. No lights, no sound but the wind tugging at the weather stripping around the windows. A note on the refrigerator door told me what I'd already guessed:

> *Hi, sweetie — Ice cream in fridge for you and Spencer — I'm at Paul's, be home LATE!!!*
> *Love, Mom.*

Alone in my room, I stared at the phone and willed it to ring. It didn't. Desperate to know where Spencer was, I called his house, but I hung up when Mrs. Adams answered.

Her voice was so cool, so calm, I couldn't imagine asking her if I could speak to her son.

In the morning, the motorcycle was parked beside the dumpster. During the night, Spencer had come and gone without trying to see me.

Casey drove me to school, but Spencer wasn't waiting for me. I didn't see him at my locker, I didn't see him in the hall, I didn't see him at lunch. His desk was empty in Walker's class.

After school, Vanessa stopped me in the hall. "Where's Spence?"

"I don't know." Too upset to face her, I stared at the floor.

"Walker is a total jerk," Vanessa said. "What he did yesterday, the way he treated Spence. Doesn't he care how he makes people feel?"

I looked at her, and her face reddened. "I'm just worried about him, we all are. You don't own him, Mouse."

Before I could say anything, Vanessa saw Kevin. Without looking at me, they walked away together.

Casey was at work and I didn't have to go to the library, so I jogged home, sure Spencer would be there. I pictured him working on the motorcycle, sitting on the steps reading, kicking a soccer ball with the kids who lived in my court — things I'd seen him do before.

From the top of the hill, I saw the station wagon parked in the motorcycle's place by the dumpster. While I'd been in school, Spencer had come and gone again.

Ignoring the boys, I walked right through their soccer game. If the ball had hit me on the head, I don't think I would have noticed. My mind was miles away, roaming the back roads, searching for Spencer. Worrying about him. Picturing trees and telephone poles, curves and hills, oncoming dump trucks and loose gravel. A boy with a face like a mask — pale, tense, leaning into the wind, going fast, faster, too fast.

Scared by my own thoughts, I waited on the steps in front of my building. Even if Spencer didn't want to see me, he had to get the station wagon. From where I sat, I read the faded bumper sticker: PROUD PARENTS OF AN HONOR STUDENT AT STEVENS FOREST HIGH. It looked like someone had tried to rip it off. Spencer probably. It was the sort of thing he'd do.

Minutes passed, maybe an hour. Every time I heard an engine, I looked up the hill, expecting to see Spencer. When I'd almost given up hope, he crested the hill, his face hidden by his helmet, and steered past the soccer players. I watched him brake to a stop between the dumpster and the station wagon. He took off his helmet, and the boys gathered around him.

Without looking at me, Spencer sat on the bike and joked with them as if it were an ordinary afternoon. Tony tried to blow the horn, Robert perched on the passenger's seat, Daniel grabbed the helmet and did his Darth Vader routine.

Finally, Spencer noticed me. When I was a couple of feet away, I stopped, unsure of what to say, what to do. Turning to the boys, Spencer told them to scram. Robert whistled at me, and Spencer gave him a friendly shove. Laughing, he ran after his friends. In a few seconds, the game was on again.

"Where have you been?" Jamming my fists into my pockets, I tried not to cry.

"No place special." Spencer took an oilcan out of the saddlebag and squatted down to squirt the motorcycle chain.

"I was worried about you."

He looked up. The wind scalped his hair back, and his face seemed suddenly defenseless. "I'm sorry, Lauren," he said. "I just didn't want to be around anybody for a while."

"What Walker said wasn't fair." I knelt on the asphalt beside him. I wanted him to put his arms around me, to kiss me, but I was afraid to touch him. He was made of glass. He'd break.

"I saw you write that paper," I said. "You didn't get your idea from any critic. Walker owes you an apology."

Busy with the oilcan, Spencer shrugged. "I don't give a damn about that S.O.B. or his stupid class."

"Don't say that," I said. "You heard what he said, you were the only one in class who saw what Frost was really saying."

"The only one *weird* enough," Spencer muttered. "The only one *disturbed* enough."

"No," I whispered, "Like Walker said, poetry's almost always about death."

"Lauren, just drop it, will you? I don't want to talk about it. I wish I'd never handed the paper in. It was a dumb thing to do, trusting that asshole." Spencer glared at me as if it were all my fault.

The ball flew past our heads, bounced against the dumpster, and rolled to our feet. Spencer kicked it back to the boys and turned to me. "I have to go home," he said. "I promised Mom I'd take my brother to soccer practice."

"Will you be in school tomorrow?" My voice was high-pitched, tight, mousey. *Don't whine,* I thought, *don't let him see he's hurting you.*

Spencer sighed and looked at the sky. The April wind blew a long low line of clouds over our heads. "I wish I could drop out," he said, "never go back there, never see the place again. Ted, Kevin, Vanessa — everybody watching me, wondering what the hell's wrong with me. Jesus, I wish *I* knew."

"There's nothing wrong with you, Spencer."

"You don't know me, Lauren, you don't have a clue." His eyes were as cold and hard as stones. He'd hidden himself so well, I didn't know what he was feeling. Anger, sorrow, fear — maybe all three.

Spencer turned his head and hunched his shoulders against the wind. "I knew I'd let you down, I warned you, didn't I? I disappoint everybody — ask my parents, ask my ex-girl friends, ask Ted, ask Kevin."

I didn't know what to say, what to do. Without looking at me, he went on talking. His voice rose. "I try to be what you want me to be, Lauren, I try to be what everybody wants me to be, but it never works. I'm just no good. You'd be better off without me, everybody would."

"Don't say that, Spencer, please don't. I love you," I sobbed. "I love you."

Pulling me close, Spencer kissed me over and over again. His teeth bumped mine, hurt my lips, his hands felt as if they were made of iron.

Suddenly, he released me, stepped back, stared at me. I thought he was going to ask me to go to bed. My heart pounded, my knees went weak. Mom wasn't home, wouldn't be home for hours. There was nothing to stop us. I waited, knowing I wouldn't say no. I couldn't. He needed me.

For a moment, his eyes widened, opened up, but, almost immediately, a curtain dropped. Glancing at his watch, he said, "Jesus, I'm late. I'll be in deep shit if Jeremy misses practice."

Before I could stop him, he was in the station wagon,

126

revving the engine. He backed out so fast, the boys scattered, shouting, raising their fists. A blast of the horn, a wave, and Spencer was roaring uphill, bouncing over the speed bump, disappearing.

I went to the motorcycle, touched the seat, the handlebars. The sun was low, the air was soft, but the wind was edged with cold. Behind me, the boys shouted, cursed, kicked the ball, ran after it, hurling their bodies at one another. Their voices were sharp and hungry, like the cries of circling gulls. They echoed from the walls and rose to the sky.

Totally depressed, I trudged up the steps to our apartment. No Spencer, no Mom. Just a reminder on the refrigerator door that she was meeting Paul for dinner again.

~Chapter Sixteen~

THE NEXT DAY, Spencer was waiting for me in the school parking lot. He'd called late the night before, long after I'd cried myself to sleep. He was sorry, he hadn't meant to rush off, hadn't wanted to, but the GSF was mad at him. All week he'd been on his back about his irresponsibility, immaturity, unreliability. Track, grades, his general attitude — in his opinion, Spencer was worthless, no good, ungrateful, lazy.

By the time he hung up, things were all right again. He wasn't mad at me, I wasn't mad at him. We loved each other. But I hadn't slept well, I'd dreamed about Spencer falling from the bridge, and I'd woken up worried and uneasy, staring into the dark, too tense to sleep.

Now Casey was squeezing my arm to stop me from running to meet Spencer. "He looks terrible, Lauren."

She was right. Spencer was paler than usual. His hair was shaggy, uncombed, his clothes wrinkled.

"See if you can get him to talk to Shaw," she said.

Pulling away from Casey, I ran to Spencer. Before I could say a word, he began apologizing all over again.

"It's okay," I told him, "it's okay, I understand."

For a moment, his eyes sought mine. "I'm such a moody S.O.B., I don't know why you put up with me." He was forcing humor into his voice, and his smile made the muscles in my face ache in sympathy.

Tipping his head back, he watched a long line of birds zigzag across the sky. "How do they do that? It's like they have the same brain, it tells them when to dip, when to soar."

"Spencer," I said, but he wasn't listening. Talking too fast for me to interrupt, he leapt from one subject to another haphazardly. First it was something he'd read in the morning paper, then it was the weather, then it was the motorcycle, then it was a song he'd heard on the radio. It was like listening to an actor trying to feel his way into a role. How should he say his lines, what should he reveal, what should he conceal?

I wanted to ask him about yesterday and the day before, but he left no openings. The script was written for one voice. His.

At the side door, Spencer hesitated and grabbed my hand. Holding it tightly, he led me inside. Ted and Kevin were standing by their lockers. When he saw them, Spencer tightened his grip on my hand. For a moment, he was the Prince of Jocks again, light on his feet, full of smiles and jokes. "Hey," he said with exaggerated goodwill, "how's it going?"

His old buddies looked at him. Their eyes lingered on his long hair before sliding to me, the girl who didn't belong. Mouse.

Ted was the first to speak. "I thought you'd been suspended."

"You heard wrong." Spencer drew me so close, I felt his heart beating.

The three of them stood in the hall, blocking the flow of students. People stepped around them, some paused to stare, others ignored them. No one spoke, no one moved. We might as well have been stones in a swiftly flowing river.

Finally, Ted mumbled something about a teacher he had to see. Taking Kevin with him, he edged into the crowd.

As soon as they were gone, the energy escaped from Spencer's body like air rushing out of a balloon. "Let's get out of here," he said. "I'm not in the mood for school."

We left the building just as the bell was ringing. Sure we'd be seen, I looked over my shoulder, but the school's windowless walls protected us. No one called us back. No one saw.

I climbed into the station wagon beside Spencer, and he started kissing me with a desperate urgency that scared me and excited me at the same time.

"Let's go to my house," he whispered.

"Won't your mother be home?"

He shook his head. "She teaches history at the community college. Nobody will be there."

His eyes lingered on my lips, drifted downward to take in my breasts, rose again to meet my eyes. The look in them made my heart beat faster. There were things to talk about, things I needed to know — the poem, Walker, Goldstein's class, Shaw — but they seemed unimportant now. *Later,* I thought, *we'll talk later.*

Turning the key, Spencer roared out of the parking lot. As the tires squealed, I grabbed the strap over the door and hung on. Taking side roads through the farmland between Adelphia and High Meadow Estates, Spencer pulled into his driveway ten or fifteen minutes later.

"Are you sure your mother won't mind?" I stared across

an expanse of landscaped lawn at his house. Built of pinkish brick, it reminded me of pictures I'd seen of English country manors, very symmetrical, very large, very imposing. It spoke of custom design, of money, of security — the perfect home for a perfect family.

Spencer took my hand and pressed my fingers to his lips. "Why should she care? She won't even know we've been here."

I followed him up a curving brick sidewalk bordered with carefully tended boxwood and waited for him to unlock the front door. The entrance foyer was two stories high and illuminated by a skylight. Ahead was a flight of polished wood steps leading to the second floor. To my left was the living room, to my right the family room.

Thoroughly intimidated, I tiptoed down the hall behind Spencer, afraid to raise my voice above a whisper.

The kitchen was bigger than our whole apartment. Its tiled floor shone, the cupboards were solid wood, the countertops were free of clutter, the sink, clean and empty.

"It's like a magazine," I said. "*House Beautiful* or *Southern Living,* the kind my mother daydreams over."

Spencer glanced at me. "Mom's a perfectionist. She can't stand dirt or disorder. Everything has to be just right. Including me."

Pointing through the sliding glass doors, he said, "See Zack? He's not allowed inside anymore. Not since he developed a bladder problem and peed on the rug."

An old golden retriever got up slowly and looked through the door, his tail wagging. Spencer let him in, hugged him, fussed over him. "How's my best old buddy?" he whispered and laughed when Zack licked his nose.

With Zack padding behind us, Spencer led me upstairs.

I followed him uneasily, breathing silent air, empty air. Despite its beauty, the house had a deadening effect on me. It was all surface, a one-dimensional reflection in a mirror with nothing but a blank wall behind it.

"Get ready," Spencer said, "you're about to enter the black hole where the teenage son lives."

It was definitely Spencer's room. His clothes hung on the backs of chairs, his shoes were scattered on the floor. The bed was unmade, the computer surrounded by heaps of paper and discs. Shelves overflowed with books and sport trophies.

In contrast to the room's disorder, neatly framed posters and prints covered the walls. Three by Escher — a hand drawing itself, monks simultaneously descending and ascending an impossible staircase, geese turning into geometric patterns and back. They were flanked by two fantasy figures — a woman with an armadillo in her lap and a woman with an owl on her wrist. Opposite them, I saw "The Scream" by Munch, Van Gogh's "Starry Night," a map of Earthsea, a portrait of Walt Whitman.

"The GSF hung those for me," Spencer said. "He didn't approve of most of them, but he made sure they were perfectly symmetrical."

"What does your father do?" I was thinking of Casey's and my guesses about the houses in High Meadow Estates. I was sure Mr. Adams wasn't a drug dealer, but I was willing to believe he wouldn't be above harming the earth to pay for a house like this.

"My father?" Spencer drew himself up like an actor and laid one hand on his heart. "Alas, my father does nothing. He keeps company with worms, my lady."

I laughed again, but I didn't understand what he meant.

Like many of Spencer's remarks, his joke was a little strange. "Don't be silly," I said, "he must do something."

Spencer turned away. "He's a corporate lawyer," he mumbled. "Very boring job, but he makes big bucks."

"I thought he was an engineer. Didn't you tell Mom he went to Lehigh?"

Biting his thumbnail, Spencer frowned. "Did I say that?"

"I thought you did." Puzzled by Spencer's nervousness, I tried to remember what he'd said. "No," I corrected myself. "Your mother met your father at Lehigh, that's what you told her."

"Right," Spencer agreed. "The GSF couldn't earn enough as an engineer to keep us in the baronial splendor which surrounds you."

I looked at him, but he was flipping through a pile of compact discs. Uncomfortable with the atmosphere my questions had created, I studied the trophies crowded together on the bottom shelf of his bookcase. Swimming, soccer, track — they were all engraved with Spencer's name. Most of them were Firsts.

When he saw me pick one up, Spencer took the trophy out of my hand and dropped it in his wastebasket. "A souvenir," he said, "of the days when I still thought I could please my parents, be the perfect boy. Now I leave that to Jeremy."

He kicked at the other trophies and they toppled over, rolled across the floor, came to a stop in corners and under the bed.

"The hell with them." Spencer flopped down on his bed and looked at me. "Come here," he said softly. "Sit down next to me. No, better yet, lie down next to me."

I hesitated, my head still full of questions. I wanted to

know why he'd stopped trying to please his parents, I wanted to know why he was so bitter, but it wasn't the right time. Not when he was lying there smiling at me, his eyes soft, his mouth tender.

When Spencer reached up and seized my hand, I let him pull me down beside him, let him silence my questions with kisses. From far away, I heard a branch tap against a window, heard the wind nudge the house, heard Zack scratching fleas, but the noise of Spencer's heart was the loudest sound of all. It thumped against mine, echoed in my ears, drowned out everything else.

I don't know how long we'd been lying there before I became aware of other sounds. A car engine, a slamming door, footsteps downstairs, voices. Spencer heard them too. Sitting up, he stared at his watch.

"Oh, God," he said, "I forgot — it's Wednesday. Jeremy and Brooke didn't have school today, teachers' conferences or something. Mom was taking them to the dentist this morning."

Leaping to his feet, Spencer tucked his shirt in, smoothed his hair, handed me a comb. While I yanked the tangles out of my hair, he put a CD in his player and motioned me toward a chair. Sitting down, I tried to look relaxed while Spencer went into the hall and leaned over the railing.

"Mom?" he called. "Is that you?"

Behind him, classical music welled out of the speakers. Mozart, one of the piano concertos. Like most of his music, it was happy on the surface, but sad underneath. It warned you to enjoy life while you could, because tragedy was just ahead. Poverty, disease, death, maybe burial in a pauper's grave.

Spencer was doing his best to sound natural, but his

mother wasn't fooled. Like me, she heard something arti-
ficial in his voice.

"What's going on?" She was coming upstairs. I heard her
high heels click on the polished wood. "Why aren't you in
school?"

Pausing in the doorway, Mrs. Adams stared at Spencer
and me. Although I'd seen her at a distance, I'd never noticed
how much she and Spencer resembled each other. The same
pale skin, the same straight dark hair, the same cat's eyes.

Uncertain what to say or do, I got to my feet and tried
to smile as Spencer introduced me. Acknowledging me with
a nod, Mrs. Adams turned back to Spencer.

"You cut school, didn't you?"

Evading her eyes, he shrugged like a little kid caught
doing something wrong. For a moment, I thought Mrs.
Adams was going to hit him. She seemed angry enough.
Instead, she seized his shoulder to make him face her.

"You know perfectly well I don't want you bringing girls
home when I'm not here," she said. "I thought I made that
perfectly clear the last time this happened."

Feeling my face flood with embarrassment, I stared at the
floor and tried not to think of the other girls Spencer had
brought to his room. Foolish me to imagine I was the first.

"We were just listening to music." Spencer's voice was
as cold as hers. He was a stranger again, the boy I'd glimpsed
on the bridge, not the boy who laughed and told funny
stories.

Ignoring him, Mrs. Adams looked at me again. Under
her scrutiny, I wanted to check my buttons, but I knew if
I as much as touched the front of my shirt I'd confirm her
suspicions. Praying I'd done them up straight, not skipped
any, I glanced at Spencer. I'd never been in a situation like

135

this, but I got no help from him. Avoiding my eyes, he leaned against the doorway, head lowered, hair hiding his face.

Mrs. Adams turned her gaze back to Spencer. "In the future, listen to music downstairs," she said, adding, "when I'm here. We'll talk about school after your father gets home."

"That'll be the day," Spencer mumbled.

Something in his voice made Mrs. Adams go white with anger. Without another word, she left the room. Since she obviously expected us to follow her, I started toward the door, but Spencer stopped me. "I'm sorry," he whispered.

Kissing my tears away, he apologized again. "All I do is screw things up."

"Spencer," his mother called. "I want you and that girl down here now! Bring Zack too — you know he's supposed to be outside."

Muttering a word he rarely used, Spencer pushed a button and cut the concerto off. In its place, strange, eerie music filled the room, not Mozart, but something else, something full of despair. With a quick twist, Spencer turned up the volume. The bass shook the walls and windows, the organ reverberated, the violins wailed.

With funereal chords booming in my ears, I followed Spencer and Zack downstairs. Something was going on here, something unspoken between Spencer and his mother — something that had nothing to do with me, but everything to do with the scary music welling out of Spencer's room.

136

~ Chapter Seventeen ~

AT THE BOTTOM OF THE STEPS, I saw Brooke and Jeremy staring at us from the family room. His eyes on Spencer, Jeremy drew a finger across his throat.

"You're dead," he whispered.

Towing me into the family room, Spencer introduced me to his brother and sister. "Wait here, Lauren," he said. "I have to talk to my mother."

With Zack behind him, Spencer left the room. I heard Mrs. Adams say something about the music. Jeremy must have heard it, too, because he jumped to his feet and ran upstairs. In a moment, the dirge was silenced, and Jeremy was back.

Ignoring me, he returned to the Nintendo game he'd been playing. Despite the difference in his coloring, I recognized Spencer in the shape of his face, in his long fingers, in the texture of his hair.

"I never saw you before," Brooke said to me. "Do you live in High Meadow?"

There was nothing of Spencer in Brooke except her eyes.

But even they weren't the same. Unlike his, they had no shadows. Brooke was a child without secrets.

When I told her I lived near the ice skating rink, she smiled. "I go there for figure-skating club."

Leaping to her feet, Brooke jumped around the room, trying to demonstrate things like axels and camels.

Finally out of breath, she collapsed beside me. "I've won three blue ribbons in competitions," she said. "Mom might take me to Philadelphia for the regionals this summer. Want to see my skates? They're custom-made."

"Brooke," Jeremy said. "Stop showing off."

Making a face at her brother, Brooke turned to me. "I'm doing a solo in the ice show next month. If you come, you can see my costume. It's beautiful."

While Brooke described her outfit, I listened to the voices from the kitchen. There was a very low one, full of anger, and a louder one, also full of anger. Between Brooke's chatter and the beeps from Jeremy's Nintendo, I couldn't hear a word either Mrs. Adams or Spencer said. Which was probably just as well.

Jeremy looked at me once and shook his head. "They fight all the time," he said. "Me and Brooke are used to it."

Brooke sighed. "When Daddy comes home, it'll be worse." Jumping to her feet again, she smiled at me. "Want to go to my room? I'll show you my Barbies."

Before I could follow her, Spencer appeared in the doorway and slung my jacket at me. "Come on, Lauren."

"Oh, can't she stay a little while longer?" Brooke asked. "I want her to play Barbies with me like Vanessa used to."

Ignoring his sister, Spencer opened the front door. "Do you want a ride or not?" He stared at me, his face cold, unfriendly.

Without looking back, I ran outside. By the time I caught up with him, Spencer was already in the station wagon, revving the engine. I jumped in and slammed the door as the car rolled backward toward Woodbine Lane.

Spinning tires, Spencer accelerated. The road was curvy and narrow. The posted limit was thirty, he was going forty-five, fifty. Hypnotized, I watched the needle climb.

"What's the matter?" I was trying not to cry, but losing the battle. Things were wrong again, his good mood was gone. It was his mother's fault, she'd spoiled everything. Hating Mrs. Adams, I grabbed the strap over the door and hung on.

Staring ahead, his face grim, Spencer whipped around a corner, slinging me against his side and then bouncing me back to the door. He drove as if we were being pursued.

As the car slid around a corner, I realized we weren't going toward Mayfaire Court. We were on Ten Oaks Road, heading for the reservoir. It was one thing to ride downhill on the back of the motorcycle. I was used to it, knew what to expect, but the station wagon was heavy, cumbersome, the back wheels fishtailed. Pushing imaginary brakes, I clung to the strap and willed Spencer to slow down, to stop, to look at me.

Spencer must have read my mind, because he lifted his foot from the gas pedal, let the car coast across the bridge, and pulled onto the shoulder where we often parked the motorcycle. Staring straight ahead, he said, "We have to talk, Lauren."

My first thought was, he's going to end it, he's going to tell me he can't see me anymore. I gripped my hands in my lap, bit my lip till it hurt, braced myself for a pain so intense I didn't think I'd survive it.

Spencer looked at me. Tears filled his eyes, spilled over, rolled down his cheeks, but he didn't bother to wipe them away. I don't think he even noticed them.

"Suppose I told you my whole life is a lie, a fake, that nothing about me is real, not even my name?"

"What do you mean?" My voice shook.

Without answering, Spencer opened the car door and got out. I followed him to the middle of the bridge and stood as close to him as I dared. Flushed with pale pinks, reds, and greeny golds, the trees rimming the reservoir duplicated themselves in the still water, creating an upside-down forest. Except for birds singing in the woods, it was very quiet.

"Remember the day we talked about 'Thanatopsis'?" Spencer was gazing across the water, his shoulders hunched against the breeze. His profile was sharp against the blue sky.

I nodded, but I couldn't see what Bryant's poem had to do with Spencer not being who I thought he was. He was confusing me, changing subjects too fast for me to connect them.

"The death wish, the urge to destroy yourself," Spencer said. "Richard Cory putting a bullet through his head one calm summer night. I told you I thought about it, but you weren't really listening to what I was saying. Well, you better listen now."

Without looking at me, Spencer bent down, picked up a stone, and dropped it into the reservoir. Its splash disturbed the water's surface. The reflection quivered, broke apart into bits and pieces of trees and sky, then quietly re-formed.

He glanced at me. The wind lifted his hair, and his earring glittered in the sunlight. "It can happen that fast."

Unable to follow his thoughts, I stared down into the water as if the answer were there. "What can happen?"

140

"Jumping," he said. "Throwing yourself in. Dying."

"Do you mean suicide?" The word was cold in my mouth, it froze my lips, made them stiff and clumsy. I held the rail so tightly, my fingers ached.

"Don't you ever wish you were dead?"

"Everybody does sometimes," I said slowly. "You have a bad day, you're really depressed, but then things get better. They always do, so you go on."

"But suppose things don't get better? Suppose you never have a nice day, a day when you're happy, a day when you feel good. Suppose day after day, week after week, it's just the same old thing." Spencer looked at me. "Would you go on then? Or would you start planning ways to end it?"

There was an intensity in his voice that scared me. I was afraid to look at him, to move, to speak.

"I could jump off this bridge right now," he said. "It would happen so fast, you couldn't stop me, I couldn't stop me, not even if I changed my mind in mid-air."

Leaning over the railing, Spencer stared into the water as if he were watching himself sink. Down, down, down to the bottom with the weeds and the old tires and the tree stumps rising up to meet him.

I grabbed his arm, pulled him back, but he paid no attention to me.

"One minute you're alive," he said, "the next minute you're dead. Where do you go? What happens to you? How can you disappear just like that?"

Spencer snapped his fingers in my face. "Dead forever, forever dead. Isn't it weird? You can't live forever, but you can be dead forever."

I put my arms around him, holding him as tight as I could. "You wouldn't do anything like that, Spencer, you wouldn't."

"How do you know? How do I know? How does anybody know what they might do next year, ten years from now, twenty?"

"You just wouldn't." I felt stupid, inarticulate, helpless.

"You have no idea, Lauren," Spencer said. "It's always on my mind. It flashes through my head when I'm driving — *Cross the yellow line, hit that dump truck, crash into that tree. Do it, get it over with.*" He struck his fist against his palm. "Gone, finished, kaput. No more hurt, no more pain."

"Don't, Spencer, don't say any more. You're scaring me." Pressing my face against his shirt, I began to weep. "If you died, I'd die too, I couldn't live without you."

His arms tightened around me. "It's not like I want to die — I just can't stop thinking about it, worrying about it, wondering about it. What's it like? Does it hurt? Is there anything afterward?"

Far below, the water lapped against the bridge pilings, whispering its secrets. From the woods, a mockingbird called.

"Keep me safe, Lauren," Spencer whispered. "Don't let anything bad happen. Tell me everything's going to be okay, tell me I'm not nuts, I'm not going to kill myself. Tell me you love me, oh, God, please tell me you love me."

The pain in his voice cut into me like a dull-edged knife. "I love you, Spencer, I love you," I whispered. "You're okay, I know you are, nothing bad will happen."

He clung to me and wept like a child, and I was scared, so scared. Scared of letting him down, scared I couldn't handle this, too scared even to cry.

"Tell me what's wrong," I begged. "Talk to me, Spencer, please, talk to me. What happened to make you feel like this? What did they do to you?"

Without speaking, he took my hand and led me across

the bridge to a trail we'd climbed before. It led steeply uphill, through the trees. Our feet slipped on loose stones, we stumbled on roots. Ahead of us, almost close enough to touch, three deer bounded across the path and vanished into the woods.

Nothing was real to me at that moment except Spencer's hand. Without it, I was sure the world would turn to dust and ashes and I would be alone.

~ Chapter Eighteen ~

AT THE TOP OF THE HILL, Spencer pulled me down beside him on a sunny ledge of rock. For a few minutes we sat quietly, side by side, breathing hard after the climb. The trees on the other side of the reservoir were misty with new leaves. They looked close enough to touch. I knew how they'd feel — soft and warm, like a cat's furry side.

After a while, Spencer put his arm around my shoulders and drew me close. "I didn't mean to scare you, Lauren, but it's true. Nobody knows himself or anyone else. We all have secrets."

He paused a moment to clear his throat. "Like that poem, 'Richard Cory,' " he went on. "The people in town, the ones who envied him, they didn't see past his glitter, his mask. They didn't know how scared and lonely and unhappy he was."

Turning away, Spencer rested his head on his raised knees and hid his face with his arms. In hope of drawing him back to me, I touched his shoulder, kissed the exposed nape of his neck, so white and vulnerable, but he didn't look at me. His voice muffled, he was still talking about "Richard

Cory." Although the poem's significance was lost on me, I knew it was important to Spencer. He was using it to explain something about himself.

"They never dreamed Richard Cory would kill himself," Spencer was saying, "but he might have been thinking about it for years, hiding it from everyone. His secret, his way out. Maybe he just got tired of worrying about it. One day he sat down in a chair and put a bullet through his head. *Bang* — peace and quiet forever. Nothing to be worried about, nothing to be scared of, no mask to put on every morning."

Frightened again by his intensity, I stared at Spencer. *What chair,* I wanted to ask, I didn't remember a chair in the poem. What was he trying to tell me? It was like receiving a crucial message in a code I couldn't break.

Suddenly Spencer raised his head. His cat's eyes probed mine. "If I tell you a secret, can I trust you not to tell anyone else? Not your mother? Not Casey?"

I nodded, but it wasn't enough. He gripped my shoulders, his face so close, all I could see were his eyes. "Promise," he said, "promise you'll never say a word about this."

"I promise I won't tell, Spencer, I swear to God."

"Nobody knows," he said. "Nobody. My own mother won't even admit it happened the way I remember it."

He shook his head. "But I can't forget it and neither can she. It's always there. It's in her eyes when she looks at me. Every little thing is a sign, something to worry about. *Am I like him,* she's thinking, *will I do it too?*"

Who was he talking about? What did his mother think he'd do? I wanted to ask, but I was afraid to interrupt. If I said the wrong thing, he might clam up, get mad, yell at me, walk away. It was better to sit still and listen.

"I've tried so hard to make Mom believe I'm okay," Spencer was saying. "All those trophies, they were for her. The running, the good grades, everything. Even my friends. Just so she wouldn't worry. But it didn't work, nothing I did was good enough. She's never stopped expecting the worst. Checking to make sure I'm not drinking, smelling my breath after a party, looking for drugs."

Hugging his knees to his chest, he gazed past me, past the rocks and the trees. In the sky, high above the earth, three buzzards drifted lazily on air currents, their wings translucent in the afternoon light. Round and round they circled as if they were tethered to one place by an invisible cord.

"She's always pushing, pushing, pushing — run, get good grades, pick the right friends, the right college, the right career." He glanced at me. "Do you know what that's like?"

I shook my head. Mom never pushed me to do anything. "It's up to you, Lally," she always said when I asked her for advice. "If you want to major in English, fine. Just remember I can't afford to pay your tuition." Good grades, bad grades — she didn't care what I did in school. She'd hated it herself, didn't see any reason to take it seriously. It was all a scam, she said. You could get straight A's and still end up working at Stockman Electronics.

"This year I said the hell with it," Spencer muttered. "Nothing pleased Mom or the GSF anyway. I quit track, quit studying. Dumb games, that's all it is. Kid stuff. Like it really matters what you do in high school. Or afterward."

He picked up a stone, hurled it into space, watched it arc against the blue sky and disappear soundlessly. Reaching for my hand, he said, "Do you really want to hear this?"

When I nodded, he swallowed hard. "I don't know what

you'll think, how you'll feel. You might walk out on me, I wouldn't blame you if you did."

A tear ran down his cheek and he wiped it away with the palm of his hand.

"I love you," I whispered. "There's nothing you could say or do that would make me stop."

Huddled close to Spencer, I felt him draw a deep breath. He seemed to shrink, small and tight, compact, as hard as marble. And just as cold. I shut my eyes for a moment and prayed I'd say the right thing, do the right thing. No matter what he told me, I mustn't let him down. I had to help him, protect him, love him. Our whole future depended on what he said and what I did.

"First of all," Spencer said, "the GSF is my stepfather. Does that surprise you?"

I stared at him, but without giving me a chance to say anything, he rushed on. "He adopted me after he married my mother. Reluctantly, I think, but that's another story. Mom acts like he's my real father, but I was seven years old on that momentous day. Does she actually believe I've forgotten?"

The image I'd once cherished shifted and changed into a new pattern as fragile as pieces of glass in a kaleidoscope. The perfect family had never existed. Mrs. Adams divorced, remarried — no wonder Spencer understood me so well, no wonder he was unhappy, moody. He'd been deserted, too. Like me, he had a father out in the world somewhere, a stranger who didn't care about him.

"I learned to write *Adams* on my school papers," Spencer was saying. "I learned to tell people my last name was Adams, I learned to pretend the GSF was my father. I lied to please my mother."

In a voice laced with sarcasm, he added, "God forbid

there should be any scandal. Mom couldn't bear it if our neighbors knew what my father did."

"I don't understand," I said, "Lots of people divorce and remarry. It's nothing to be ashamed of."

The expression on Spencer's face warned me to stop talking. "Believe it or not, Lauren, there are worse things than running away with a woman you met in Kmart. Much worse."

The sarcasm in his voice made me wince. I glanced at him, but he was watching the buzzards. "Jesus," he muttered, "I've never told anybody this."

While Spencer searched the sky for words, I tried to imagine what awful thing his father had done. Maybe he'd committed a crime. Embezzled money, gone to jail, left the country.

"My father killed himself," Spencer said. "One ordinary winter afternoon, he sat down in a chair and put a bullet through his head."

For a moment, the words made no sense. Was Spencer talking about Richard Cory again? He couldn't have told me his father committed suicide. I must have misunderstood.

Spencer stared at me, his eyes gauged my reaction. Maybe he misinterpreted my silence, maybe he thought I was disappointed in him. His face closed like a fist.

"That's the kind of person you've gotten mixed up with," he said bitterly. "The son of a suicide. My genetic makeup, my heredity. Not what you expected, is it? Spencer Adams, superachiever — what bullshit."

Silently, I put my arms around him and held him tight. What he'd experienced was so awful, I had no words for it. His father killed himself. Put a bullet through his head. It was too horrible to think about.

"Oh, Spencer, Spencer." I whispered his name over and over again. If only his life had been as I'd once imagined it. Golden and sunny and happy. "I'm so sorry."

His body was rigid, unresponsive. It was like hugging a dead man. "Children of suicides often kill themselves," he said. "I learned that in psychology. Alcoholism — same thing. If your father's a drunk, you'll probably be one, too. That's why my mother watches me, waits, holds her breath. It's like I'm doomed, Lauren. To be like him, to do what he did. I'm his son."

Spencer began to sob — awful, ragged, gulping sobs from deep down in his gut. I held him tighter. Over his head, the blue sky, the clouds, the buzzards dissolved in tears.

A long silent time passed before Spencer spoke again. "Can I tell you about it, Lauren?"

While I clung to his hand, he let the words tumble out. A torrent of memories, some good, most bad. Typical family stuff — vacations, trips to the zoo, picnics, the kind of things I vaguely remembered from the days before Daddy left. His father playing games with him, reading to him, building block towers and knocking them down.

But something went wrong, Spencer didn't know what. His father started drinking, he lost his job. Pretty soon he stayed home and drank all day. His mother cried, his father yelled, they fought constantly.

"I'd come downstairs in the morning," Spencer said, "and Daddy would be sitting at the kitchen counter, a bottle of gin beside him, staring out the window. I never knew what he'd say, what he'd do. Maybe he'd kiss me. Maybe he'd shout at me. I was scared of him."

He stopped talking for a moment. Something in the way he hunched his shoulders told me he was coming to the worst part, and I found myself praying his father had gone somewhere far away to shoot himself. Don't let Spencer tell me he saw him do it. Please God, don't let him say that.

"One day when I was in first grade," Spencer said slowly, "the school furnace broke and they sent us home before lunch. Mom was teaching at the high school then, and I was supposed to walk to my sitter's, but she wasn't there, she didn't know school closed early. So I went down the street to my house. I knew Daddy was home, his car was in the driveway, but he didn't answer when I called him."

While I listened, I pictured Spencer tiptoeing from room to room in a house I'd never seen. A little boy with dark hair. Six years old. Frightened of the silence, knowing something was wrong.

His father wasn't in the kitchen, he wasn't in the bathroom, he wasn't asleep on the living room couch. Spencer went to the top of the basement stairs, he looked down, he heard faint music coming from the family room. Slowly, slowly, one step at a time, he crept to the bottom.

I knew what he was going to find. I wanted to cover my ears with my hands, I wanted to jump up and run away. Instead, I sat very still, scarcely breathing, and listened.

"Daddy was sitting in a chair," Spencer said. "The stereo was on, but the record was scratched. The same notes were playing over and over. I moved the needle, and the music went on."

He looked at me. "The CD I played before we left my room. That's what he was listening to when he pulled the trigger. Albinoni's 'Adagio.' "

I remembered the scary music swelling out of the speakers, so loud it seemed to shake the walls. Why did Spencer own that disc? What made him buy it? Play it?

"There must have been blood." Spencer sounded so detached, he might have been describing a movie he'd seen.

150

"But I don't remember it. I don't remember what Daddy looked like, either. The gun was on the floor beside him, I saw that, but I just left everything the way it was and went upstairs to my room. By the time Mom came home, I'd built a big wall of blocks around myself. A fort like Daddy used to make for me."

He was silent for a moment. When I whispered his name, he went on talking. His mother had been angry at him, she'd scolded him, he wasn't supposed to be alone with his father.

"Where is he?" she'd asked. When Spencer didn't answer, she searched the house. She heard the Albinoni. She went down the basement steps.

"I stood at the top," Spencer said, "and waited to see what would happen next." He leaned forward as if he were still waiting, and stared into space. His eyes unfocused, he was in another time, another place, a house he'd lived in long ago, listening to his mother scream.

After that, everything was a jumble in his memory. Police, rescue workers, an ambulance, his grandmother arriving, taking him to her house, telling him his father was in the hospital. Later, his mother said he'd died of a heart attack.

"Nobody knew I'd seen him," Spencer said, "so they lied. They didn't want me to find out what really happened, they didn't want me to know my father killed himself."

I stared at him in disbelief. "Do you mean you've never told your mother you saw your father's body?"

Head down, Spencer avoided my eyes. "You don't understand, Lauren. She's been protecting me for years. How can I tell her I've known all along?"

"Spencer, you've got to talk about it. Maybe she knows why he did it, maybe he left a note, an explanation. You can't just bottle it up inside. You'll drive yourself crazy."

He looked at me, his hair lifted in the wind, his eyes shining with tears. "Don't you think I want to? I've tried dozens of times, hundreds of times, but when I mention his name, she clams up, turns her back, walks out of the room. If the GSF hears me, he's all over me. Next thing you know, everybody's in an uproar and guess who gets blamed for it?"

Taking my hand, Spencer kissed each finger. "Let me tell you about my mother, Lauren. Maybe you'll see what I mean. It's like she's wrapped round and round with golden wire, holding herself together with strands so fragile, anything could shatter them. Sometimes I want to break them myself, force her to talk to me, tell me about him, but I can't, I just can't do it. I'm scared she'll fall apart."

Although I didn't dare say it, I thought Mrs. Adams was made of iron. She'd survived a bad marriage, a suicide, she'd remarried, had two more kids. She didn't need Spencer's protection. What's more, she didn't deserve it. Couldn't she see what she was doing to him? How she was hurting him? Biting my lip to keep from saying the wrong thing, I smoldered with anger.

"I'm such a rotten son," Spencer was saying, laying all the blame on himself. "Like today, I hurt her on purpose — I shouldn't have played the Albinoni, she can't stand to hear it, but she pissed me off. The way she talked to me, the way she treated you, the things she said. I hated her. Now I hate myself for doing it."

He gnawed at his nails, head turned away, profile stony-sharp against the sky. The sun was low, and the clouds had turned purple, sullen, ugly, the color of an old bruise. The buzzards had broken free of their invisible tether and disappeared.

152

"Don't hate yourself," I whispered, "don't. It's not your fault, none of it's your fault."

Suddenly, Spencer buried his face in his hands. "The older I get, the worse it is, Lauren. I feel him growing inside me, moving in my blood, burrowing through my bones, tunneling into my brain. He's always sitting in that chair, holding that gun, getting ready to pull the trigger, but it's me he's aiming at now, me. I run and I run and I run, but I can't get away from him. No matter how fast I go, he's right behind me."

Spencer grabbed me, pulled me close. His heart thudded against mine. His hands were cold. He was crying again.

"Let me stay with you tonight," he whispered. "I can't go home, not now. Please, Lauren, please, hold me, don't let me think about him, make him go away."

Yes, I said, yes, he could stay, he could sleep in my bed. It would be okay, he'd be safe. I'd hold him in my arms all night, I'd keep him from thinking about the man in the chair. I wouldn't let him hurt Spencer, I wouldn't let him come near us.

~Chapter Nineteen~

WITHOUT TALKING, Spencer and I climbed the stairs to my apartment. From behind closed doors, we smelled dinners cooking, heard snatches of TV shows, arguments, a baby crying. When I put my key in the lock, my fingers shook.

"Where's your mother?" Spencer asked.

"At Paul's. She told me not to wait up for her — which means she'll probably be at his place all night."

Embarrassed by the implication of my words, I edged away from Spencer, unsure what to say, what to do, as tense and uncomfortable as the first time I'd brought him home to an empty apartment.

Spencer brushed his hair aside, cleared his throat, opened his mouth to speak, but closed it again, swallowing whatever it was he was going to tell me. As uneasy as I was, he walked to the window and stared at the dull sky. Not day, not night, but that gray in-between time when you look for the first star.

I wasn't hungry, but I went to the kitchen anyway. Eating

would give us something to do, a chance to change our minds, think, talk. Opening the freezer, I contemplated its contents — forgotten souvenirs of Paul's meals wrapped neatly in aluminum foil, Budget Gourmet dinners, pizza, an almost empty pint of Ben & Jerry's Cherry Garcia ice cream, and unidentifiable things furred with ice.

Suddenly, Spencer was beside me. Sliding his arm around my waist, he rested his cheek against mine.

"Do you want something to eat?" I asked him.

"As long as it isn't frozen gerbil."

"Oh, God," I said, "I hoped you'd forgotten that."

"Not on your life, Lauren. How many mothers would let a kid keep her dead gerbil in the freezer till the ground was soft enough to bury it?"

It was true. My gerbil had died in the winter when I was in eighth grade. Mom and I put him in a little box, wrapped it in aluminum foil, and kept it in the freezer till spring. Then we'd taken him to a clearing in the woods and buried him with a ceremony befitting a gerbil named Sir Walter Raleigh. It was the kind of thing I didn't always remember about Mom — the times she was there, the times she did just what I needed her to do.

"You thought Sir Walter should have a Viking burial at the lake," I said.

"Why not?" Spencer nuzzled my ear. "You could've built a little boat, put him aboard, set it on fire, and shoved it out to sea. It would have been fantastic."

Our laughter shattered the tension. Suddenly, he was Spencer again, not a fragile stranger. I knew how to act, what to say.

Giving him a kiss, I pulled a package out of the freezer. "How about lo-cal pizza?"

Spencer toyed with my earrings. As usual, the chains were tangled. Standing close to me, he separated them from my hair. His breath tickled my ear.

"Pizza's fine," he murmured.

After I put the box in the microwave, I opened a couple of diet sodas and lit the candles left from Paul's last dinner at our place. While I set the table, Spencer sat down and put his head on his folded arms. Gently, I stroked his hair, and he turned to me with a sigh. Pressing his face against my body, he held me tight.

We stayed like that, as still as kids frozen in a game of statues, until the microwave beeped. The sound was so loud in the quiet apartment that we jumped apart, as startled as if Mom had come home. Away from the warmth of Spencer's body, I shivered.

I put the pizza on our plates and turned out the kitchen light. The candles illuminated the table, but the rest of the apartment was dark. It was easy to pretend we were sitting down to dinner in our own place, just the two of us, a married couple.

Before I lifted my fork, Spencer grabbed my hand. "Maybe I shouldn't have told you about my father," he said, "maybe you're sorry you got mixed up with me."

I shook my head. The image I'd once had of Spencer was gone, torn to pieces like an old photograph, but his true self had already replaced it. "I just wish I knew what to say, how to help you feel better."

"You're doing all I want, Lauren. Listening to me, letting me stay with you, putting up with all my crappy bad-ass moods. If I didn't have you, I'd go crazy."

We stared into each other's eyes. In Spencer's pupils, the flames of the candle burned, two tiny lights.

"I love you," I whispered.

156

"I love you, too." Spencer held my hands so tightly, my bones ached. "Do you really want this pizza?"

I stared at my plate. The cheese was waxy, the tomato sauce was thin and dry, the crust was limp and soggy. I shook my head slowly.

Spencer pushed his chair back and stood up. Pulling me to my feet, he kissed me. "Let's go to your room."

I hesitated. "Shouldn't you call your mother? She'll be worried if you don't come home."

He frowned and pushed his hair out of his eyes. It was much longer now. Very straight, very black. I loved the soft, silky feel of it, the way it moved when he ran.

"What would I tell her?" he asked.

When I didn't answer, Spencer blew out the candles. With his hands on my shoulders, he guided me down the hall. While I scurried about picking up dirty clothes, Spencer roamed around looking at my things as if he'd never been in my room before. Squatting down to read the titles on the bottom shelf of my bookcase, he pulled out a tattered copy of *Rain Makes Applesauce*.

"This used to be my favorite book," he said. For a few seconds he examined the cover — the children in the apple tree, the rainbow, the storm clouds. Turning to the first illustration, he stopped and looked into my eyes.

" 'The stars are made of lemon juice,' " he said.

" 'And rain makes applesauce.' " I sat down beside him. Not because I needed to see the words, but to be close to Spencer.

He put his arm around my shoulders and kissed my nose. " 'Oh, you're just talking silly talk.' "

Shaking my head, I turned the page: " 'I wear my shoes inside out.' "

" 'And rain makes applesauce.' "

157

" 'Oh, you're just talking silly talk.' "

We stared at each other, amazed that we both knew the same book by heart. If I hadn't already fallen in love with Spencer, I would have done it then. He was my other half, I thought, the person I'd looked for all my life. My best friend. The one who listened, who understood, who made me laugh, who made me cry. The one who loved me. The one who'd never leave me, never desert me.

The one who needed me.

"My father used to read this to me." Spencer was staring at a picture of a man playing bagpipes. Behind him, borne on currents of air, things streamed away into darkness. A chair, balloons, children, a tricycle. Even the houses tilted as if they might tumble helter-skelter across the sky.

" 'The wind blows backwards all night long,' " Spencer said slowly.

" 'And rain makes applesauce.' "

" 'Oh, you're just talking silly talk.' "

I started to turn the page, but Spencer put his hand on mine to stop me. "Is he good or bad — that piper?"

"His eyes scared me when I was little," I admitted. "And I didn't like the children blowing away with no one holding on to them. Their parents asleep, letting them go, not caring."

Spencer pointed at the little girl holding a pinwheel. "But look at her smile. She's not scared, Lauren, none of them are. It's a big adventure. Maybe they're going to Never-Never Land."

Spencer kissed me, and we went on to a picture of monkeys in a jellybean jungle, candy, more monkeys, tigers and elephants, and so on, till we came to the end. Smiling at each other, we said the words on the last page:

158

Oh, you're just talking silly talk.
I know I'm talking silly talk . . .
But rain makes applesauce.

Resting my head on his shoulder, I said, "I wish we didn't have to grow up, I wish the wind could blow us to Never-Never Land, I wish we could talk silly talk forever."

"Who says we can't?" Spencer asked.

The only light came from the high-intensity lamp on my desk. There were dark shadows in the corners, dark shadows hiding our eyes.

Drawing slowly apart, we stared at each other. "What do you want to do, Lauren?" Spencer's voice was low, thick with emotion.

Confused by my own feelings, I didn't dare look at him. I knew what I wanted to do, but I was scared to say it, scared to think about it.

Spencer reached out and turned me toward him, so gently you'd think he was afraid I'd break. Slowly, so slowly, he kissed me. My bones felt as if they were melting.

After a long time, he drew back and stared at me. My shirt was unbuttoned, his hands were warm and sweet on my bare skin, but his eyes were dark with worry. "I've never slept with a girl before," he whispered.

I stared at him, too surprised to answer. I'd assumed he'd been with dozens of girls — girls like Vanessa with big breasts and full lips, girls who knew how to be sexy, girls who weren't ashamed of their bodies.

"I came close lots of times," Spencer said, "but it was never right. It seemed to me I should love them, and I didn't." He paused. "You're the only girl I've ever loved."

I caressed his face, stroked his hair, ran my hands over

his smooth, perfect skin. "You're the only boy I've ever loved. Right from the first time I saw you."

"I remember," Spencer said. "You walked into Mrs. Berkowitz's class. I was reading *The Tombs of Atuan,* and you looked like I imagined Tenar — so pretty, so sad. I wanted to make you smile."

"You did."

Spencer frowned and stared into the shadows behind me. "It seems to me I haven't given you much to smile about. Not lately. Certainly not today."

"I'm happy now." To prove it, I kissed him.

After a while, he looked at me again. "Are you scared?"

I knew what he meant. Scared to make love, scared to lose my virginity, scared of being hurt.

"Yes," I whispered, ashamed to hear my voice. It was as squeaky as if the old Mouse had spoken.

"We don't have to do anything, Lauren. We can just lie together all night."

"I want to." I'd said it, I meant it.

Spencer must have seen something in my eyes, heard it in my voice, because he started kissing me again, harder and harder. We wriggled free of our shirts and fumbled with our shoes. There was a knot in one of my laces. I picked at it, made it worse. In movies, women never had problems like this. They slipped out of their clothes like snakes shedding skins, they fell backward gracefully on beds, countertops, tables, floors, they made love quickly and easily.

"Here, let me try." Spencer undid the knot and yanked off my shoe.

We stood up then, and I turned out the light. In the dark, we rid ourselves of the rest of our clothes and got into bed. Our knees bumped, Spencer's elbow poked my eye, his feet were lumps of ice.

160

"Wait," he said. "I forgot." Sitting on the edge of the bed he fumbled through the pockets of his jeans. When he found what he was looking for, he turned his back and told me not to look.

In the silence, I heard foil tear. Realizing what he was doing, I pulled the blanket over my head, as embarrassed as he was.

After a few seconds, Spencer pulled the covers back and slid into bed beside me. He was trembling and so was I, but he held me tightly. "I love you, Lauren."

"I love you, too."

Hearing his voice whispering in my ear, feeling his hands on my skin, his lips on my mouth, I forgot to be scared, forgot everything except how much I loved him. I wanted to be his, I wanted to give myself to him. Not just my body. All of me. My whole life — my loneliness, my sadness, my happiness. Everything. There was no going back. Not for me. Not for him.

Afterward, when we could breathe, we lay close together and stared silently into each other's eyes. There were no words big enough or grand enough to express my feelings. Holding Spencer close, I caressed his back, his sides, his chest, and he nestled into my body like a freezing person seeking warmth.

"I didn't hurt you, did I?" he asked.

"Just a little," I said. "Next time it won't hurt at all."

"Next time," Spencer whispered. "Next time. There really will be a next time, won't there? Oh, God, Lauren, I can't believe you love me." In the dim light, tears shone in his eyes like stars.

"I can't believe *you* love me."

He kissed me on my mouth, my shoulders, my breasts,

my stomach. "I'll make you happy, Lauren, I swear I will," he said. "I'll be strong for you."

Murmuring promises, Spencer drifted away from me. His eyes closed, his body relaxed. As trustful as a child in a strange bed, he fell asleep.

Wide awake, I gazed at his face. We'd lost our virginity together. It had been strange and wonderful — more than I'd expected and less, too. Something had changed, I knew that, but not the entire universe. Just the part of it where Spencer and I lived.

Watching him sleep, I vowed to protect him. I'd love him so much, he'd forget his father and what he'd done. I'd love him as no one ever had. Love, that was all Spencer needed. Love would make him happy, keep him from worrying, give him peace. Love was stronger than death. Stronger than fear. Stronger than hate.

Beside me, he sighed in his sleep, twitched, moaned as if he were dreaming, and I held him even closer, sheltering him with my body. There was nothing I wouldn't do for Spencer Adams. Nothing.

~Chapter Twenty ~

WHEN I OPENED MY EYES in the morning, the first thing I saw was Spencer's face. His eyes were closed, he breathed deeply, peacefully. Careful not to wake him, I touched him gently. His skin was warm, his body solid, real. I hadn't dreamed it. We'd spent the whole night together, Spencer and I. All the barriers between us were gone, the secrets, too. His father was my father, his memories were my memories. My body was his body. His body was my body.

Lying close to him, loving him, I wanted to wake him, but he lay as still as an enchanted prince. If I kissed him, the spell would break. He'd open his eyes, he'd smile, he'd tell me he loved me.

But that could wait. Right now, I was happy to lie still and listen to the gray rain falling. Soon enough the day would claim us.

Lost in morning dreams, I was vaguely aware of footsteps in the hall. Suddenly my bedroom door opened, and Mom was telling me to get ready for school. The sight of Spencer stopped her in mid-sentence.

"What the hell is going on?"

Mom's voice shattered the enchantment. Wide awake, too startled to speak, Spencer pulled the covers up to his shoulders, and stared at Mom. Suddenly aware I was naked, I cowered beside him. I'd meant to lock my door before I went to sleep, but I'd forgotten. Since I hadn't heard her come home, I'd thought she was at Paul's.

Shooting me a look of pure fury, Mom said, "I don't have time to deal with this now, Lauren. I'm already late. You'd better be here when I come home tonight."

Before she turned away, Mom glanced at Spencer. "As for you," she said, "I'm very disappointed."

With that, she left the room. Her high heels clattered down the hall. The front door slammed. Without her, the apartment was suddenly quiet.

Spencer and I stared at each other. For a moment, neither of us spoke. If I'd been watching a movie, the expression on Spencer's face would have been funny. His hair stuck up in uncombed spikes, his eyebrows rose in dismay, his lips were pinched. In reality, it wasn't the slightest bit humorous — he was genuinely distressed.

"First my mother," he said, "now yours. I'm ruining your life, Lauren."

Putting my arms around him, I pulled him close. I felt the bones in his spine, his shoulder blades, the soft fuzz of hair on his back.

"Don't worry," I said. "My mother doesn't have any right to get mad at me. Not the way *she* acts."

I was talking fast, letting the words spill out, working up a lot of anger against Mom. She'd shattered the spell, she'd upset Spencer, she'd scared me. My heart was still pounding from the shock of seeing her in the doorway.

To calm me, Spencer caressed my skin, stroked my face,

kissed my lips. Gradually, the worry in his eyes softened, darkened, changed into something else. "You're right," he whispered, "let's not worry about your mother. Not now." I peered over his shoulder at my clock. It was almost eight. "What about school?"

Spencer nuzzled my throat, moved closer, covered my body with his. "The hell with school," he murmured, "the hell with everything except you and me."

Giving in to my desire for him, I forgot my fears and worries, his father, my mother, school, teachers. Safe in Spencer's arms, I shut my eyes and let the wind blow them away, all of them, backward into the past.

Late in the afternoon, I told Spencer he had to leave before Mom came home. I didn't want him to witness the scene she was sure to make, but I had a hard time convincing him he wasn't deserting me. It was his fault, he said, his idea — he couldn't just walk out on me.

I ended up practically pushing him out of the apartment. Even then, he lingered in the doorway, still uncertain. "You won't regret this, will you?" he asked. "You won't be sorry you slept with me?"

For an answer, I hugged him as hard as I could. "I wish you could spend every night here. Don't you know how much I love you?"

Spencer smiled then. "Oh, I was just talking silly talk," he whispered. "Silly, silly talk."

The moment the door closed behind him, I wanted to call him back. Running to the living room window, I watched him drive away. As the station wagon bounced over a speed bump and vanished into the gloom, I pictured Spencer walking into that big cold house of his and confronting his mother. From what he'd said about her, she'd be furious, she'd lash out at him, she'd say things to hurt him.

He'd wanted to stay here and protect me, but it was Spencer who needed protecting. It scared me to think of him facing that woman.

Turning away from the window, I went to my room and flopped down on the bed. My pillow still smelled like Spencer. I pressed my face against it, breathing in the woodsy fragrance, wishing he were still there.

Outside, the rain fell steadily. A dreary April day was sinking into an even drearier night. Without Spencer, I felt as gloomy as the weather. It was a long time till morning. Till school. Till I saw him again.

When I finally lifted my head, I noticed a little heart on the wall. Spencer must have drawn it when I wasn't looking. Inside he'd written, "Je t'aime, Lauren." Just above my pillow, it was the first thing I'd see in the morning and the last at night.

Touching it gently, I whispered, "Je t'aime, Spencer, je t'aime."

When Mom came home half an hour later, I was sitting at my desk trying to look busy. Actually, I'd been staring at the same calculus problem for fifteen minutes. I was too nervous to concentrate on anything.

Mom stalked across the rug and sat on my bed. I'd changed the sheets and tidied the spread. It looked as virginal as a nun's cot.

"I can't believe you let Spencer stay here all night," she said. My mother didn't believe in preliminaries. It was best to jump in feet first.

Closing my book, I took a deep breath. I'd had time to

166

prepare my defense — more of an attack, actually. "Why are you making such a big deal of it?" I asked. "Plenty of guys have spent the night in your bed."

Jumping to her feet, Mom strode toward me. For a second, I thought she was going to slap me. "Are you saying it's okay for you to sleep with Spencer because I've had a couple of lovers? Is that what you think?"

"A couple?" I tried to laugh, but it came out shrill and false. "That's a slight miscalculation."

Hoping she wouldn't notice it was shaking, I held up my hand and started counting on my fingers. "The first one I remember was Andy, then there was Greg, and Dwayne and — "

Smacking my hand away, Mom said, "Don't try to turn this back on me, Lauren. I'm an adult. My life isn't in question right now. Yours is."

"*My* life," I repeated. "What do you know about *my* life? What do you care? You leave me alone night after night. Don't you think I get lonely? Don't you think I need somebody to talk to?"

My rage turned to tears. Unable to speak, I dropped my head onto my folded arms and wept. It was too much. Spencer's problems, Mom's anger — I couldn't cope with it.

I heard her come closer. Standing beside me, she touched my shoulder, but she didn't say anything.

"He loves me," I sobbed, "he cares about me."

"And you think I don't." It wasn't a question. Mom's voice was flat, drained of emotion.

"To you, I'm this accident, this kid who ruined your life. If you hadn't gotten pregnant, you wouldn't have married Daddy, you would've finished school, you'd have a good job."

"Oh, my God," Mom said. "I know I haven't been the

world's best mother, but I was never sorry I had you. I've always loved you, Lally."

"Oh, sure, Mom, sure. That's why you spend so much time with me." Old hurts rose in my throat, words tumbled out, I didn't even try to stop them. By the time I got to her birthday, Mom had her arms around me.

"Lally, Lally," she said, "I'm sorry. I didn't think you cared that much."

"Well, I did. I cared a lot." I blew my nose, wiped my eyes, tried to stop crying, but everything was such a tangle — Mom and Spencer, his father, his mother, love and desire, sadness and fear. Resting my head against Mom's hip, I let her stroke my hair as if I were a little girl.

After a while, Mom drew back and stared down at me. In the harsh light of my desk lamp, her face looked older. She wasn't angry anymore.

"I should have seen it coming," she said. "Joanna warned me, she told me this would happen, but you never had a boyfriend before, and I thought, I thought . . ."

Silently, I finished the sentence for her — *you thought I was a bookworm, you thought I wasn't interested in sex.*

Unaware of what was going on in my head, Mom said, "I thought I could trust you and Spencer to have more sense."

"We love each other."

Mom looked at me across years of experience. "That's not always enough, Lally."

I opened my mouth to argue, but she wasn't finished. "How long have you been sleeping with Spencer?"

"Last night was the first time." I looked at Mom — could I tell her how worried I was? Would she listen, would she understand, give me advice? Tentatively I added, "Spencer was upset, unhappy, and it just kind of happened."

168

" 'Just kind of happened'? Lally, when sex 'just kind of happens,' girls get pregnant."

Stung by her sarcasm, I told her not to worry. "I didn't sit through all those boring sex ed classes for nothing."

"You used precautions?"

"It was as safe as sex can be." To avoid her eyes, I stared at the cover of *Rain Makes Applesauce*. I didn't want to talk about Spencer now. Not to her. Not to anyone. What we'd said and done was private, just for him and me to know and share.

"I called my gynecologist," Mom said. "You've got an appointment to see her next week. Get the pill, stay on it, use condoms, don't take any chances."

I stared at Mom, she stared back at me. In the silence between words, I heard the rain falling.

"It changes everything, you know," Mom said at last. "You can't go back to who you were before." With one finger she touched my picture book. "Nobody gets to talk silly talk forever, Lally."

When Mom was gone, I went to my window and watched the rain. Why was I so disappointed? She wasn't angry anymore, she hadn't yelled or screamed or cursed, she hadn't called me names, hadn't forbidden me to see Spencer. But she hadn't really listened, asked the right questions, or told me one thing I didn't already know.

What I felt for Spencer Adams couldn't be measured out in condoms and birth-control pills and visits to gynecologists.

~ Chapter Twenty-one ~

THE NEXT MORNING, Casey was waiting for me at the top of the hill. "Where were you yesterday?" she asked. "I was late because of you."

"Sorry." I busied myself with the seat belt, hoping she wouldn't notice anything different about me. Just because Casey gave me the details of her and Jordan's relationship didn't mean I had to return the favor.

Casey lit a cigarette and glanced at me through a haze of smoke. "Were you sick or what?"

Avoiding her eyes, I said, "I had the flu — one of those twenty-four-hour stomach bugs. I'm fine now."

"That's funny," Casey said. "Spencer must have had the same problem. He wasn't in school, either."

Instead of answering, I fiddled with the radio. Casey had it tuned to one of those stations where the disc jockeys act like they're hopped up on drugs. Their stupid jokes were getting on my nerves.

"I hope it's not the kind of bug that puts you in the hospital nine months later," Casey said.

"Don't be stupid." I turned up the volume and let an old song by the Pretenders flood the car with noise. The last thing I needed was more motherly advice.

Casey touched my hand. "Hey, don't get mad — it's okay with me if you sleep with Spencer."

When I didn't respond, she sighed and changed the subject. For the rest of the way to school, it was Jordan this and Jordan that — which was fine with me. It left me free to think.

When we pulled into the parking lot, I saw Spencer leaning against the baseball backstop, hands in his pockets, head down, kicking at a knot of weeds.

"The Prince of Gloom awaits your ladyship," Casey said.

Ignoring her, I jumped out of the car. When Spencer saw me running toward him, his face lit with a happiness I didn't often see. He held out his arms and I threw myself against him so hard, he almost lost his balance. Holding me tight, he kissed me till I wished we could skip school again.

"What was it Whitman said?" Spencer whispered in my ear. "I want to become undisguised and naked — I am mad for you to be in contact with me."

He kissed me again and then drew back to look at me. "Was your mother mad? Did she give you a hard time?"

"Not really." I smiled at him. "We ended up eating moo goo gai pan and watching a couple of Laurel and Hardy videos. Next week, I see a gynecologist and get on the pill. That was all there was to it. More or less."

"I was afraid she'd turn you against me, make you hate me, tell you not to see me."

"Nobody could do that. Not my mother, not anyone." To show him what I meant, I kissed him as fiercely as I dared.

"Oh, God, Lauren, if you ever stop loving me, I'll die."
The desperation I'd heard before was in his voice again, in
his hands. I could taste it on his lips.

"How about *your* mother?" I pulled back to see his face.
"What did she say?"

Spencer's hands tightened on my shoulders. "No more
car for starters. Not that I care. We've got the motorcycle."

"Is that all?" I was thinking we'd gotten off fairly lightly,
but Spencer had more to tell me.

"She said I was out of control." He tried to make it sound
like a joke, the ultimate parental accusation, the one they
hurl at you when they don't know what else to say.

"She actually threatened to send me to Tyler Manor."
The laughter faded from his voice, and his shoulders sagged.
Tyler Manor wasn't funny. I knew kids there, and so did
Spencer. Some of them stayed for a long time. "Disturbed
adolescents" — that's what they were called.

"She can't send you to Tyler Manor," I said. "You don't
have a drug problem, you don't drink."

"It was just a threat," Spencer said uncertainly, "her way
of telling me to shape up."

We stared at each other. In the parking lot, kids blew car
horns, yelled at one another, laughed, but they might have
been actors on a stage. They had nothing to do with us.
Our reality was different.

"Have you ever thought about talking to somebody?
Shaw for instance, he seems nice — "

Spencer cut me off in midsentence. "I'd never talk to a
shrink, never."

"But — " The look in Spencer's eyes warned me to shut
up. Swallowing hard, I stared at our feet, frayed running
shoes almost toe to toe on the asphalt. *Don't get mad,* I begged
silently, *don't turn cold and scary.*

172

I felt his finger lift my chin. Our eyes met, and he smiled. "I have you to talk to, Lauren. After last night, I don't need anyone else. I told you I'd be strong for you, and I meant it."

His mood lifted, changed so swiftly he caught me off guard. "The last one through the door buys the gas for our next motorcycle trip," he said.

With my book pack bouncing against my back, I chased Spencer across the parking lot, dodging in and out of rows of empty cars. The sun made oil rainbows on the puddles left from last night's rain. On the south wall of the school, forsythia blazed with yellow light, and the grass was green and tall, ready for its first cut.

Ahead of me, Spencer turned and ran backward, laughing at me. Lit by sunlight, his hair sparkled. He was perfect, I thought, beautiful. If only he could always be as happy as he looked now.

At the end of the day, Spencer sat quietly beside me. It was the first time he'd been in Walker's class since the "Stopping by Woods" incident. From the other side of the room, Meg and Vanessa were watching him, their heads together, whispering. If he noticed, he paid no attention.

When Walker called roll, he paused at Spencer's name. "I want to see you after class, Adams."

Pressing his leg against mine, Spencer nodded without looking up.

After a discussion of E. E. Cummings's style, Walker chose "my father moved through dooms of love" to read aloud. I felt Spencer tense, heard the breath catch in his throat. While Walker talked of God as father, creator, comforter, Spencer doodled complicated geometric designs on his notebook paper. It wasn't God Spencer saw in Cummings's poem. Lost in his own "motionless forgetful where," he saw the man in the chair, his father, his "ghostly roots," his "dooms of feel," his "sorrows as true as bread."

And it wasn't Cummings's last stanza Spencer believed. It was the one before: "maggoty minus and dumb death all we inherit, all bequeath . . ."

When the buzzer signaled the end of class, Spencer stayed where he was, and I sat beside him.

"Lauren," Walker said, "you may go. This doesn't concern you."

I started to leave, but Spencer grabbed my hand. "She can stay," he said.

Walker's eyes bored into mine. Before he spoke, I realized what he thought, and my face burned with denial. "Are you telling me Lauren wrote the paper for you?" he asked Spencer.

"If that's what you think — " Spencer jumped to his feet, but Walker stepped in front of him.

"Tell me if I'm wrong." It was me Walker was speaking to, me he'd believe, not Spencer.

"I saw him write it." My voice shook, but I forced myself to look Walker in the eye. If he thought I was lying, he could flunk both of us. "Spencer didn't copy it, and I didn't help him. It was all his, every word of it."

I wanted to tell him that Spencer's interpretation came from his soul, from something he'd seen that Walker couldn't even imagine — a father moving through dooms of love to his own death. To stop myself from saying more, I gripped Spencer's hand.

Head down, hair sliding over his eyes, Spencer shrugged. "Like I said, it was my own idea. Lauren would never cheat, never lie, not for herself, not even for me."

"I apologize." Walker spoke as if he had to force the words through living tissue. "I was wrong."

174

Spencer shifted his weight and squeezed my hand. "I accept the apology." A flash of his old confidence gave his voice strength.

"More work like that," Walker said, "and you might pass this course."

Leaving school, Spencer muttered, "What a pompous ass."

"It almost gave him a coronary to admit he was wrong," said, "but at least you have a chance of getting a C out of him."

We walked slowly toward the library. Unlike yesterday, it was a working afternoon for me. If I'd had the nerve, I would've called Mrs. Jenkins and told her I was sick, but I was too scared of losing my job to take a chance like that.

"Maybe I should pull up my grades, instead of taking the GED," Spencer said. "It might get Mom off my back."

He sat on the rail of a footbridge and I leaned against his shoulder. For a few moments, we watched the creek swirl under the bridge, carrying leaves and bits of trash with it.

Turning to me with a sigh, Spencer said, "I don't want to end up in Tyler Manor."

He was still worrying about his mother's threat. No matter what I said about drugs and alcohol, he was convinced it was an easy way for parents to get rid of kids who didn't turn out right — like sending a dog you couldn't housebreak to the pound. All they had to do was convince themselves they were doing it for the kid's own good. Maybe he was a danger to others, maybe he'd kill himself — away he went to Tyler Manor, and presto! No more loud music, no more arguments, no more scenes. The troublemaker was gone, the house was peaceful.

"Think about it, Lauren. Mom has two perfect kids — what does she need me for? Every time she looks at me, she sees my father. She'd be a hell of a lot happier if I weren't there to remind her of him — and so would the GSF."

"You don't believe that."

"No, no, of course not. I'm just talking silly talk, silly silly talk." There was no humor in his voice, no hope in his eyes — just bitterness and a dull despair that made me hate his mother.

Slipping my arms around him, I said, "I wish we had our own place, just you and me."

Responding to my hug, he held me tightly. "When we go to California, we'll find a cheap apartment, a room even, right on the beach. I could get a job as a mechanic and you could go to college."

The sound of running feet interrupted us. Looking up, we saw the cross-country team coming around a curve in the path. Kevin was in the lead. The others followed in a ragged line like unevenly strung beads. Before they reached the bridge, Spencer and I crossed to the other side and stepped off the path to let them pass.

Kevin glanced at Spencer and nodded. His T-shirt was dark with sweat, his face shone, he was breathing hard. Ted and Jordan were close behind him. Grinning at Spencer, Jordan touched his hand to his forehead in a mock salute, but the others ran doggedly, paying no attention to us.

Spencer watched them vanish around a bend. Taking my hand, he peered into my eyes, full of doubt again. "Do you think my life's out of control? Am I going over the edge, am I losing it?"

I shook my head. "Your father did something terrible to you, something awful, something most people can't even think about. Look at your mother — she won't even admit it happened."

Chewing his thumbnail, Spencer studied the path as if it

were mined. One misstep, and it would blow up in his face.

"You're not crazy," I said. "And you'd never do what your father did."

"How do you know?"

"Because he hurt you so much. You couldn't cause anyone that much pain."

Spencer made an effort, but his smile didn't quite reach his eyes. "I wish I were as sure of myself as you are," he said.

~ *Chapter Twenty-two* ~

ONE SATURDAY AFTERNOON IN MAY, Mom and I went to the mall to shop for my graduation dress. The big event was only a week away, and I needed something to wear, not just for the ceremony itself, under the gown, but for the party Spencer was taking me to afterward at Mount Washington Country Club. Neither of us wanted to go, but it was a High Meadow tradition and his parents were adamant. Spencer had to be there.

In the Laura Ashley shop, Mom held up a pale blue and white flowered dress. "I know it's expensive, but this would look so nice on you," she said. "Maybe I could charge it and pay if off a little at a time."

I wanted that dress so badly it was all I could do not to agree, but it was way beyond our budget. Shaking my head, I made her return it to the rack. The dresses swayed and whispered together, little silken giggles of fabric. They weren't for me.

Ignoring the saleswomen huddled at the cash register, Mom and I left the shop and headed for Woodward and Lothrop's. Surely, a big department store would have something we could afford. But I was wrong — hundreds of dresses, but not one in our price range.

Finally, I found an Indian gauze dress in a little boutique. Pale beige, full-skirted, bare-shouldered, and inexpensive, it was perfect. I spun around to show Mom the way the skirt flared, and she smiled. Even though she preferred the class of a Laura Ashley label, she admitted it was very becoming — romantic, exotic, artsy. "You look like a Gypsy princess," she said.

To celebrate the dress, we stopped at the Food Court for a seven-grain special veggie sandwich. Paul's cooking had converted Mom. She genuinely liked vegetables. No more hot dogs, no more hamburgers. A steak on the sly once in a while, that was it.

"Spencer seems happier," Mom said. As usual, no preliminaries — she could be talking about the weather one minute, and the most intimate details of your life in the next, without even taking a breath.

I had a mouthful of alfalfa sprouts, so all I could do was nod and chew. Mom was right, Spencer was happier. At least on the surface. Ever since the Tyler Manor threat, he'd worked harder in school. It was too late to bring his grades up to more than C's and D's, but he was pretty sure he'd graduate.

Sliding by wasn't enough to please his mother and the GSF. He avoided scenes by spending as much time as possible at my apartment.

I glanced at Mom. She must have known Spencer spent the night whenever she stayed at Paul's, but she never mentioned it. Once I was on the pill, she seemed to lose interest in my sex life.

"Have you given much thought to the future?" Mom asked. "Like getting married?"

"Married?" I almost choked on a chunk of avocado. "How could we get married? What would we live on? Besides, we have to go to college, maybe graduate school."

Mom shrugged. "I got married when I was only a couple of years older than you."

I sipped my soda to keep myself from blurting out the wrong thing. Did she actually think I wanted to follow her example?

"But it was a mistake," Mom added. "That's what I was trying to say. Live with him if you want, but don't marry him. Spencer's a sweet boy, I like him a lot, but . . ."

Mom's sentence trailed off unfinished. She sipped her coffee and eyed me over the rim of the cup.

"But what?"

She shrugged. "I don't know. He's so fragile. Don't you worry sometimes?"

I didn't answer right away. Knowing what I did about Spencer — of course I worried. Every time he rode off on the motorcycle without me I worried. Every time he held me tight and talked about his mother, what she'd said, what she'd done to show her disappointment in him. Every time he woke me at night tossing and moaning in his sleep. Every time I looked at his fingertips swelling over his bitten nails. Every time he plummeted down into one of his dark moods.

I spent so much time worrying about Spencer, it was a wonder I had the energy to do anything else. In the beginning, I'd been so sure love was the answer. If I loved him enough, his pain would dissolve. He'd be whole and happy and healthy. But I was beginning to think Spencer needed more than love.

Mom reached across the table and patted my hand. "Listen," she said, changing the subject. "They're playing Bob Dylan. When I was your age, I never imagined I'd hear 'Blowin' in the Wind' on the mall music system."

By the time we finished eating, Mom was telling me about her high school hippie days. Bell bottoms and tie-dyed T-shirts and smoking pot behind the gym.

"How I got a kid like you is absolutely amazing," she said. "Maybe your father was smarter than I thought."

On the way back to the parking lot, we took a short cut through Hecht's, and Mom paused to admire a display of puppets. Before I realized what she was doing, she had a furry white rabbit on her hand. Wiggling its nose, she said, "Watch out, here comes Wicked Wabbit."

She lunged at me and made the puppet bite my nose. In self-defense, I grabbed a shaggy gray dog. "Woof, woof," I barked and shook him at the rabbit.

As our puppets scuffled, I noticed someone walking toward us. Flanked by Jeremy and Brooke, Mrs. Adams was staring at Mom and me. Mortified, I dropped my hand, but Mom was really into her rabbit role. Without noticing my loss of interest, she lisped, "Come on, you widdle coward, you nasty widdle fing, you bad bad widdle doggy boy!"

Her puppet grabbed my puppet and shook it. "Take dat, take dat, and dat! Wicked Wabbit's got you now and he's gonna make you sowwy for all your sins!"

Jeremy and Brooke grinned, and Mrs. Adams stood beside them looking elegantly puzzled. I hadn't seen her since the day she'd found me in Spencer's room, but it was obvious she hadn't forgotten who I was.

Aware that something was happening behind her back, Mom released my puppet and turned around, still holding Wicked Wabbit.

"Mom, this is Spencer's mother," I said. "Mrs. Adams."
When Mrs. Adams extended her hand, Mom fumbled with the puppet. By the time she'd gotten it off, it was too late to shake hands. "I'm Joyce Anderson," Mom said. "And this is Wicked Wabbit. Isn't he the cutest thing you ever saw?"

While our mothers sized each other up, I looked at the two of them. It was hard to believe they were members of the same species. Beside me was Mom, her long hair haloing her face and cascading down her back in a tangled perm. She was wearing a baggy T-shirt with the words DAMN, I'M GOOD printed across the front. How had I failed to notice she was wearing that? Her jeans were fashionably faded, and on her feet were a pair of oversized Birkenstocks, a gift from Paul.

Facing me was the tall and sophisticated Mrs. Adams, a model from a high-priced fashion catalog — polo shirt, tailored slacks, stylish flats, perfect blunt-cut dark hair framing her pale face. She had the sort of poise I'd never have, not even after ten reincarnations. It was genetic, I thought. Bred in the bone. Way beyond Mom and me.

"Aren't puppets great?" Mom was saying. "They're so therapeutic. I'm going to buy this and take it to work. Whenever I get pissed at my boss, the rabbit can make a rude remark."

Mom laughed at the thought, and so did Brooke. Jeremy stared as if he didn't know what to make of the situation. Mrs. Adams looked uncomfortable. And I found myself wishing I had heart trouble. Nothing fatal. Just a minor attack to get us out of the mall before Mom said anything else.

"Where is Spencer?" Mrs. Adams asked me. "I thought he was with you."

"He's at the library," I said, "studying for his calculus exam." We'd left Spencer in the parking lot happily working on his motorcycle, but Mom didn't say a word.

"If you see him," Mrs. Adams said, "tell him it would be nice if he showed up for dinner tonight."

"He's such a sweet boy, your son," Mom started to say, but Mrs. Adams was already walking away, trailed by Jeremy and Brooke.

When the Adams entourage was at a safe distance, Mom wiggled her puppet at their backs. "Stuck-up snobs," she said in a squeaky voice. "You better watch out or Wicked Wabbit will get you!"

I grabbed at the puppet as if it were causing all the trouble. "She already hates me. Please don't make it worse."

Mom looked at me, suddenly serious. "Poor Spencer," she said. "No wonder he's so moody. It must be awful to have the Ice Queen for a mother. And those two kids. Perfect little marionettes. Does she pull strings to make them talk?"

When Mom and I drove into the parking lot, Spencer looked up and smiled. He had his tools fanned out neatly on a piece of chamois cloth, but he began gathering them up.

"All finished," he said. "Want to go for a ride?"

I handed Mom the bags, and in a few minutes Spencer and I were roaring through the green-gold countryside to the reservoir. We zoomed across the bridge and skidded to a stop in a shower of gravel. Hand in hand, we climbed the hill and spread the blanket we always carried on a carpet of tiny purple wild flowers. In the tree over our heads a mockingbird sang, and a chipmunk watched us from a log, ready to run if we threatened him. The sky was hazy blue, wisped with clouds, and the air was soft and warm on our skin. Spencer took off his shirt.

"This is our own private Eden," I told him.

"Well, you know what happened to Adam and Eve —"

"Hush." I pressed my fingers against his lips, but he didn't smile. "No gloomy talk," I whispered. "Not now."

The sun cast a mottled pattern of moving shadows across his face and chest, dappling him like a fawn. I ran my finger down his bare side, feeling the armor of ribs beneath his skin. "You're so beautiful, Spencer."

" 'Oh, you're just talking silly talk.' " He smiled then and pulled me down beside him for a long kiss.

Much later, we climbed downhill toward the bridge. It was early evening, and the color was fading from the sky. A mockingbird sent its song after us, as sweet and clear as a nightingale.

Before we got on the Honda, Spencer said, "What'll we do about the graduation party?"

"I bought a dress this afternoon," I said.

"That must mean we're going."

"Does your mother know you're bringing me?"

Spencer kissed me. "I told her you're part of the deal. I won't go without you."

"I saw her at the mall," I said. "She was with Jeremy and Brooke."

While he listened, I told him about Mom and Wicked Wabbit and the DAMN, I'M GOOD T-shirt. By the time I was finished, we were both laughing so hard, we had to hold each other up. Like a lot of things, it hadn't been funny when it happened, but now every detail was hilarious.

After I'd repeated Wicked Wabbit's lines a couple of times,

I leaned my head against Spencer's shoulder. "Your mother said it would be nice if you came home for dinner."

"Nice for who?" Spencer turned away and stared down at the darkening water. Putting my arms around him, I tried to keep him from drifting back into a bad mood. Why had I mentioned his mother?

For a long time, we stood together on the bridge. We didn't talk, we didn't kiss, we just held each other. Gradually, I felt his body relax.

Letting me go, Spencer looked up at the sky. "I see the moon," he sang, "the moon sees me."

Sure enough, the moon, wearing its usual bewildered expression, was gazing down at us. Remembering the words from Girl Scouts, I sang all the verses with Spencer. Then we made up our own words. Our version was a little too raunchy for a Scout campfire, but it made us laugh.

"Don't you wish we could walk down that path and climb up into the sky?" Spencer said.

He was pointing at the moon's reflection, a silver road sparkling on the black water's surface. "Where would we go?" I asked.

"To the forever place," Spencer said. "Otherwise known as Earthsea, Narnia, Middle Earth, Never-Never Land, Sesame Street. Take your choice, Lauren, and I'll buy the tickets — one way, if you like."

Hearing something dark in his voice, I hugged him hard. "Let's stay right here," I whispered, "and love each other forever and ever."

"Sounds good to me." Spencer kissed me. "Is your mom spending the night at Paul's?"

I nodded. "And you're spending the night with me."

Hurtling homeward on the motorcycle, I held on tight.

185

In the headlight's beam, the trees crowded close to the road. For a moment, they seemed to reach out for us, hungry for blood.

I closed my eyes and pictured the empty apartment waiting for us. We'd order pizza, we'd eat by candlelight, we'd watch a Pink Panther video and laugh at Peter Sellers's misadventures. Then we'd go to bed. We'd be safe.

~Chapter Twenty-three~

ON GRADUATION DAY, Casey dragged me to the girls' room before the ceremony began. She was going to Ocean City with Jordan and a bunch of other kids, but she was worried about me.

"Are you sure you can't talk Spencer into coming with us?" Casey knew I was dreading the party at Mount Washington. In her opinion, I was putting myself through purgatory just to please Spencer.

Avoiding her eyes, I told Casey it wouldn't be so bad, might even be fun. "If nothing else," I finished up, "I'll get a good dinner. I hear the food's great at the club."

"You get pretty good food at wakes, too," Casey said.

I made a face at her reflection, and she laughed and crossed her eyes. "Seriously though," she said, refusing to let me distract her, "what are the Prince of Gloom's plans for the summer? Is the motorcycle trip still on?"

Pretending to look for something, lipstick maybe, I groped in my purse. Ever since he'd seen the Honda, Spencer had talked about going to California after graduation, but I'd never been able to get him to name a date. His plans were so vague — he couldn't decide what route to take, what to see. Sometimes he played leapfrog all over the map, trying to figure out a way to visit everything from Niagara Falls to Mount Saint Helens. He didn't want to miss a thing — including back roads and offbeat places like Cadillac Ranch just outside Amarillo.

When I'd told him it would probably take two or three years to cross the country his way, he'd just shrugged and said, "So what." Lately, I'd begun to think it was all a fantasy, the whole thing, even California.

Casey tapped my forehead. "Earth to Lauren, Earth to Lauren — are you there?"

"I guess so," I said.

Casey adjusted her mortarboard and scowled at her reflection. "I bet Spencer hasn't even told his parents," she said.

I played with my new earrings, big gold hoops, a gift from Spencer. Of course he hadn't told his parents. They didn't even know he had a motorcycle.

"He's scared to tell them, isn't he? He knows they'll raise hell."

"They won't like it," I said, "but he's eighteen. They can't control his life."

"I bet you don't go," Casey said. "Spencer doesn't have the guts to cross the Potomac, much less drive all the way to California."

Stung by the scorn in her voice, I glared at Casey. "I thought you liked him, I thought you cared about him."

"Don't get mad, Lauren, don't cry, please don't cry. You'll make me start and my mascara will run."

Casey tried to laugh, to make it into a joke, but she didn't succeed. "I'm just giving you some advice, that's all. You're my best friend — I don't want anything to happen to you."

I slumped against the sink, sniffling, wiping my face with a wet towel. If she only knew, I thought, if she even had a glimmering of what Spencer was struggling against, she'd be more sympathetic. But I couldn't tell her. I'd promised to keep his secrets.

Suddenly, Casey slung her arms around me, "Stay here this summer, make him sell that stupid motorcycle."

Her familiar red hair tickled my nose — I smelled cigarette smoke and perfume and chewing gum, Casey's own special aroma. I didn't know whether to laugh or cry or yell at her, so I hugged her back as hard as I could.

"Hey, you two," someone called from the door. "The processional's about to start."

We sprang apart, straightened our caps, and rushed down the hall to join the line. "I'll talk to you after I get back from Ocean City," Casey said. "Maybe I'll lock you in a closet to keep you off the bike from hell."

During the ceremony, Spencer sat two seats away from me, almost close enough to touch. Throughout the principal's long, boring speech, we gazed at each other, not listening to a word Mr. Parker said. We'd heard it all before at countless assemblies.

Two more speeches followed. Meg gave the valedictory, a long string of crowd-pleasing clichés, artful, but signifying nothing, and the president of the community college spoke about the importance of continuing our education, warning us of hard times to come in the adult world.

Finally, we rose one row at a time to receive our diplomas and a handshake from Mr. Parker. I'd expected to feel a pang of regret to be leaving high school, but all I was thinking about was Spencer. After the party, we planned to spend the night together. Mom was going to be at Paul's and the apartment would be ours.

When the ceremony ended, Spencer and I peeled off our robes and went in search of Mom. At the sight of me, she burst into tears. "You looked beautiful," she wept, "so serious, so grown up."

While Mom dabbed at her eyes with a tissue, Paul put his arm around her. "Your mother wept through the whole thing," he told me. "Especially at the end, when you marched out."

"It was the music," Mom said. "*Pomp and Circumstance.* All that hope and glory. It gets me right here." She thumped her heart and tried to laugh.

Turning to Spencer, Mom hugged him and told him how handsome he looked. "I've never seen you in a jacket and tie."

Gathering a fold of material in Spencer's sleeve, she rubbed it gently between her thumb and fingers. "It's silk, isn't it? The soft nubby kind."

When Spencer admitted it was, Mom flipped open his jacket. "I just have to see the suspenders Lauren gave you," she said. "Pink paisley. See Paul? They match his shirt and the print in his tie. I think I'll buy some for you."

Paul swore he wouldn't wear them, Spencer blushed, and Mom kissed his cheek. "Have a wonderful time at the club," she said. "Tomorrow night, Paul and I will treat you to dinner at Clyde's. Would you like that?"

Spencer glanced at me over Mom's head, and I nudged her. "Here, take these home for us, okay?" I gave her our caps and gowns. "We have to meet Spencer's parents."

"Not so fast." Mom stopped me. She had her camera, and there was no escape till she'd shot a roll of film. We

190

had to put our robes on, we had to pose with her, with Paul, with each other. When she'd taken a picture of every possible combination, in cap and gown, without cap and gown, she grabbed a passing stranger and got a group shot — all four of us, a family.

After another round of hugs and kisses, Mom let us go, and I followed Spencer into the crowd. I'd never met his stepfather, and I wasn't looking forward to seeing Mrs. Adams again. The Wicked Wabbit incident was still fresh in my memory.

While I was waving at Casey, Spencer gripped my hand hard and introduced me to his stepfather. Mr. Adams was tall and handsome in a blown-dry way, and thoroughly intimidating. He wore a dark suit, his hair was silvery, his eyes were the color of shadows on snow. It was truly like meeting the Great Stone Face in person.

At her husband's side, Mrs. Adams smiled politely and offered her congratulations, but I knew she wasn't pleased to see me. Beautiful, perfectly dressed in tailored beige linen, the Ice Queen was much too polite to reveal her feelings. Making a few well-chosen remarks about the weather (hot and muggy), the speeches (too long), and the seats (too hard), she led us to the car.

Squashed between Brooke and Jeremy, Spencer and I sat in the middle of the BMW's backseat, joined at the shoulder, arm, and thigh. Rigid with tension, Spencer's body was as hard as marble and just as still.

On my other side, Brooke smoothed her dress carefully over her knees, trying to keep it free of wrinkles, and Jeremy looked out the window, a portable tape player plugged into his ears. From a couple of feet away, I heard the tinny voices of a top-forty pop rock group.

Eyeing us in the rearview mirror, Mr. Adams frowned

at Spencer. "I told you to get your hair cut this morning," he said, "but I see you didn't follow instructions. No surprise there."

Thrusting a comb at Spencer, he added, "Do something with it. This isn't 1970."

Mr. Adams's eyes slid over me, taking in my long hair, my gauzy dress, my earrings, my sandals. If I'd been his daughter, he would have said something about my appearance, too.

To my surprise, Brooke touched the hoops dangling from my ears. "These are pretty." For a six-year-old, she had a deep and carrying voice. "When I get big, I'll buy some just like them."

While Brooke examined the flowers I'd braided into my hair, I saw Mrs. Adams glance at her in the mirror and frown. Her perfect blond daughter better not grow up to look like a Gypsy. No flowers in her hair. No dangly earrings.

"Dad," Jeremy said, "can I get my head shaved this summer?"

"Absolutely not." Mrs. Adams turned around and frowned at him. The BMW swerved a little as Mr. Adams also looked at Jeremy.

"Well, you don't like long hair," Jeremy said, "so why can't I have mine short? It's much cooler. Mark's mother let him. And so did Todd's."

Jeremy leaned forward, his voice rising to a whine, and Spencer squeezed my knee, a gesture observed with obvious displeasure by Mrs. Adams.

Despite the car's air conditioning, I was beginning to feel very warm. Turning my head, I watched the green Maryland countryside roll past in a blur. White fences, barns, horses, mailboxes leaning together companionably. With every turn of the BMW's wheels, I wished Spencer and I were on the motorcycle, heading toward the reservoir, instead of sitting in this car getting closer and closer to the club.

At Mount Washington, Mr. Adams parked deftly under a tree and led us toward the terrace at the back of the building. Falling into step beside me, Brooke told me about her friends, her favorite singers, her ballet class.

"Do you like my dress?" she asked. "If I spill anything on it, I'll be in big trouble."

"It's beautiful," I said. "You look like a princess at a garden party."

"I do?" Brooke smiled and tossed her short hair. "You're a princess, too," she said. "A sort of magical one, maybe a fairy."

" 'Oh, you're just talking silly, silly talk,' " I said.

" 'I know I'm talking silly talk . . . ,' " Brooke said, " 'But — rain makes applesauce.' "

Taking my hand, Spencer said, "It's her favorite book. I used to read it to her every night."

In a singsong voice, Brooke recited another line: " 'Candy tastes like soap, soap, soap.' "

"And rain makes applesauce," Spencer and I said.

Jeremy glanced over his shoulder, wondering what the joke was, but Mr. and Mrs. Adams walked on without noticing the laughter behind them.

~ *Chapter Twenty-four* ~

SOMEWHERE IN THE FLUTTER of summer dresses on the crowded terrace was Vanessa. Meg, too. Ted, Jeff, and Kevin, all the kids Spencer had known since fourth grade, were at this party. Men in suits and women in expensive outfits gathered around him, shaking his hand, patting his shoulder, smiling. Their names ran together, their faces blurred. I couldn't think of anything to say to them, so I smiled. And smiled and smiled and smiled till my jaws ached.

"Spence, we haven't seen you for so long," a blond woman said. "Where have you been keeping yourself, sweetie?" She threw her arms around him, hugged him, kissed his cheek, laughed.

Her husband pumped Spencer's hand. "Kevin told me you quit track this year. Why the hell did you do that? You were a champion, boy, a champion. I loved to watch you run."

"Oh, Hank." The woman gave her husband a playful little slap on the wrist and smiled at Spencer. "Don't pay any attention to him, Spence. He's got the social presence of a flea."

She paused a moment, still smiling, ignoring me. "We'll be going down to Ocean City in July. We've got the condo for a whole month. Come see us, okay?"

Spencer encircled my waist, drew me closer to his side. "Have you met Lauren?"

Mrs. Edwards extended her hand, and I shook it. "Nice to meet you," she said. "Lovely dress. Just right for a hot day."

"Thank you," I whispered.

Flashing her teeth, Mrs. Edwards turned back to Spencer. "You remember what I said, honey. July. Ocean City."

Spencer nodded and edged away, pulling me with him. I felt invisible, unable to cope. My dress was wrong, my shoes were wrong, everything about me was wrong. I didn't speak the language, didn't know the customs.

"Well, what a surprise." Vanessa stepped out of the crowd and stopped a few inches from Spencer, close enough to graze his chest with her breasts. She was wearing the dress Mom had admired in the Laura Ashley shop. The color matched her eyes, and the low neck revealed cleavage I'd never have. Thank God I hadn't let Mom talk me into buying it.

"Good to see you, Spence." Kevin put his arm around Vanessa's waist and drew her close to his side. Like Vanessa, he didn't look at me. Someone in the crowd bumped me, and I moved closer to Spencer.

He squeezed my hand. "I just saw your folks," Spencer said to Kevin.

"Dad's already three sheets to the wind," Kevin said. "He started celebrating early. If I know him, he'll be totally out of it by dinner. And Mom will be furious."

"How about you, Spence?" Vanessa asked. "Have some champagne. Nobody's checking I.D."

She touched her glass to his lips, her face close to his. "To old times."

His body tense, Spencer backed away. "No, thanks."

"Well, excuse *me*," Vanessa said. She was aiming for sarcasm, but I knew Spencer had hurt her feelings.

When Spencer didn't say anything, Vanessa pressed her lips to Kevin's and kissed him so hard, he staggered and slopped champagne on her dress. Losing her balance, Vanessa took a little step toward Spencer and steadied herself by putting a hand on his shoulder. Her face close to his, she brushed his hair out of his eyes. "Cut this stuff, it's awful. You look like a freak."

Glancing at me, Vanessa ran her eyes over my hair, my clothes, my sandals. Under her scornful gaze, I felt my dress sag and my flowers wilt.

Without saying a word to me, Vanessa glared at Spencer. "What are you trying to prove? You don't belong here anymore. I wish you'd just go away. It makes me sick to see you."

Leaving Kevin with his mouth hanging open, Vanessa pushed into the crowd and vanished.

"She didn't mean that, Spence," Kevin said. She's had too much champagne or something. You know how she gets."

Spencer shrugged, and Kevin mumbled something about finding Vanessa. We watched him elbow his way through a group of parents and teachers.

"I'm sorry, Lauren." Spencer's lips touched mine, warm and soft. "Van's right, it was a mistake to come. I shouldn't have let my mother talk me into this."

For a moment, I clung to him and tried to forget the look

of pure hatred Vanessa had directed at me. "I thought she broke up with you," I said. "I thought she didn't care."

"Forget it," Spencer said. "You heard Kevin. She's been hitting the champagne."

Pushing me gently ahead of him, Spencer moved toward the refreshment table. It was almost five o'clock. Beyond the terrace, the sun sent shafts of golden light through the thunderheads looming above the trees. On the lawn, Brooke and her friends turned cartwheels, their fancy dresses forgotten. Hearing their laughter, I wished I were their age. As far as I could see, they were the only ones having fun.

After several minutes of handshakes and greetings, we finally reached our goal — the hors d'oeuvres. Laid out on the linen-draped table were platters of fruit, cheese, tiny sandwiches, and all sorts of fancy concoctions. While the guests heaped their plates, white-jacketed servers replenished things as needed.

After we'd taken what we wanted, Spencer looked at me. "Have you ever tasted champagne?"

I shook my head, and the flowers braided in my hair tickled my back. The champagne fountain sparkled in the sunlight. The bubbles looked cold and fresh. Tempting on a hot afternoon.

Beside me, Kevin's father was filling glasses for himself and his wife. Catching Spencer's eye, Mr. Edwards handed one to him.

"Here, Spence," he said, "celebrate your escape from school. The future's yours, kid. Live it up."

Spencer looked at me. "Why not?" he asked. "This is a special occasion." Giving me a glass, he raised his and we clinked them together. "Here's to you and me, Lauren — and our trip."

Anxious to escape the crowd, we carried our plates across

the lawn and found a bench under an oak tree. Far from everyone else, we watched the party without being part of it. Voices no louder than a chorus of cicadas on a hot August afternoon drifted toward us. Vanessa and Kevin, Meg and Ted, parents, relatives, neighbors moved in and out of view. They weren't so frightening from a distance.

We sipped the champagne and picked at our food. Although I hadn't eaten anything since breakfast, the heat stole my appetite. None of the little sandwiches tasted as good as they looked, and the flies landing on the deviled eggs and steamed shrimp didn't increase their appeal.

"How do you like it?" Spencer eyed me over the rim of his glass. He hadn't eaten much, either.

"The champagne?" I took another sip and let it wash the inside of my mouth. "It's kind of sweet and sour at the same time and it tickles my nose like ginger ale."

We emptied our glasses, and Spencer walked back and got two more. Watching him cross the grass, the sun back-lighting his hair, I loved him so much it hurt. He saw me looking at him and did a little dance step. Behind him, the party was a moving backdrop, and Vanessa was no more than a bright thread woven into it.

"Your champagne, my lady." Spencer kissed my hand as I reached for the glass. Then he bent down and kissed my lips, long and lingering, his mouth sweet on mine.

In the woods behind us, a mockingbird sang. The clouds piled up, darker, purpling, sending shadows to chase the sunlight across the lawn. Hearing distant thunder, a rumble so slight it might have been a truck bouncing over a rough place in the road, we looked at the sky.

Raising his empty glass toward the clouds, Spencer murmured, "It looks like the end of the world is near."

Something in his voice sent a little shiver down my spine,

198

and I poked Spencer's side. "Just remember, 'Rain makes applesauce.' "

"I hope you have your umbrella." He hugged me. "How about another champagne?"

The warm, muggy air clung to me, made me light-headed, thirsty. "Sure," I said. "We don't graduate every day, do we?"

After the third glass, my mouth felt as if I'd had a shot of novocaine, and I had trouble saying words that started with S. This struck me as so funny, I couldn't stop laughing. Spencer started laughing, too. his face was flushed, his eyes sparkled, and I leaned close, caressing his thigh with one hand.

"I wish we were alone right now," I said between giggles. "Just you and me, Spence. In my room."

"Me, too," Spencer whispered. He stroked my face and kissed me. "Maybe we could sneak off, hide in the woods, nobody'd see."

"I'm invisible anyway," I told him. "Haven't you noticed? They all see you, but nobody sees me. I'm the girl who wasn't there."

" 'Oh, you're just talking silly, silly talk,' " Spencer whispered, and we started laughing again. I threw my head back and the world spun for a moment.

We hugged each other, laughing harder and harder. The sun disappeared behind the trees, and a breeze riffled the leaves, flipping them up to show their white sides.

"Look at those people." Spencer pointed at the terrace. "They're all drunk, I bet. Except my mother and the Great Stone Face, of course. Not them, boy, not them."

"Not us either," I said.

"No, not us," Spencer agreed. "In fact, I think we should have another glass of champagne."

I giggled again, but I wasn't sure I wanted any more to drink. I was so dizzy, nothing stayed still when I looked at it, and, when Spencer pulled me to my feet, my knees felt like they might bend the wrong way. Scared of falling, I grabbed his arm.

Holding each other up, we strolled toward the terrace, singing the words from *Rain Makes Applesauce* to a tune we made up as we went along. Everything we said was funny, everything we looked at made us laugh.

Grabbing my waist, Spencer suddenly spun me round and round. "I love you, Lauren, I love you forever."

"I love you, too, Spencer, forever and ever and ever."

If I'd been directing a movie, I would have freeze-framed us at that moment. We were happy, so happy — I wanted it to go on and on.

But we weren't in a movie, we were trapped in real life, and Spencer's mother was striding across the lawn toward us. We stopped, our arms around each other, and all of a sudden, nothing was funny. Nothing at all.

~ *Chapter Twenty-five* ~

ON THE DARKENING LAWN, Mrs. Adams's beige dress fluttered in the breeze. Peering first at Spencer and then at me, she said, "You've been drinking, you're drunk, both of you!"

Spencer wavered from side to side, staggered backward, leaned forward, and finally found a balancing point. "It's my graduation, isn't it? My special day? Isn't this how people celebrate?"

"You know how I feel about alcohol," Mrs. Adams said. "How could you behave like this? How could you?"

Spreading his arms wide in mock surprise, Spencer said, "I'm just Daddy's little boy doing what you always expected."

"I won't tolerate this." Mrs. Adams's voice was cold with fury. "Lower your voice, behave yourself. People are looking."

I glanced at the terrace. She was right. Several guests were staring across the lawn at us.

"Is that all you care about?" Spencer spoke louder. "Who sees, who hears? That's why we never talk about my father, isn't it? You don't want anyone to know about him, what he did. Let's glitter when we walk, let's keep up the perfect family act."

"Stop it, Spencer, stop it!" Mrs. Adams gripped his arms, shook him. "How much champagne have you had?"

"Not enough!" he yelled. "Not nearly enough, goddamnit!"

The wind blew harder, ballooning my dress, ruffling the striped canopy over the tables of food, sending paper plates cartwheeling across the grass. Lightning flashed on the horizon, and, a few seconds later, thunder rumbled. As the first drops of rain fell, the people on the terrace forgot us and scurried for shelter.

Mrs. Adams's hand shot out and struck Spencer's cheek with a loud clap. "I'll be inside with the others," she said. "Take a few minutes to get yourself together and join us. There's a sit-down dinner and I expect you to behave, to sober up. I want that hair combed, too."

Glancing at me, she added, "Maybe you were brought up in a home where this kind of behavior is acceptable, but Spencer knows better."

Without looking back, she strode across the lawn. For a moment, we stood and watched her vanish through the French doors.

"Come on." Spencer grabbed my and and ran, not toward the club but toward the parking lot. It was raining harder now, and the ground was wet. We skidded, slipped, fell, had trouble getting to our feet.

Finding the BMW, Spencer searched his pockets and produced a key. "My copy," he said, jamming it into the lock and opening the door.

I stared at him. The rain was pouring down, soaking me to the skin.

"Get in." Spencer ran around the car to the driver's side.

"But what about your family?" I stared at him across the roof of the car. Raindrops bounced between us, making it hard to see his face.

"The hell with them," Spencer said. "Let somebody else take them home. They're not my family anyway. You're my family now, just you."

He got into the car and I bent down to look at him. The dome light made his skin ashen. His hair, black with rain, clung to his face. Starting the engine, he said, "Goddamnit, Lauren, get in!"

Wet and shivering, my dress clinging to my skin like cheesecloth, I slid into the BMW beside him. He dragged me toward him, kissing me frantically, hugging me, whispering into my ear, my hair, my eyes. Frightened, I clung to him while the thunder boomed over our heads and lightning bolts zigzagged down from the clouds.

Releasing me, he threw the car into reverse and then drove out of the parking lot. For all we could see, we might as well have been driving through a car wash. Sheets of rain sluiced over the windshield, flashes of lightning blinded us, in places the BMW was up to its hubcaps in water.

Too scared to speak, I didn't ask Spencer where we were going or why. He was too drunk to drive, I knew it, he knew it, but neither of us dared say it.

When we pulled into a parking place at Mayfaire Court, Spencer opened the car door and stepped out into the rain. "Let's go."

We were home, we were safe. All we had to do was go upstairs to my room. But, instead of heading for the apartment building, Spencer pulled me toward the motorcycle.

"We're out of here," he said. "California. Mexico. Timbucktu. I don't know, I don't care. Someplace different, someplace better. She's seen the end of me, she can't talk to me like that."

"We can't leave now, not tonight." I stared at him, searching for reasons. "Look at the way we're dressed. It's raining, we don't have any money."

"I've got a thousand dollars' worth of checks in my wallet," Spencer said. "Graduation presents from my relatives. When it runs out, we'll get jobs. McDonald's, Hardee's, Wendy's, whatever we find. We'll have each other, that's all that matters."

The good champagne feeling was gone — I was cold and sick, depressed and scared. This wasn't a good idea, not tonight, not without any planning, not when it was raining and we'd drunk too much and I couldn't think straight.

Seizing Spencer's arm, I said, "Please, let's go inside. Mom's at Paul's, we'll have the apartment to ourselves. We can talk, make plans."

He pulled away from me "We're going now, Lauren! Don't you get it? I don't want to see my mother again, I don't want to live in that mausoleum anymore."

"We can't, Spencer, not in this rain, not after all that champagne."

"I thought you loved me!" Spencer straddled the motorcycle. "I thought I could count on you, I thought you understood!"

"I do love you, I do!" I grabbed at him, but he shook me away and kick started the engine.

"Come to bed with me," I cried. "Don't leave me like this, Spence, please don't. I love you, I love you."

But he was revving the engine, his face cold and hard and deathly white. Running in front of the motorcycle, I grabbed the handlebars. "Wait till morning," I begged. "I'll go with you in the morning."

Wresting the handlebars away, Spencer tried to steer around me. "Goddamn you!" I screamed. "Put on your helmet, at least put on your helmet!"

Scowling at me, he grabbed the helmet and pulled it on. With the visor in place, I couldn't see his face. Before I could stop him, he opened the throttle and roared away.

I chased him all the way to the top of the hill, crying, telling him to wait, I'd changed my mind, I'd go, but he didn't look back, didn't hear. By the time I reached Thunder Valley Road, all I saw was his red taillight disappearing in the rain.

I thought he'd come back, I was sure he would. I stood on the curb, watching, listening. The rain pounded down, the thunder rumbled like artillery. Small branches and clusters of leaves lay in soggy heaps on the road, witnesses to the storm's violence.

Minutes passed, hours it seemed, but Spencer didn't return. Fighting tears, I walked slowly downhill toward home. With every step I hoped to hear the motorcycle behind me, but nothing followed me except the wind and the rain.

When I unlocked the door, I saw Mom sitting at the table, drinking a cup of coffee and smoking a cigarette. She was as surprised to see me as I was to see her.

"What are you doing here?" I asked.

"Paul and I had a fight," she muttered, "and I walked out. I told him I wanted a commitment, you know, is he serious or not? He just slid away from the question, got all evasive. I'm so sick of that crap."

She looked at me, and her eyes widened. "My God, Lauren, you're soaked to the skin. Where's Spencer?"

Turning away from her, I leaned against the wall and cried.

I felt Mom's hand on my hair, stroking the remains of the flowers, the tangles. For once, I didn't pull away. Instead, I put my head on her shoulder and let her try to comfort me.

"Oh, Mom, Mom," I wept. "He's gone, he's left me."

I heard her suck in her breath and suddenly I was telling her everything, letting the words tumble out, not caring whether they made sense or not.

When I was finished, Mom steered me to the bathroom, helped me peel off the sodden ruin of my dress, and turned on the shower. Alone, I stood in front of the mirror and gazed at my reflection. Slowly, I undid my braid. One by one, the wilted flowers dropped from my hair. They lay on the floor like dead butterflies.

Standing under the hot water, I shampooed my hair, scrubbed my body, watched the mud swirl away from my toes. Then, tired and unhappy, I leaned against the tiled wall and sobbed. The shower poured down on me, harder than the rain, but not so cold. It had happened, what I'd always feared — Spencer had left me, he didn't love me after all, and I didn't see how I could live with the pain.

When I came back to the kitchen, Mom fixed me a cup of tea and I sank into a chair beside her. Like a zombie, I felt nothing. My insides were gone, I was hollowed out. Without Spencer, I had nothing to live for.

Outside, the rain fell as if it would never stop. Someone came running up the steps, and I stared at the door, hoping, but a key turned in a lock across the hall, and all was quiet again.

"I'm glad you didn't go with him, Lauren." Mom's face mirrored my unhappiness. Reaching across the table, she took my hand. "No matter how much you love someone,

206

you can't save him from himself," she said. "Spencer has problems only he can solve, Lauren."

The phone rang so loudly, we both jumped. Sure it was Spencer, I ran to answer it, but, when I put the receiver to my ear, it wasn't his voice I heard. It was his mother's. I stared at the wall, my heart bumping in my chest like a wild thing, my throat so tight with disappointment, I could barely speak.

"Is Spencer there, Lauren?"

"No," I whispered.

"You can tell me the truth," Mrs. Adams said. Her voice was cold in my ear, so cold it hurt.

"He's not here." I twisted the phone cord round and round my finger.

"Who is it?" Mom asked.

"But you know where he is," Mrs. Adams went on.

"No." I was crying now.

Noticing my tears, Mom walked toward me. "Who is it, Lauren?" she asked again.

"Don't lie to me," Mrs. Adams said. "You and Spencer left without a word of explanation, you took the car even though my son was in no condition to drive, you left us stranded at the club. Do you have any idea how humiliating it was to face our friends, to ask for a ride home?"

"I'm sorry," I whispered. "The car's here."

"The car's there, but Spencer isn't?"

"Yes, no." Her questions confused me, her voice froze my brain. I looked at Mom. She was standing a few inches away, frowning. Putting my hand over the mouthpiece, I said, "It's Mrs. Adams. She thinks Spencer's here."

Snatching the phone, Mom said, "This is Joyce Anderson. Can I help you with anything?"

She listened for a moment. "My daughter wouldn't lie to you. She has no idea where Spencer is, and she's worried sick. He left on the motorcycle a couple of hours ago. Lauren begged him not to go, but he went anyway. He was upset, angry, unreasonable."

There was another period of silence, longer this time. Mom frowned, shook her head. "No, you can't talk to Lauren," she said. "It was Spencer's motorcycle, he bought it last winter. I thought you knew he kept it here."

While Mrs. Adams talked, Mom looked at me. "I'm sorry," she said. "I know you're worried, we are, too. If Lauren hears from Spencer, I'll see that she calls you."

After giving Mrs. Adams our address, Mom hung up and leaned against the kitchen wall. "So," she said, "the motorcycle was a secret."

"His parents didn't want him to have it."

"And you lied to me."

I nodded, and Mom lit another cigarette. We sat together for a long time, watching the phone, expecting it to ring. I picked up the receiver once or twice, thinking it might be out of order, but the dial tone hummed in my ear like a message from the dead.

Finally, Mom yawned and put her hand over mine. "It's past two, honey," she said. "He's probably safe in bed right now. Why don't you get some sleep yourself?"

"You think so?" I looked at her, wanting to believe her, desperate to be convinced that nothing had happened to Spencer.

"He's not stupid enough to run away to California like a spoiled child," Mom said. "Riding in the rain for a few miles probably brought him to his senses. You'll see, he'll call you tomorrow and apologize."

Something in Mom's voice worried me. She didn't believe her own words, she was trying too hard to sound sincere.

"He went off on the motorcycle once before," I said uncertainly. "He didn't call me then, either."

Mom looked relieved. "That's just his way then," she said a little too brightly.

"I guess so." I kissed Mom goodnight and walked slowly down the hall to my room.

Still hoping the phone would ring, I stood at my window and stared at the dark woods at the bottom of the hill. The rain had almost stopped, the thunder rumbled in the distance, and the lightning flickered on the horizon. Spencer had gone with the storm, and I'd never felt more alone in my whole life.

~ Chapter Twenty-six ~

THE NEXT MORNING, I expected the motorcycle to be in its usual place, but all I saw when I ran to the window was the BMW, parked crookedly, too far from the curb. I stared at the car until Mom woke up and found me.

Putting an arm around my waist, she looked at the BMW. "I suppose his parents will be over sometime today to get that," she said.

"Mom, why hasn't he called?" I was crying again, and she hugged me.

"Men are such S.O.B.s," she said.

Turning away, she went to the kitchen and tried to make Mr. Coffee start, but the little light wouldn't go on, the water wouldn't heat. The machine sat on the counter, brain dead.

"What did I tell you?" Mom said. "You can't depend on a man to do anything right." Unplugging Mr. Coffee, she said, "Next time, I'll buy *Ms*. Coffee!"

While Mom and I sat at the table, drinking instant coffee, the phone finally rang. I rushed for it, but once again, it wasn't Spencer. Thrusting the receiver at Mom, I flung myself down in my chair and stared at the rain. Where was he? Surely he'd come to his senses by now. Why didn't he call?

When Mom hung up, she said, "Well, well, what do you know? Paul wants me to come over and talk."

"I guess you'll have to quit smoking again," I said.

Mom scowled and took a long drag. Exhaling slowly, she watched the smoke rise before she put out the cigarette. Jumping to her feet, she crumpled the pack and tossed it into the trash can. "Don't let me root it out of there tonight, Lauren."

Pausing on her way to the bathroom, she said, "What are you going to do today?"

When I shrugged, she put an arm around my shoulders. "Would you like to come with me?"

I shook my head. Spencer would call, I knew he would. Unless, unless — I shook my head, forcing the thought away. Nothing had happened to him. He was all right. Mad maybe, disappointed in me, in one of his moods. Soon he'd call. This wasn't one of Mom's boyfriends, this wasn't my father we were talking about. It was Spencer. Spencer who loved me, loved me forever. Spencer who wouldn't walk out on me.

At two o'clock, Mom left. Alone with a silent telephone, I picked up the Sunday paper, but I couldn't concentrate. Words didn't make sense, they turned into meaningless patterns, and I found myself reading the same paragraphs over and over again, trying to make sense of the story.

Hours passed. The phone didn't ring. Out in the parking lot, the BMW sat where Spencer had left it. One of the court's stray cats sat on its roof, its fur bedraggled, and glowered at the scudding clouds.

In desperation, I went for a run, but everything I saw

reminded me of Spencer. The bridge where we sat and talked, a certain grove of trees, a pond, empty swings in a tot lot. Under the gray sky, all the places we'd been were sad and gloomy reminders of his absence. If I were Owl, I'd soon have enough tears to make a whole pot of tea.

An hour later, I sat on a bridge railing and watched the creek swirl past, higher and faster because of the storm. Closing my eyes, I saw Spencer's pale face, black hair plastered to his skull by the rain, begging me to go with him. With all my heart I wished I had, couldn't understand now why I hadn't. He'd left thinking I didn't love him.

In my head, Spencer's voice went on and on, repeating the same thing over and over again like a scratched record — *"I'm my father's son, he did it, I'll do it, do it, do it . . ."*

No, I shook my head, *no.* He couldn't have. We were so close I'd know, I'd share his pain like a twin. I couldn't have slept last night, couldn't have gotten through this long dreary day if, if . . .

Frightened, I slipped off the railing and jogged home. Surely he'd called while I was gone. Running faster, I imagined Spencer in a phone booth somewhere, lonely, lost, needing me.

It was past seven when I sprinted up the stairs to our apartment. As I fumbled with the key, I heard the telephone ringing. Heart pounding, I threw open the door, ran to the kitchen, and snatched the receiver off the hook.

"Lauren? Oh, thank God, I was so scared," Casey shouted in my ear. "I've been calling you all afternoon. I thought you must have been with him."

I gripped the phone, felt my mouth go dry, my knees turn to water. The receiver was so heavy I could barely hold it. "What are you talking about?"

"Oh, my God," Casey said. "You don't know. You haven't heard."

I wanted to hang up, but I stared at the receiver instead. Out of its little holes came a tinny voice, an insect's buzz.

"Lauren," the voice was saying, "Spencer wrecked the motorcycle. Kevin told Jordan when we got back from Ocean City."

"No," I said, "no."

"He hit a tree."

"Is he — ?" I whispered, "Is he — ?" I couldn't say the word.

"He's in Shock Trauma at Grace Hospital," Casey said. "That's all I know, Lauren."

I couldn't cry, couldn't breathe, couldn't let myself believe Casey's words. She was mistaken, it was a trick, a lie. Someone else was in Shock Trauma, a thief maybe, a boy who'd stolen the motorcycle. Not Spencer. Not Spencer. Please God, not Spencer.

"Lauren? Lauren?" The insect voice chirped, louder and louder, insisting I pay attention, answer.

"Drive me to the hospital," I sobbed. "Please, Casey, please."

I hung up and rushed out the door just as Mom reached the top step. Paul was right behind her, carrying a big bag of Chinese take-out. The odor of egg rolls filled the warm air in the hall.

"Where are you going?" Mom grabbed my arm and spun me around. "What's the matter?"

"It's Spencer," I sobbed, "he's in Shock Trauma. Casey's driving me to Grace Hospital."

"Oh, no, Lauren, no." Mom put her arms around me, but I beat at her with my fists.

"Let me go! Let me go!"

Mom staggered and clung to my arm. "Honey, they don't allow visitors," she said, "not in Shock Trauma."

I pulled away from her, but she ran after me and caught me again. "Calm down, think it through. You can't help him now, Lauren. You'll just upset yourself."

Breaking free, I raced down the rest of the steps two, three at a time. Above me, Mom leaned over the railing and begged me to come back. Ignoring her, I pushed open the vestibule door and raced out into the rain, running wildly toward Casey's apartment.

At the top of the hill, I saw Casey getting into her car. Yanking open the passenger door, I slid in beside her and burrowed into her arms. She held me tight, she let me cling to her and sob.

"It's all my fault," I wept. "If I'd gone with him, he wouldn't have done it."

"What do you mean?" Casey asked.

"At the party," I sobbed, "his mother, she was awful to him. We were drunk, the champagne, we shouldn't have had so much, we just kept drinking it, I don't even know why, and he, and he, he told her, he — "

Casey stared at me. It was obvious she didn't know what I was talking about, so I babbled on. "His father, his real father, he was an alcoholic, he killed himself, and Spencer's so scared, he worries all the time, like it's hereditary or something."

I was crying too hard to talk. Casey drove with one hand, patting my arm, trying to hug me, pulling my head over to rest on her shoulder.

"I should've gone with him, he begged me to, I let him down, he thought I didn't love him," I sobbed. "He did it

214

on purpose, I know he did, and it's all my fault — I might as well have killed him."

Casey was talking, but I wasn't listening. Staring at the rainy Interstate, at the trucks and cars, at the streaky patterns of red taillights ahead of us, I saw Spencer. Saw him laughing, saw him turn his head to watch a bird soar across the sky, saw his face when we made love, the look in his eyes. Saw him running, his body slim and strong and graceful, his skin white and smooth, his hair shining in the sun.

"You can't be dead," I whispered, "you can't be, I won't let you be dead."

I turned to Casey. "Maybe he's conscious now, maybe he's out of Shock Trauma, maybe it's not even him, just a mistake, someone who looked like him."

We were on the Capital Beltway, and Casey was too intent on driving to talk. She gripped the steering wheel, squinted at the exit sign for Connecticut Avenue, flipped on her turn signal.

In my head, I played out a little fantasy. Spencer joking with the nurse, the nurse saying, "You really had us worried for a few minutes, young man, but I knew you were too beautiful to die."

Then I'd come through the door, maybe I'd have flowers or a balloon or a book. Something to make him laugh — *Curious George Goes to the Hospital* — that would be just right. Spencer would look up, see me, smile. He'd have a cast on his arm, a few bruises, nothing serious. *It was an accident,* he'd say, *a mistake, I'd never do something like that on purpose.* Oh, the picture in my head was so real, I was sure that was how it would be.

Slowing for a traffic light, Casey peered into the darkness, trying to remember which street led to Wisconsin Avenue.

Making a decision, she turned at the next light. We passed the expensive stores in Chevy Chase, restaurants, movie theaters, the National Cathedral. Knowing we were nearly there, my heart started beating harder, faster. By now, I was sure Spencer was waiting for me, wondering where I was, thinking I didn't care, didn't love him.

Following signs for the hospital, we turned right on Reservoir Road. For a few frustrating minutes, we were lost in a maze of narrow streets. One-way signs, no-parking signs, no-right-turn, no-left-turn. Where was the hospital?

Finally, Casey pulled up in front of what she hoped was the main entrance. "Do you have any money?"

Money, I hadn't thought of money. I opened my purse, got out my wallet. Two dollars. And some change.

Casey thrust a twenty at me. "Pay me back later."

She put her arms around me, held me, let me weep all over her. "Don't you want me to stay with you?" she asked.

"I'll be okay," I said. "As soon as I see him, I'll be okay."

Not giving her a chance to say anything else, I thanked her, jumped out of the car, ran up a flight of steps and across a brick terrace. My feet beat out a rhythm, *Don't die, don't die, don't die.*

The light in the lobby was dim. A man sat at the information desk, his face in shadow, reading a book.

"Someone told me a friend of mine is here." My voice shook, my knees shook, I had to hold the edge of the desk to keep from falling down. "They said he's in Shock Trauma."

"No one is allowed to visit Shock Trauma," the man said softly.

"I know, but can you tell me if he's here? And how he is?" I hesitated. "Maybe he isn't in Shock Trauma, maybe I heard wrong, maybe . . ."

"His name?"

I bit my lip, afraid to tell him. Just saying Spencer's name in this silent lobby seemed to put him in peril. The man waited, his face kind.

"Spencer," I whispered, "Spencer Adams." I clasped my purse, committed now to hear the truth.

The man checked a file. When he looked up, his face was graver than before, more sympathetic. "He was admitted last night," he said, "in critical condition."

The room tilted, the man multiplied into many men, his voice ran on and on without stopping, repeating endlessly "critical condition, critical condition, critical condition."

Steadying myself, I gripped the edge of the desk. "What does that mean?"

"It's all I'm permitted to say, all I know."

"Is there someone I can talk to? A doctor, a nurse?"

He shook his head. "It would be best for you to go home."

"No," I said. "I'll stay here till someone tells me how he is, till I see him."

The man sighed. "There's a lounge in the Shock Trauma Unit, but I don't think it's advisable. If you aren't a family member, no one on the staff will tell you anything."

When I insisted, he told me which elevator to take, what floor. I walked down a hall lined with photographs of the Middle East. Starving children, hollow-eyed women, refugees from war hiding in the bombed-out ruins of their homes, pictures taken by a surgeon helping the Kurds, brought back to show us how lucky we are.

In the elevator, I folded my arms tightly across my chest and tried to breathe normally. I was cold, so cold I thought I'd never be warm again.

The doors slid open, and I stepped into a silent gray world.

217

The carpet was gray, the furniture was gray, the walls were gray, the air was gray. Directly ahead was a lounge partitioned into small sections. A silent couple faced each other on gray chairs, a man slept under a gray blanket on a gray couch, a woman sat alone in a gray corner and wept. The room had the appearance of an airport where passengers had been stranded overnight.

Somewhere, not far away, was Spencer. How could I find him?

Minutes passed, flowed into hours. Finally, a doctor walked up to the elevator and pushed the button. He was young, nice-looking. While he waited, he glanced at me.

"Do you know where Shock Trauma is?" I asked him.

"It's at the end of that corridor and to the left," he said, "but visitors aren't allowed."

The tears I'd been fighting spilled out of my eyes and ran down my cheeks. "My boyfriend," I sobbed, "he's in there, and I don't know how he is."

"What's his name?"

"Spencer, Spencer Adams."

"The young guy, the motorcycle accident." The doctor frowned, and the thought flashed through my mind that Spencer was dead. While I'd been sitting here, so close, he had died.

"I'm sorry," he said, "he's in critical condition."

"But what does that mean?" Surely he knew more than the man at the information desk.

"I'm just an intern," he apologized, "but the fact he's still alive is a good sign."

He patted my shoulder. "I haven't seen him," he said. "I wasn't on duty when the Med-Evac helicopter brought him in. His parents are here somewhere, maybe they can give you the details."

When the elevator came, he told me he was sorry he couldn't tell me more. He stepped inside, the doors slid shut, and I was alone again.

Even though I couldn't see Spencer, I wanted to be close to him. Trembling with cold, I walked down the corridor and turned left at the end. The air was totally dead. A chemical odor, faint and unidentifiable, burned my nostrils and left its taste in the back of my throat.

Ahead were closed double doors posted with restrictions — SHOCK TRAUMA. My mouth went dry, my heart hammered. Spencer was on the other side of those doors. What had happened to him, to his body, to his mind that was so awful no one could see him?

~ Chapter Twenty-seven ~

TOO TIRED TO DO ANYTHING ELSE, I sat on the floor with my back to the wall and stared down the hall at the closed doors. I'd wait for Mr. and Mrs. Adams. Surely, they'd come this way.

An hour passed, but I was afraid to leave for even a moment. I might miss them. Ignoring my bladder, the pain in my back, the hard floor, I waited and waited and waited. No one came or went.

At last, I heard footsteps. Turning my head, I saw Mr. and Mrs. Adams. She was crying, he had his arm around her, they walked slowly.

Scrambling to my feet, I faced them. For a moment we stared at each other, his mother and I. We didn't move, we didn't speak. The distance between us, two or three yards at most, was impassable.

The expression on Mrs. Adams's face told me I'd made a mistake. Instead of running to her and begging for news, I backed away.

"What are you doing here?" Mrs. Adams bore down upon me. "Haven't you caused enough harm?"

Behind her, Mr. Adams tried to stop her. He reached out for her, said something in a low voice, but she paid no attention to him.

"Please," I whispered. "Please tell me how he is."

Mrs. Adams's eyes glittered with frozen tears, but her voice was taut with fury. "How could you let my son go off by himself on that motorcycle? What were you thinking of?"

Mr. Adams touched her shoulder, but she ignored him. "Spencer has had other girlfriends," she went on. "Nice girls from decent homes. He never drank, never behaved this way. What sort of influence did you have on him?"

"I tried to stop him," I sobbed, "I begged him not to go, but he wouldn't listen, he went anyway."

"For God's sake, Eleanor, it's not Lauren's fault," Mr. Adams said.

Too angry to listen to him, to me, to anyone, Mrs. Adams insisted I was responsible for everything — the motorcycle, the champagne, Spencer's grades. I'd ruined him, she said. If he died, it was my fault.

Her words slapped me, hurt me, made me say things I hadn't meant to. "It was you he was running from," I cried. "you and his father."

Mrs. Adams's face paled. "What do you know about Spencer's father?"

"He shot himself."

A nurse passed, her head swung toward us, but I didn't care who heard, who saw. "Spencer found the body, he's known all along."

Turning away, I pressed my face against the wall and wept. I expected Mrs. Adams to say something, but I heard nothing. When I finally turned to face her, she and her husband were gone. The corridor was empty.

Suddenly exhausted, I slid down the wall and sat on the

floor. Clasping my knees to my chest, I hid my face. What had I done? Why had I spoken like that to Spencer's mother? She'd never forgive me, never.

Worse yet, she had every right to be angry. I shouldn't have let Spencer keep the motorcycle at Mayfaire Court, shouldn't have let him drink so much champagne, shouldn't have let him leave without me. I should have gone with him, I should be in Shock Trauma, too. Or dead.

I felt someone touch my shoulder. Thinking Mrs. Adams had returned, I looked up. It was the nurse who'd walked past earlier.

"Are you all right?" she asked.

I shook my head. Of course I wasn't. She was a nurse — why did she have to ask?

She helped me up, she led me back to the gray lounge, she told me to lie down and rest. I was a child in her hands. Obedient, unquestioning.

The long night passed, one gray hour after another. I slept, woke, slept again, dreamed. Spencer and I were riding the motorcycle through a desert toward a vanishing point on the horizon. I was holding a red heart-shaped balloon and laughing. I was so happy that he was alive, well, himself again. Suddenly, the balloon's string broke. I grabbed for it, tried to catch it, but I couldn't close my hands. I pawed at the air. It was too late. The heart rose into the sky, shrank, turned black. Clouds closed around it, it was gone.

Spencer looked at me. "You let my heart go," he said. His face turned to a skull, his body collapsed, and I was left clutching his empty leather jacket.

I woke up gasping. When I stood up, the lounge spun and my heart thudded. I was as dizzy as if I'd been drinking champagne again.

*   *   *

Late in the afternoon, I saw the intern who'd talked to me when I first arrived. "Don't you ever go home?" he asked.

When I started crying, he took my arm and guided me toward the elevator. "There's a canteen in the basement," he said. "I'm taking a break. Come with me."

Too tired and hungry to resist, I watched him push the down button. "My name's Michael Doyle," he said. "What's yours?"

"Lauren Anderson." It was too much effort to say more, but Michael seemed to understand. He leaned against the side of the elevator and watched the numbers change as we dropped down, down, down, leaving Shock Trauma behind.

In the canteen, I got a couple of things from vending machines and carried them to a small table. Peach yogurt, an apple, a cup of coffee — a still life, something to paint, not to eat.

"I know this is hard for you," Michael said, "but Spencer's young and strong. He made it through the first twenty-four hours, the most critical time."

I nodded, but I couldn't look at him, couldn't bear to see the knowledge in his eyes. I sipped the coffee, but it was too black and bitter to drink.

"I understand his mother is angry with you," Michael said.

Too ashamed to raise my head, I stirred sugar into my coffee. The nurse must have told him about it. Part of the night's activity. A screaming match outside Shock Trauma.

"It's a common reaction," Michael said. "We see it all the time — people blaming other people, shouting, crying. Shock Trauma's a very emotional place."

Behind me, someone dropped coins into a machine. The sound startled me so much, I upset my coffee. Without moving, I watched Michael mop it up with a napkin. The dark liquid spread, dripped on the floor, stained the white paper.

He turned away to throw the napkin into the trash. Afraid he was getting ready to leave, I grabbed his sleeve. "Can you tell me how Spencer is? Have you seen him?"

Michael frowned. For a moment, I thought he was going to repeat what I'd heard so often. "I know he's in critical condition," I said. "Is he conscious? Does he have head injuries? Spine injuries? For God's sake, tell me what's wrong with him."

"I talked to one of the nurses." Michael said slowly. "You may not believe this, but Spencer was lucky. He was wearing his helmet, his leg took most of the impact, he was thrown into bushes instead of the road. Someone saw the accident and called for help right away."

"*Lucky* — " an odd word to describe someone in Shock Trauma. Michael was right. It was hard to believe Spencer had been lucky.

"No head injuries, no spinal damage," Michael went on, "but he lost a lot of blood, damaged his liver and spleen, fractured his leg in several places."

"Is he conscious?"

Michael shook his head. "He's made a lot of progress, Jane says he's a real fighter, but he's not out of the woods yet. At the moment, his chances are fifty-fifty, much better than they were when he arrived Saturday night."

I don't know what else Michael would have said if his beeper hadn't sounded. "I have to go." Handing me a tissue, he added, "Keep your chin up, we're doing all we can."

Alone in the canteen, I poked at my yogurt, but I couldn't

eat it. Fifty-fifty, he'd said, fifty-fifty — Spencer's chances. Maybe it had been better not to know.

I walked back to the elevator, rode to the seventh floor, sat down on the bench. Michael's words repeated themselves endlessly — *Not out of the woods yet, not out of the woods, the woods, the woods* . . .

I remembered Frost's poem, the man and his horse, the frozen pond, the snow. Spencer had entered the woods, the lovely woods, the dark and deep woods where Thanatos waited. He'd forgotten his promises, he'd forgotten the miles he had to go, he'd fallen asleep too soon.

I pictured Spencer riding down Ten Oaks Road. It was dark, it was raining, he was drunk. He accelerated, he went faster, faster. He flew over hills, he leaned into curves, he saw the tree, I knew he did. He headed straight for it.

What was he thinking about? Why had he done it? Why hadn't I gone with him? The same images, the same questions over and over again.

But no answers.

~ Chapter Twenty-eight ~

AROUND SEVEN-THIRTY, the elevator doors slid open, and Mom stepped out. "My God, Lauren," she said, "you look terrible."

Without giving me a chance to protest, she grabbed my arm and towed me out of the hospital. I struggled, I argued, but she was insistent. "You can come back in the morning, you can stay all day, but you're not sleeping here at night."

An hour later we were in Adelphia. I felt like Rip Van Winkle returning after a hundred years' absence. The houses, the streets, the trees, the green lawns — they belonged to a time when Spencer and I were together. It hurt to look at them, to see the empty place by the dumpster, the asphalt stained with oil from the motorcycle.

Alone in my room, I turned on my tape player and lay on my bed. The moment the music began, I remembered Spencer had left a cassette in it. The adagio. He'd wanted me to listen to it, to help him understand what his father had been thinking about when he pulled the trigger.

Closing my eyes, I let Albinoni's music wind through my head, twist into my blood, cramp my heart with despair.

226

The organ throbbed in the background, the violins shivered, moaned, wailed, sank down into gloom.

Lost in visions of death and darkness, I opened my eyes and saw the little heart Spencer had drawn long ago just above my pillow: "Je t'aime, Lauren."

Since then, he'd written many things on my graffiti wall. His calligraphy was good, better than mine or Casey's, easy to find. "The wind blows backwards all night long," filled in the empty space between Casey's Erica Jong and my Emily Dickinson. "Silly talk, silly talk, Lauren talks silly talk" swirled around a verse I'd copied from Edna St. Vincent Millay.

Among declarations of love, I discovered quotes from Whitman I hadn't noticed before, recent additions squeezed into small spaces, hiding among longer and larger scribbles: "All goes onward and outward, nothing collapses, /and to die is different from what anyone supposes, and luckier."

A couple of inches away, Spencer had written the next line: "Has anyone supposed it lucky to be born?/I hasten to inform him it is just as lucky to die, and I know it."

Near the baseboard, in tiny letters I found more Whitman: "The suicide sprawls on the bloody floor of the bedroom, / I witness the corpse with its dabbled hair, I note where the pistol has fallen."

A sudden fury poured through my veins. Death, suicide, self-destruction — was that all Spencer thought about?

Leaping to my feet, I ejected the cassette and threw it against the wall so hard, the case cracked and the tape spilled out in a tangle of vinyl. Music to die by, suicide's music, that was what the adagio was. I hated it, I never wanted to hear it again.

Not satisfied, I hurled *Rain Makes Applesauce* across the room. In a flurry of pages, it struck my Baryshnikov poster and crashed to the floor. After it, I flung *Leaves of Grass*, Robert Frost's poetry, my Earthsea books, *Bedtime for Frances*. Everything that reminded me of Spencer hit the wall. Never, never would I open those books again. I despised them. I despised him.

Suddenly, my door opened. Mom took one look, crossed the room, and put her arms around me. Holding me tight, she whispered, "It's okay, Lally, it's okay, let it out, get rid of it."

"I hate him, I hate him, how could he do this to me?" Words tumbled out, doubts, fears, things I'd wanted to tell her before. This time, she let me talk, she listened, she comforted me. Clinging to her, I wept until I was dry and trembling and weak and totally empty of everything.

She wiped my face with a warm washcloth, she stroked my hair, she led me to the table and made me sit down.

Too tired to move, I watched her open a can of chicken rice soup and dump it into a pot. The familiar smell reminded me of childhood illnesses and Mom taking time off from work to sit by my bed and read *Mary Poppins*.

I started crying again. "What's wrong with me?" I sobbed. "Am I going crazy?"

Mom put a bowl in front of me and patted my hand. "You're exhausted, Lally. You haven't slept, you haven't eaten."

"Do you think he did it on purpose?"

Mom stirred sugar into her coffee. "Spencer's the only one who can answer that question," she said slowly.

"What if he doesn't wake up? What if he dies?"

Mom's eyes filled with tears and she squeezed my hand. "He won't," she said fiercely. "He can't. He just can't."

We stared at each other. The apartment was very quiet.

The summer night pressed against the window screens, bringing the sweet smell of honeysuckle into the room. Where Spencer lay, the air was cold and odorless. He slept undisturbed, far from the waking world, unaware of grief.

Mom cleared her throat and blew her nose. "Please eat your soup Lally," she said. "You'll make yourself sick."

Lifting my spoon, I forced myself to swallow one mouthful, two. When the bowl was empty, I carried it out to the kitchen.

"Remember the gerbil?" I asked Mom.

She stared at me. "Gerbil?"

"Sir Walter Raleigh — he died and the ground was too cold to bury him so you let me freeze him till spring."

Clapping her hand over her mouth, she laughed. "I'd forgotten about that. Joanna wouldn't eat here till we'd had the funeral. She was sure she'd find him on her plate." Remembering, we leaned against the stove and laughed.

We'd had goldfish and guppies too, Mom reminded me. They'd all died, and we'd had funerals for every one of them.

Suddenly we looked at each other. "Oh, Lord," Mom said, "what are we talking about?"

Turning her attention to the dishes in the sink, she ran hot water, poured in soap. She washed, I dried. The golden-oldies station blared an old Gordon Lightfoot song about a shipwreck.

When the kitchen was tidy, Mom sent me to bed. Not to mine, but hers. If anyone understood ghosts, she did.

The next morning, Mom woke me around seven, made me shower, dress, eat breakfast. Ordinary things, things I used to do every day without thinking about them.

After a second cup of coffee, she offered to drive me to the Silver Spring metro stop. "You can walk to the hospital from Foggy Bottom," she said.

When she pulled into the Kiss and Ride parking lot, I hugged her hard. "Thanks, Mom," I whispered, "thanks for everything."

She kissed me on both cheeks, mingling her tears with mine. "Look at us," she said, trying to laugh, but only managing a kind of snort. "We're a pair, aren't we?"

After making me promise to meet her at seven, she handed me a small bag. "I picked these up at the drugstore. You might want them."

When Mom was out of sight, I found a seat on a crowded car and watched the graffiti-covered buildings slide past the window. Cool Disco Dan's name was scrawled on every wall. Spencer and I used to look for it, wonder about him, make up stories to amuse ourselves. He was a legend, Spencer said, a modern John Henry.

Finally, I opened the bag and took out the photographs Mom had taken at graduation. There we were, Spencer and I, capped and gowned. His tassel hung in the middle of his face, and he'd crossed his eyes to focus on it. Unaware he was clowning, I stared seriously into the camera. In the next one, we had our arms around each other. We were smiling, the sun backlit our hair. Spencer's jacket was open to show his pink shirt and his matching paisley suspenders and tie. The last time I'd seen those clothes, they were soaking wet. What had happened to them when he crashed?

Tears dropped on the photo. Without looking at the others, I put them in my purse. Graduation had been years ago, it had taken place in another lifetime, a different world. The boy and girl in the pictures no longer existed.

At Foggy Bottom, I rode the escalator up to the street

and walked toward Georgetown. On the bridge over Rock Creek Park, I stopped and looked down. Below me, traffic snaked along the road. The treetops were soft and green. What would it be like to jump? To free-fall through space? For a few seconds, it would be glorious, but then the flight would end, you'd hit the ground. Had Spencer realized how much it would hurt?

Mesmerized by height and airy space, I clung to the railing. For the first time, I knew what he'd meant when he said death fascinated him, tempted him. Scared of my own thoughts, I backed away from the railing, crossed the bridge, and jogged up M Street toward Wisconsin Avenue.

In my memory, Spencer ran beside me, making up silly stories about the people we saw, laughing, feeding pigeons, giving money to the man playing a flute on the corner.

I passed the Key Theatre, where we'd watched foreign films that never made it to the suburbs. Across the street was Olsson's, our favorite bookstore. Ice cream places, Vietnamese carryouts, exotic boutiques, the shop where Spencer had bought my earrings. How could these things be here, unchanged, when he wasn't with me?

Dodging tourists, taking chances with cars and buses, I ran up Reservoir Road toward the hospital. I'd been away from Spencer almost twelve hours. Suppose something had happened to him while I was gone?

~ Chapter Twenty-nine ~

NOTHING HAD CHANGED. The moment I stepped out of the elevator, the gray silence wrapped itself around me again. Sitting on my bench beside the elevator, I waited.

And waited and waited — for days, for weeks. I took the Metro, met Mom or Casey in Silver Spring, and returned in the morning. Even though I was nervous about doing it, I called Mrs. Jenkins and told her I wouldn't be coming back to the library. She was more sympathetic than I'd thought she'd be — she actually said she'd be happy to re-hire me in the fall.

"The picture book section hasn't been the same since you left," she said.

At the hospital, I often saw Mrs. Adams, but she never saw me. Or, if she did, she pretended not to. Keeping her face averted, she hurried past me. Once or twice, Mr. Adams nodded to me, but that was as far as it went.

Every time the Adamses walked by, I swore I'd stop them, ask them questions, make them tell me how Spencer was, but I never had the courage. Often they were surrounded by white-coated doctors clasping clipboards. They spoke in low voices filled with urgency; I overheard words like respirator, infection, complications, internal bleeding.

Four weeks after the accident, I saw Michael in the canteen. Ever since the first time we'd talked, he'd taken time to tell me how Spencer was doing. Interns picked up a lot of scuttlebutt, he said, and he shared what he learned. The news was always the same — Spencer was unconscious, he was still in Shock Trauma, his chances were improving, but . . .

Today, Michael had good news: Spencer had regained consciousness. It looked like he was out of the woods at last. "Barring complications, he'll be moved to Critical Care sometime in the next few days."

My heart was pounding so loud I could barely hear Michael. Spencer was awake, he was going to be all right. "Will I be able to see him?"

Michael nodded. "The head of the medical team wants to get you into CCU," he said. "Spencer insists you were on the motorcycle, and we can't convince him you're alive. Seeing you would set his mind at ease, but there's one problem. You're not a family member. We have to get Mrs. Adams's permission."

My eyes filled with tears. "She hates me, she won't even speak to me."

"Dr. Sugarman's aware of the situation," Michael said, "but he's sure he can persuade her. After all, it's in Spencer's best interest."

He patted my shoulder. "Believe me, Lauren, Sugarman lives up to his name. He's the most charming guy in the world."

As soon as Michael left, I called Mom and begged her to let me stay overnight. I couldn't leave, not now. Spencer was awake, he was calling for me. At any moment Michael might appear and take me to him.

I slept in the lounge, waking every time I heard a voice, but a couple of days passed before Michael came looking for me. Spencer was in Critical Care, he said, and Mrs. Adams had reluctantly agreed to let me see him. It had been a true test of Dr. Sugarman's charm.

Michael paused in front of the doors leading to the Critical Care Unit. "Don't expect Spencer to be his old self," he warned me. "He's been through a hell of a lot, he's still in pain, he's groggy from medication. But compared to the way he looked when the Med-Evac helicopter brought him, he's in great shape."

He studied my face. "Do you understand what I'm saying, Lauren?"

Tears splashed down my cheeks. I understood.

"Let me level with you then. It won't do Spencer any good to see you cry. If you can't smile and put up a good front, we'd better wait a few days."

I swallowed hard and wiped my eyes with the tissue he handed me.

"Blow your nose, too," he said.

When he thought I'd controlled my tears, he opened the door. The Critical Care Unit was large, complex, impersonal, overwhelming in its efficiency. In the middle was an enclosed area where at least half a dozen people worked at desks, watched monitors, answered phones, paged doctors.

A nurse looked up from the file she was reading, and Michael introduced me. "This is Lauren Anderson, the girl I told you about. She's here to see Spencer."

The nurse took my hand and smiled. "My name is Jane. I've been Spencer's primary care nurse since he came in."

Glancing at Michael, she said, "Don't be disturbed by his

appearance, Lauren. Spencer's a survivor if I ever saw one. A miracle. When he arrived, I didn't think he'd make it."

As Michael started to lead me away, she added, "Just take it easy, smile at him, treat him the way you always have. He's not as fragile as he looks."

My legs shook, but I followed Michael. Behind glass, I saw people in beds with high sides. The only sound was the beep and gurgle of machines. The air was cold and deadly still. Doctors spoke in hushed voices, nurses read charts, no one smiled.

Michael drew me into a small room. Lying in bed was a person surrounded by hospital equipment. A stranger, no one I knew, not Spencer.

Thinking we'd made a mistake, I stepped back, but Michael led me closer. Under a white blanket, Spencer lay as still and pale as an effigy on a tomb, a knight who'd died young. His eyes were shut, and his dark eyelashes brushed his cheeks. His mouth and nose were covered by a transparent oxygen mask, but his chest rose and fell naturally. On a stand by the bed hung four plastic bags. A tube ran from each one into Spencer's body. Other machines beeped softly. Some pumped things into his body, some pumped things out. On a monitor over his head a confusing pattern of red and green lines zigzagged rhythmically across the screen.

"Tell him you're here," Michael said. "And remember to smile."

Slowly, I reached out, afraid I'd hurt him, and put my hand on his cool, white cheek. "Spencer," I whispered, "Spencer, it's me — Lauren."

I waited a moment, but he didn't respond. Bending closer, I put my lips to his ear and whispered his name again. All I heard was the rush of oxygen through the tube leading to his mask.

Finally, his eyes opened and he stared at me. "Lauren?" he whispered. "Is it you?"

Pulling at the oxygen mask, he tried to yank it off, but his hand was weak and fumbly. Jane had come into the room. Now she stepped forward and eased the mask away from his mouth. "You can get along without it for a while," she said. "When Lauren leaves, we'll put it back on."

His eyes filled with tears and I watched them run unchecked down his face. "I thought you were with me," he said. "I was sure you were dead."

I held his right hand. The left was strapped to a board. Tubes from the IV unit pierced the veins. Remembering what Michael said, I smiled till I thought my face would crack, I bit my lip, I willed myself not to cry.

"Oh, God, it's good to see you, Spencer." I stopped, unable to go on without crying.

He gazed at me. "So sorry, Lauren, can't tell you how sorry. Forgive, please, sorry . . ."

His eyes closed, he drifted into sleep. For a moment, I stood by the bed, unwilling to leave. "There's nothing to forgive," I said. "You're alive. I love you."

Michael touched my shoulder. "That's enough for now," he said softly. "He tires easily. You can see him again in a few hours."

Taking my arm, he led me away. From the doorway, I looked back, but Spencer hadn't moved. Lost in dreams, he slept peacefully.

"Is he really all right?" I asked Michael.

"Just make sure he doesn't get another motorcycle. I don't want to see him in here again."

I stared at Michael. Surely he was joking. The last thing Spencer would want was a motorcycle.

*　*　*

When I left CCU, I didn't notice Mrs. Adams until it was too late to avoid her. She was standing at a large window staring at the pad where the Med-Evac helicopter landed. Unsure what I'd say, what she'd say, I walked toward her. She might yell at me, she might turn her back, she might blame me all over again, but I had to face her.

She saw me when I was a few feet away. Our eyes locked and we stared at each other silently.

I was the first to speak. "Thank you for letting me visit Spencer," I said. It was Mouse's voice I heard, squeaky and high, a wavery quavery child's voice.

"Dr. Sugarman recommended it." Her cat's eyes were cold, her voice icy. When she turned her head, her hair swung forward like Spencer's and hid her face. She had said all she wanted to say, but I hadn't.

"I'm sorry I yelled at you that night."

She glanced at me. Behind her, a helicopter was dropping slowly from the sky. Waiting on the ground was a team of doctors and nurses. Their white coats fluttered in the wind kicked up by the whirling blades.

"I'm sorry, too," Mrs. Adams said suddenly. "I had no right to speak so harshly, but I was upset, frightened. I thought my son was dying."

It wasn't easy for her to apologize. There were spaces between her words, silences that separated them like beads on a string. She twisted her hands, she frowned, but she stared straight at me the way Spencer did when he was trying to make me understand something.

The rest of my apology rushed out in a flood of tears. "You were right about the motorcycle, I shouldn't have let him keep it at my apartment. I'm sorry about the champagne, I'm sorry I let him drive away without me. I tried to stop him, I tried."

"What happened that night began years ago. It had nothing to do with you." Running her hands through her hair, Mrs. Adams pushed it back from her face in a gesture that reminded me sharply of Spencer. Like his, her skin was so transparent I could see the same faint tracery of blue veins at her temples.

"I lost my temper," she whispered, "I struck him. What would I have done if my son had died? How could I have forgiven myself?"

Covering her face with her hands, she began to weep. If she'd been my mother, I would have put my arms around her and we would have cried together, but I was afraid to touch Mrs. Adams.

Making an effort to control her emotions, Mrs. Adams blew her nose and wiped her eyes. To my surprise, she took my arm. Her fingers were icy cold on my bare skin.

"I appreciate what you've done," she said. "You've given up a great deal to sit here in the hospital day after day. It can't have been easy. Or fun."

"I love Spencer," I said.

"I know you do," she said, "but you're very young, and so is he."

We looked at each other silently, measuring, considering. Outside, the helicopter sat on the ground, its blades still. As the Shock Trauma team ran toward the hospital, we drew closer together.

"The staff wants Spencer to begin seeing a psychiatrist while he's here," Mrs. Adams said. "They told me it's standard procedure in cases like his — a single-vehicle crash. There's always a question of intention."

Mrs. Adams lowered her head as if it shamed her to tell me Spencer needed help. "I spoke to Dr. Gruenwald, the psychiatrist. She feels Spencer has been obsessed with his father's death since it happened. He's thought about killing himself for years. Feared he would. Did he talk to you about it?"

Her eyes probed mine. Unable to bear her scrutiny, I fidgeted with a thread hanging from the hem of my T-shirt. "Yes," I admitted, "but I never thought he'd do it."

She nodded as if I'd confirmed her own suspicions. Wiping her eyes with a tissue, she said, "I wanted to protect my son, I didn't want him to know, I never dreamed he'd seen his father's body. He was only six years old, Brooke's age, sweet, sensitive, quiet. How do you explain suicide to a child?"

It was a rhetorical question. Mrs. Adams didn't expect an answer, so I merely shrugged and went on tugging at the loose thread. *You could have tried when he was older,* I thought, *you could have made it easier for him to ask questions. He needed to know.*

I glanced at her, but she was watching the helicopter rise up into the cloudless sky. When it was gone, she thanked me again for helping Spencer, and shook my hand.

I watched her walk down the hall and push open the door to CCU. Tall, slim, straight, impeccably dressed — who would ever guess she'd once been married to man who killed himself?

Alone in the empty corridor, I allowed myself to feel sorry for Mrs. Adams. She hid hurts as deep as Spencer's — "heavenly hurts," Emily Dickinson would have called them, the kind that leave no scar, the hardest to heal. The man in the chair had aimed a bullet at himself, but it had split into fragments, ricocheted, and found other targets. Bits of it were buried in Spencer's mind, others in his mother's. Smaller pieces still traveled through time and space seeking new victims — Jeremy and Brooke, grandchildren, maybe even great-grandchildren. Who knew where the bullet would stop?

~ *Chapter Thirty* ~

I SPENT THE NEXT FOUR or five weeks visiting Spencer in CCU. In and out, in and out — fifteen minutes, four times a day, that was the schedule. At first, he tired easily. Jet lag, he said once — you don't take a round-trip to the edge of the forever place without suffering a few side effects. But gradually, the tubes and bags and catheters disappeared, the machines vanished, he grew stronger.

By the time he was ready to leave CCU, and go to rehab he was down to one IV in the back of his hand. He was sitting up, making jokes, feeding himself. Except for the cast encasing his left leg from hip to toe, he looked like Spencer again — a little pale, a little thin, but definitely himself.

As Jane said, he was a miracle. He had rough days ahead, but he'd survived internal injuries, fractured bones, shock, infections. She had no doubt he'd recover completely. But it would take time, maybe a year, depending on his leg. He'd need physical therapy. And counseling.

"Come back some day," she said as an orderly wheeled Spencer out of CCU. "I want to see you on your feet."

Raising his head, Spencer smiled at her. "I'll waltz you down the hall," he promised.

When Spencer had been in Wing G for a week, he finally told me about the crash. We were talking idly the way you do sometimes, leapfrogging from movies to books to music, remembering things we'd done together, laughing, pausing to kiss.

Suddenly, Spencer said, "While I was in Shock Trauma, I went on and on about my father. I quoted Whitman, Frost — you know me, conscious or unconscious, the same old stuff comes out."

Guessing I wanted to say something, he touched my lips with his finger. "I've put you through so much this summer, Lauren. I owe you the truth — or at least my version of it."

I knew what he was going to say, I'd known all along, but I didn't want to hear it. I wished I could cover his mouth with mine and silence him with kisses. Instead I sat quietly and listened.

Without looking at me, Spencer said, "When I left you, I was mad. Crazy. Drunk. I had this idea I'd ride out to the reservoir, crash through the railing, fly. Nothing was real, not me, not you. Everything was an illusion. Life, death — just words, meaningless words."

He faltered, he stumbled on what he was saying, but he kept talking. "The road was wet, it was slippery, I was going fast, too fast, I knew I was going too fast, but I didn't care. The curve was just ahead, the tree was there, I'd seen it a million times before."

Releasing my hand, he chewed on his thumbnail for a moment, frowned, stared out at the window. "I put on the brakes," he said, "I'm sure I did, but it was too late. I was out of control, I was off the ground, heading for that goddamned tree, and I was thinking, 'So this is it, the hell with it.' "

He turned to me, his eyes wide. "I didn't give a shit, Lauren, I didn't care whether I hit it or not. Whether I lived or died."

"If I'd gone with you, it wouldn't have happened," I said. "You left thinking I didn't love you. I let you down, Spencer, I let you down."

Spencer shook his head. "If you'd been on the back of the bike, you'd be dead, Lauren. You couldn't have stopped me. Nobody could have. According to Dr. Gruenwald, I've been heading straight toward that tree for a long, long time."

He took my hand and held it so tightly I felt my bones grind together. "My mother was right," he said. "She knew whose son I am."

"No," I whispered, "no, you were drunk, you didn't know what you were doing."

"My father was drunk when he shot himself," Spencer said. "Maybe he didn't realize he'd actually die, but that didn't change anything, did it? No matter what he thought, the bastard's dead and buried."

"But you're alive," I whispered, "you're alive, Spencer."

He shifted his position and winced in pain. "Yes," he said, "I'm alive."

Holding him as close as I dared, I kissed him. For a long time we didn't speak, we just held each other. The room was so quiet, I could hear the IV dripping into his veins.

"Maybe talking to Gruenwald will help," Spencer said at last. "I don't want to make a habit of running into a tree every time I get mad. The Sierra Club might sue me."

He tried to make it sound like a joke, but he was too tired to put much effort into it. Lying back against the pillow, he played with a strand of my hair. "Do you hate me for what I did?"

"No," I whispered, "no."

Tears rose in his eyes. He didn't bother to hide them. They rolled down his cheeks one after another like rain drops on a windowpane.

I kissed them away, I told him I loved him. "You'd never do anything like that again," I said.

He shook his head, but the shadows I knew so well moved across his face and lodged in his eyes. While I held his hand, he fell asleep. The light streaming through the window washed the color from his face and emphasized the weight he'd lost. He looked hollowed out, tired, as fragile as a cancer patient.

Reluctant to leave, I sat beside him for a long time, trying to understand what he'd told me. It wasn't clear to me what he'd meant to do. It wasn't clear to him, either. Dr. Gruenwald must be the only person who was sure about what had happened that night.

Mom was waiting for me at the Silver Spring metro stop. Before I could say a word, she flung her arms around my neck and hugged me hard.

"Paul asked me to marry him last night." Like a kid, she seized my hands and jumped up and down.

All the way to Adelphia, she talked nonstop. It would be a September wedding (an age-appropriate month, she said), but we'd move into Paul's house at the end of July. I'd have a nice room, I'd love the yard, and just think — no more stereo booming through the wall from next door, no more hauling laundry and groceries up three flights of steps, no more yelling from downstairs.

244

"And do you know what?" Mom grinned at me. "Paul's buying a new car and giving me his Toyota. That means you get this old baby." She slapped the Beetle's steering wheel.

To celebrate, Mom took me to a little Chinese restaurant not far from home. While we waited for our food, she looked at me. "You're awfully quiet, Lally."

I smiled. What was the use of telling her she hadn't given me a chance to say anything? "I'm really glad," I told her. "Paul's the nicest man you've ever dated."

"I wish I'd met him when you were younger," she said sadly. "It's ironic, isn't it? When you're practically a grown woman, I finally find the perfect dad for you."

For a few moments, we busied ourselves pouring tea. The waitress brought bowls of wonton soup and refilled our water glasses. By the time our meals arrived, Mom was giving me a humorous account of her day at Stockman. I tried to pay attention, but it was hard to keep my thoughts from straying to Spencer.

"Is something wrong?"

Startled by the question, I looked up. Mom was leaning across the table staring at me. Without planning to, I said, "Spencer told me he was thinking about killing himself when he hit the tree."

"Oh, God." Mom squeezed my hand. "I've always been afraid of that."

"Me, too." I cradled the cup of tea with both hands. The air conditioner was set so low I was shivering. "He put on the brakes, he tried to stop, but it was too late."

"I know you're worried about him," Mom said softly, "but sometimes you just have to hope for the best, honey. Like Paul and me — our marriage might last a couple of months, a few years, forever. It could be a disaster, it could be the greatest thing on earth. There's no way to tell how anything will turn out."

Overwhelmed by the uncertainty of life, she sighed. "One day at a time, that's Paul's philosophy — corny but true. Let the future take care of itself."

Leaving me to think about that, Mom turned her attention to her Broccoli and Tofu Delight. While she experimented with her chopsticks, I poked at my vegetables. Not too long ago, Spencer's future had been measured in minutes, but now it stretched ahead, as indefinite as anyone's — blank pages waiting to be filled. What would he write on them?

When I visited him the next day, Spencer was gloomier than ever. He barely noticed the heart-shaped balloon I'd bought from a street vendor, he didn't want the Snickers bar I'd gotten from the snack bar. Instead of talking, he watched the jets drift past his window, their engines silenced by the glass. Like homing pigeons they followed the Potomac to National Airport, so low you could read the names on their tails — Delta, United, USAir.

Desperate to entertain him, I read a couple of chapters from *God Bless You, Mr. Rosewater*, but even Kurt Vonnegut couldn't make him smile. When I got to the part about Ethical Suicide Parlors, I closed the book.

" 'What are people for?' " Spencer said dully, proving he'd already read it.

That was the sort of mood he was in.

Day after day, I tried to cheer him up. Sometimes I succeeded, sometimes I failed. He swung from high to low and back again. One moment he'd be full of ideas — going to Ocean City in the Volkswagen, taking courses with me at the University of Maryland, finding an apartment, living together, getting married, traveling. But in seconds, his enthusiasm would evaporate, his smile would vanish, and he'd sink down into doom and gloom. Nothing would ever be right again, his life was ruined.

One morning he greeted me with the news that he'd talked to a bone specialist. She'd showed him X rays, explained his fractures, warned him he'd probably need more surgery in the spring. He was afraid he'd never run again, maybe he'd limp, maybe he'd be crippled. Taking it to Spencerian extremes, he muttered, "You'll be pushing me around campus in a wheelchair, carrying my books, helping me in and out of buildings."

He was also obsessed with AIDS. The transfusions he'd had in Shock Trauma, all that blood, who knew where it came from, what junkie sold it to buy drugs? I told him hospitals screened blood to make sure it was safe, but Spencer shook his head. "Five years from now, I'll probably test HIV positive," he said. "It's like having a time bomb inside waiting to go off."

When I said he was talking silly talk, he scowled. "You won't say that if I give you AIDS."

To make him shut up, I pressed my mouth against his, but as soon as I let him up for air, he started again. "What if I get you pregnant? We'd have an AIDS baby."

I'd had enough. Looking him straight in the eye, I muttered one of his favorite words.

Spencer stared at me. For a moment, he was too shocked to speak. "What did you say?"

"You heard me." Taking a deep breath, I repeated it, louder this time. "Bullshit."

His eyes widened. "You never talk like that."

"Do you want to hear it again?" I was ready to say worse things if I had to. "Because that's all it is — bullshit. You don't have AIDS, and you aren't going to spend your life in a wheelchair, and I'm sick of hearing it."

I started crying then, and Spencer put his arms around me. "I'm sorry," he murmured, "I'm sorry. I didn't mean to upset you, Lauren. I'm scared, that's all. Scared of what I did to myself, scared of what I did to you, scared I'll do something dumb again."

"You won't," I sobbed, "you won't."

I couldn't say anything else. He was kissing my words away along with my tears. "No," he said, "you're right, I won't ever do it again. I promise, Lauren, I promise."

Wanting to believe him, wanting to trust him, I felt the world shrink around us. For a few minutes, nothing existed but Spencer and me. I loved him, he loved me. We were together. We were safe, happy. Like Mom said, the future would take care of itself.

The tinkling sound of a nurse's cart shattered the spell. Red-faced, I leapt away from Spencer and jostled the IV unit. It immediately began beeping.

Miss Palumbo silenced it, but she wasn't amused. "It's time to check your vital signs," she said briskly.

"Lauren's already done that," Spencer told her. "Believe me, they're fine."

"I bet they are." Without smiling, Miss Palumbo stuck a thermometer in Spencer's mouth and began closing the curtains around his bed.

Waiting in the hall, I thought it would be a good story to share later with Casey. She'd probably find the whole thing a lot funnier than either Miss Palumbo or I did.

~ Chapter Thirty-one ~

SEVERAL DAYS LATER, I told Casey about my embarrassing encounter with Miss Palumbo. We were sitting in the swings behind Mayfaire Court, and, just as I expected, she found the part about Spencer's vital signs hilarious. In fact, she laughed so hard she choked on her soda, and I had to whack her on the back to make her stop coughing.

When Casey could talk again, she wanted to know how much longer Spencer would be in the hospital.

"He thinks he'll be out in two weeks."

Casey looked at me closely. "And then what?"

With my bare toe I drew a heart in the dust under my swing. "He wants to take a few courses at the University of Maryland this fall," I said, "but his leg will probably need more surgery in the spring."

I hesitated a moment before I added, "The biggest problem is where he'll live."

I glanced at Casey. It was almost nine o'clock, and the summer twilight made it hard to see her features. Tipping my head back to drain the last swallow of soda from the can, I waited for her to respond.

"If you're thinking what I think you're thinking," Casey said, "the answer is no."

As usual, she'd read my mind. Casey had come up with a plan to find an apartment in Adelphia. We'd get a couple of other girls to move in and split the rent with us. She'd keep working at Mister Burger, and, if Mrs. Jenkins didn't want me back at the library, she was pretty sure somebody in the mall would hire me. To save money, we'd carpool to the Catonsville campus.

"Spencer's not moving in with us," Casey added to make herself perfectly clear.

When I asked why not, she made up a string of reasons, none of which sounded credible — it was an all-girl deal, she didn't like Spencer's taste in music, he wouldn't put up with her cigarettes, she wanted to be free to walk around half-nude if she felt like it.

"No guys." Jumping out of the swing, she added "Let's go. The mosquitoes are eating me up."

We walked back to Mayfair Court in semihostile silence. Low in the sky, the evening star kept the moon company. A mockingbird sang in a spindly pear tree, and, at the bottom of the hill, the boys were kicking a soccer ball and yelling good naturedly at one another. Trapped by asphalt and buildings, the day's heat lingered. The air was so heavy with humidity it clung to your skin and clogged your lungs.

"Can't we just try it and see how things go?" I asked.

Casey shook her head. Sitting down on the steps in front of her apartment building, she lit a cigarette. "I guess you think I'm a mighty mean woman," she said. "Hard as nails, just like my mom."

I made a face and swatted the smoke away. She was like her mother, but it was the first time she ever admitted it.

"Jordan wants to move in, too," Casey added, "but I don't want him living with us either. I'm not ready for that kind of commitment."

She frowned at me through a cloud of smoke. Although she didn't say it, I knew what she was thinking — I wasn't ready, either. Neither was Spencer, neither was Jordan.

"Spencer can visit whenever he likes," Casey went on. "He can even sleep over, but if you want to live with him, you'll have to find your own place."

The next day I was saved from telling Spencer the bad news. When I stepped out of the hospital elevator, I saw Kevin and Ted walking down the hall ahead of me. For a moment, I was tempted to go to the canteen. I could drink a cup of coffee, eat a doughnut, linger till I was sure they were gone.

But I checked myself. That was the old Mouse, the girl I used to be. I was out of high school now — why should I be scared? Kevin and Ted didn't own the world. Or the hospital. I had just as much right to be here as they did. Maybe more.

Forcing my feet to move, I walked to Spencer's door. Ted was the first to notice me. As he stepped aside to let me into the room, he made a noncommittal noise which I interpreted as a greeting. It was the friendliest sound he'd ever made in my presence.

When Spencer saw me, he patted the bed and I sat down next to him. Side by side, we faced Kevin and Ted.

It was obvious they were as uncomfortable as we were. They began a fidgeting, fumbling apology for not having come to see him sooner, stumbling over words as if English were a second language, one they hadn't quite mastered.

Finally, they broke down and stared at Spencer. What should they say next? What should they do? Was it okay to laugh? Should they whisper, say solemn things?

In an effort to help, Spencer asked how the Orioles were doing. Seizing the topic with the gratitude of a drowning man, Ted launched into an account of last night's game. He and Kevin had gone to Camden Yards to see it — the Birds had never been better. Taking turns, the boys recounted every play, inning after inning, interrupting each other, correcting each other, piling on details till my eyes almost crossed from sheer boredom.

Suddenly Kevin said, "You scared the shit out of us, Spence."

"Hell, it takes more than a little tree to kill me." The prince hadn't lost his style after all. Some of the old bravado had crept back into his voice. Worse yet, he looked pleased with himself, a hero receiving tribute.

The change in him made me so uncomfortable I was tempted to leave. He was putting on an act for Ted and Kevin, and I wondered who he was fooling — himself or them.

"Are you kidding?" Kevin asked. "We drove out there the next day. You didn't hit any little tree. It was a big mother of a tree, an oak or something."

"You gouged a chunk like this out of it." Ted held his hands about two feet apart to show Spencer the size of the scar he'd made in the trunk.

The expression on Spencer's face made me feel like punching him. It was obvious he enjoyed hearing the awe in Ted's voice.

"And the bike," Kevin said. "We saw it at the junkyard. Twisted metal, that's all it was."

"I'll be more careful with the next one."

252

I stared at Spencer, too shocked to speak. It was the first time he'd mentioned buying another motorcycle.

Noticing my reaction, Spencer winked. "We have to get to California somehow, Lauren. Your poor old Beetle would never make it across the Alleghenies."

Not sure whether Spencer was joking or not, the boys laughed a little too loudly. Shifting to safer ground, Kevin asked me about college, and Ted wanted to know what Casey was up to. If she ever got tired of Jordan, he hoped she'd give him a call. He was going to Maryland, too, maybe he'd see her on campus, take her to a frat party or something.

Before they left, Kevin told Spencer that Vanessa sent her love. "She's lifeguarding at the club. Not much free time, you know? Otherwise she would've come with us."

Spencer nodded. Keeping his face serious, he said, "Tell Van not to work too hard. Sitting on your butt in the sun all day takes a real toll on people."

When the boys were gone, Spencer closed his eyes for a moment. "I thought they'd never leave. All that smiling was making my jaw ache."

Ignoring his fatigue, I leaned toward him. "You were kidding about buying a motorcycle, right?"

"I guess so," Spencer said slowly. I waited a moment, and he went on, just as I knew he would. "I really loved that bike, Lauren. Until my last ride, it was fantastic." He sighed, and I knew he was remembering the curves, the hills, the rush of air in his face.

Looking him straight in the eye, I said, "Spencer Adams, if you get another motorcycle, that's it. I'm never riding on one again. I mean it."

He stared at me, saw I was serious, and smiled. "You're turning into a real pain, Lauren. First you tell me I'm full of bullshit, then you tell me I can't have a motorcycle. What'll you tell me next?"

The expression in his eyes made it impossible to stay angry. "I love you," I said. "That's what I'll tell you next."

"I love you, too." He beckoned me closer, put his arm around me, and kissed me. "How about a Jeep instead? Just picture this, Lauren — you and me and Zack following Route Sixty-six all the way across the country, seeing everything between here and there. We'll go — "

His voice broke off in midsentence, and he fell back against his pillow. A drift of dark hair slid across his forehead and hid his eyes. "Who the hell am I kidding," he muttered. "We'll never do it, will we?"

I leaned closer, took his hands in mine, held them tight. "Why not?" I asked. "There's next summer and all the summers after that. We've got our whole lives to do it."

But Spencer's enthusiasm had evaporated like morning dew, leaving his voice dull and dry. "Dr. Gruenwald thinks I spend too much energy thinking up things like trips to California," he said. "She says I have to focus on practical solutions."

Without looking at me, he played with my fingers, bending them, admiring their length, measuring them against his. "Do you know what she wants me to do? Go home and work on my relationship with my mother, talk to her, go to family counseling, take responsibility for my own life." Spencer was obviously imitating the psychiatrist's voice.

"You can't change the past," he added, still mimicking, "but you can change the way you look at it."

He shifted his position, winced with pain, and gripped my hand so hard it hurt. "Sometimes I think Gruenwald's full of it," he said. "but she's right about one thing."

Leaning toward the stand by his bed, he grabbed the copy of *Rain Makes Applesauce* I'd bought for him, and turned to an illustration he'd shown me before. " 'The wind blows backwards all night long' — remember?"

We stared at the man playing bagpipes, and Spencer said, "All my life the wind's been blowing me back to my father, to that chair, to that gun."

He frowned. "It doesn't do any good to run away from him. My father's part of me, Lauren, he's inside me, I have to face it."

Closing the book, Spencer gazed out the window. In the silence, a nurse paged Dr. Sugarman. An old man tottered past the door pushing a walker ahead of him and towing an IV unit behind him. In other rooms, someone laughed, someone caughed, someone groaned, a TV blared.

Suddenly, Spencer pulled me close and kissed me. I tasted tears, sweet and salty. Were they his or mine? I didn't know, couldn't tell.

"I lay awake for hours last night thinking about you and me, wondering what we should do," he said. "Maybe it's not a good idea for me to move in with you and Casey. Gruenwald's right — I've got too much unfinished business, as she puts it."

Full of worry, his eyes searched mine, begging me to understand. "I love you so much, Lauren. I want to marry you and spend the rest of my life with you, but I'm scared of screwing up and ruining things. I think we should wait till I'm stronger — not just here." He tapped the cast on his leg. "But here, too," He tapped his head and made one of his crazy-man faces.

I stroked his forehead to smooth the furrows away. There was something I needed to tell him, something important, but I didn't have the words to hold it. Not sure he'd understand what I meant, I said, "The wind blows forward too, Spencer. Your whole life is ahead of you, just waiting. School, California, everything."

Hoping I was saying the right thing, I added, "Your father's dead, he belongs in the past. Can't you just let him go?"

"Let him go?" Spencer thought about it for a while. "What a weird idea — let him go, release him, free him."

His eyes strayed to the heart-shaped balloon floating over his bed, and he laughed. "Remember when you lost that balloon in Baltimore? Maybe we could let him go like that — a big black balloon full of crying gas floating up, up, up into the sky."

We looked at each other. "It would be the best balloon story of all," I said, and Spencer agreed.

~ Chapter Thirty-two ~

ALMOST A MONTH LATER, I drove over to High Meadow. Spencer had been out of the hospital for a week. The day he was released, I'd ridden home with his family and stayed for a celebration dinner. Even though Mrs. Adams was still a little cool, a little distant, she made it clear I was welcome. She didn't even object to the time Spencer and I spent alone in his room, a ground-floor addition Mr. Adams had designed to accommodate the wheelchair.

Not that Spencer would be in a wheelchair for the rest of his life — in the spring, he'd return to the hospital for more surgery — but in the meantime, he wasn't supposed to put any weight on his left leg.

It was a Saturday morning in early September, warm and sunny, a perfect day for a weddng, but Spencer and I had something else to do before we met Mom and Paul at the county courthouse.

When I pulled into the driveway, I saw Spencer waiting for me. Brooke and Jeremy were tossing a Frisbee on the lawn, Zack was leaping for it, Mr. Adams was mulching the bushes, and Mrs. Adams was watering the geraniums.

For a moment, I remembered the image I'd once had of them — the perfect family, happy, unscathed, enviable. Despite everything, they still glittered. You had to admire them for that.

Brooke ran to the car. "I wish I could come with you," she said. "I love weddings."

She'd lost both front teeth, but a new one was already poking through her gum, its edge as sharp as a saw blade. Pausing to glance over her shoulder, she put her mouth close to my ear. "When you and Spencer get married, can I be the flower girl?"

"You'll be all grown up by then," I said. "Maybe you can be a bridesmaid instead."

Brooke looked disappointed, but only for a moment. Tossing her hair back, she smiled. "I'll wear a blue dress, right down to the floor, and I'll braid flowers in my hair like you."

"Beep, beep," Jeremy said, "get out of the way, Brooke." He was pushing Spencer in the wheelchair.

Scowling at her brother, Brooke moved, and Jeremy parked Spencer beside the Beetle.

"Are you sure there's enough room in that car?" Mrs. Adams asked. "Why don't you take the station wagon? You'd be much more comfortable."

With my help, Spencer was easing himself into the passenger seat. "It's fine, Mom," he said. Closing the door, he added, "See?"

Mrs. Adams hovered by the car, watching Jeremy put the folded wheelchair on the bike rack. "Will it be safe there?" she asked.

Spencer sighed and shook his head. "Will you stop worrying? I'm fine, the chair's fine, everything's fine."

His mother didn't look convinced. Before we left, she

258

wanted to know when Spencer would be home. Staring her straight in the eye, he said, "Don't expect me till Monday."

She opened her mouth, but before she could say anything, Spencer covered her hand with his. "I'm eighteen, Mom — remember what Dr. Gruenwald said? Old enough to vote, old enough to join the army and go to war, old enough to make my own decisions."

Jeremy grinned and raised his thumbs. Unamused, Mrs. Adams put one arm around his shoulders. Although she wasn't smiling, she waved to us. "Give your mother my best wishes," she called to me.

As soon as the house was out of sight, Spencer said, "Where is it?"

"In that big bag in the backseat. I was hoping nobody would notice it."

I drove slowly, carefully. Although I'd gotten my license when I was sixteen, I hadn't had much experience. Mom had depended on the Beetle, and she'd worried I'd strip the gears, ruin the transmission, run up costly repair bills. Now that she had the Toyota, she'd given me some refresher lessons, but I still had trouble shifting. Every now and then I stalled at stop signs and made the car jump like a rabbit.

By the time I parked, I was feeling a little weak in the knees, but Spencer said I was doing great. "I never noticed how nice it is out here," he said. "The scenery was just a blur when I drove."

I unfolded the wheelchair and helped Spencer into it. He scowled and swore at his leg, but I managed to push him off the road and onto the gravel shoulder. Together we stared at the oak tree. Without speaking, we both touched the scar on its trunk. A little breeze rustled overhead, and a yellow leaf drifted down through the air, spinning idly before it landed in a clump of ferns.

"Ted was right," Spencer said. "I left my mark, didn't I?"

"It's nothing to brag about." Suddenly angry, I glared at him. "You could've died here."

He gave my hand a squeeze. "I'm not bragging, Lauren, honest."

"You sure sounded like it the day Ted and Kevin came to the hospital." Imitating his voice, I said, " 'Hell, it takes more than a little old tree to kill me.' "

Spencer sighed. "That was just an act, a habit from the old days — look strong, smile, joke, fool everybody. You should know that by now."

Gripping my hand tighter, he looked at the tree and the silent woods behind it. A bird called, its voice sweet and compelling. "Let's go," he said. "If you want to know the truth, this place scares the hell out of me. It's like looking at my own grave."

While I was helping Spencer into the car, a motorcycle sped past. A guy driving, a girl clinging to him, their faces hidden by their helmets. We watched them lean into the curve and roar downhill toward the reservoir. Glancing at Spencer, I caught a flash of pure envy in his eyes.

I slid behind the wheel, and Spencer pulled me close. He kissed me till some guys in the back of a pickup truck yelled and whistled at us. Letting me go, Spencer said, "On to the next event, driver."

The reservoir's small parking lot was packed. We waited for a Jeep to leave and took its place. Once Spencer was settled in the wheelchair, I reached into the backseat and got the balloon.

"You found a black one," he said.

"But no crying gas," I said, "just plain, old-fashioned helium."

I pushed the wheelchair along a path to a little promontory overlooking the water. Ignoring the middle-aged couple staring at us, I watched Spencer pull several folded pieces of paper out of his pocket and tie them carefully to the balloon's string.

"What are those?" I asked.

"Messages to the dead." Knotting the last one, he gazed at the balloon floating above his head. "You know, I've always felt like it was my fault. What happened to my father."

"*Your* fault? How could it be *your* fault, Spencer?"

He shrugged. "Maybe if I'd been there, he wouldn't have done it — maybe I could've stopped him."

I shook my head, but he wasn't looking at me. "I didn't go straight home that day," he said. "I sat on the baby-sitter's steps for a while, then I dawdled, fooled around, stopped to look at things — rainbows in mud puddles, a squirrel, some boys playing basketball. All that time, maybe he was still alive."

"Spencer, you couldn't have stopped him."

"How do you know?"

"He would've done it some other time, the next day maybe." I tried to make him look at me. "If you'd gone home, he might have shot you, too. You read things like that in the paper all the time."

Spencer sighed. "Sometimes I wish he had."

"No," I whispered. "No. You don't mean that. Not now, not after all you've gone through."

He didn't say anything. His eyes were fixed on the balloon and the blue sky cobbled with small white clouds.

"You've got to let him go," I said.

Still holding the string, Spencer slowly raised his arm. For several seconds he watched the balloon sway in the breeze. It tugged and pulled at the line, the messages fluttered. Opening his hand, he said, "So long, Dad. Safe journey."

The balloon sailed up and out, over the water. A gust of wind caught it and whisked it higher. When it was out of sight, I put my arms around Spencer.

"Why am I crying?" he asked. "It's just a goddamned balloon."

I couldn't think of anything to say, so I held him tighter and let him weep.

As we drove away from the reservoir, Spencer said, "This is one balloon story we'll never laugh about."

A couple of hours later, we met Mom and Paul in Ellicott City. The county courthouse was packed with wedding parties. Most of the brides and grooms had the look of veterans. Survivors accompanied by assorted children, optimists ready to go back and try it again, they overflowed the dark hall, spilled out onto the white steps and across the green grass.

While we waited for our group to be called inside, Spencer and I sat quietly in the shade of a small tree, a little apart from the others. I leaned beside him, holding his hand. Despite the heat, his fingers were cold.

Mom's laughter drew our attention to her. Wearing a new purple suit, she stood in the sunlight beside Paul. She'd never looked prettier. Armed with a camera, Joanna hovered near her, larger than life in a green-and-white polka-dot dress. Mom said something, Paul grinned, Joanna took a picture.

Slipping an arm around my waist, Spencer rested his face against my hip for a moment.

"What's wrong? Are you tired?"

He shook his head, and his hair stirred, dark and silky. "Just happy," he whispered.

When he looked up and smiled at me, my heart turned over the way it had ever since middle school.

"I'm happy, too," I said.

Mom beckoned to us. It was time to go inside and witness her marriage. Reluctantly, I let go of Spencer's hand and pushed the wheelchair toward the ramp. The wind gusted, lifted my hair, swirled my dress. It was behind us, pushing us forward. Wherever it took us, I hoped Spencer and I would go there together.